"Deeply moving, sad and haunting, *Into Captivity* [...] when he was at his most interesting; it is an intense [...] what it means to be alive and spiritual in a world ig[...] imagery, its crystal-clear prose, and its strangeness."
— Brandon Hobson, National Book Award Finalist and author of
Where the Dead Sit Talking

"Smart and gripping, *Into Captivity They Will Go* depicts a God-soaked rural Oklahoma consciousness through the perspective of young Caleb, a protagonist I rooted for from beginning to end. The love and pain of the mother-son relationship, so rarely featured in contemporary fiction, is central to Milligan's compelling story."
— Constance Squires, author of *Along the Watchtower* and *Hit Your Brights*

"Noah Milligan is a keen observer of the complexities of the human condition that make us long for family and belonging, and can also create tribalism and extremist faith. *Into Captivity They Will Go* is a story for our time, told with sometimes brutal emotional honesty and always with compassion."
— Jennifer Haupt, author of *In the Shadow of 10,000 Hills*

"For any book about end-of-the-world cults, it would be tempting to stick to archetypes, easy jokes, and well-worn cliches. Yet the characters and motivations of Into Captivity They Will Go were human, compelling, and unnervingly familiar. The second-coming of the messiah and his enthusiastic mother aren't insane or deceptive, just damaged and optimistic. How Noah Milligan manages to evoke such authenticity and compassion in a story of this kind is a literary magic trick that'll convert even the most cynical."
— Charles Martin, Owner - Literati Bookstore

"Noah Milligan commands this novel with expert instincts, a deep consideration for language, and with his feet planted firmly within a world both tragic and all too familiar. *Into Captivity They Will Go* explores family and trust and what can happen when those two things part ways. If there's a more honest book written this year, I'd like to see it."
— Sheldon Lee Compton, author of *The Same Terrible Storm*

"*Into Captivity They Will Go* is an ambitious and original novel that dares to explore—with both sharp-eyed clarity and full-hearted empathy—worlds and characters too often overlooked in contemporary fiction."
— Lou Berney, author of *November Road*

"Fascinating. Heartbreaking. Powerful. *Into Captivity They Will Go* is all that and more. This look inside a millennialist sect and the otherwise unremarkable people who participate in it is crafted with a sympathetic yet uncompromising hand. It is a story that will trouble your heart and mind long after the book is closed."
— Jeanetta Calhoun Mish, Oklahoma State Poet Laureate & Director,
The Red Earth MFA

INTO

CAPTIVITY

THEY

WILL

GO

NOAH MILLIGAN

central
avenue
publishing

2019

Published by Central Avenue Publishing, an imprint of Central Avenue Marketing Ltd.
www.centralavenuepublishing.com

Published in Canada
Printed in United States of America

1. FICTION/Literary

INTO CAPTIVITY THEY WILL GO

Trade Paperback: 978-1-77168-177-3
Epub: 978-1-77168-178-0
Mobi: 978-1-77168-179-7

1 3 5 7 9 10 8 6 4 2

For Allie.
Thank you for saving me.

Whoever has ears, let them hear:
If anyone is to go into captivity,
          Into captivity they will go.
If anyone is to be killed with the sword
With the sword they will be killed.

—Revelation 13:10

THE BOOK OF GENESIS

CHAPTER 1

THIS IS THE STORY SHE TOLD HIM.

It was before dawn when she arrived, so dark she couldn't make out her stepfather in front of her, just hear his footsteps scraping through the underbrush. The woods were still quiet. It smelled like burnt leaves and the threat of rain. Evelyn Gunter travelled the well-worn path by memory, avoiding holes and jagged limestone. She'd walked this path thousands of times before, hauling pails and shovels and rakes from the barn to the garden, from the garden back to the barn. To the east, she knew, was Bluestem Lake. To her north, the plains of Kansas. The west, the panhandle. In between were ravines, knolls, and miles of Blackjack Oak. The land was dotted by coyotes, white tail, and rabbit. Oil rigs churned in the nearby fields, and gravel roads sparkled with empty Busch cans and broken-down Chevys. She'd been raised here. She'd toiled here. She'd grown stronger here. It was the exact place she was supposed to be.

The barn was already prepared. Dried hay covered the floor like a threadbare carpet. Fluorescent lamps illuminated the room. The light was iridescent, almost purple. In the middle her stepfather had prepared a pallet underneath an old blanket, stitched together by her grandmother when she'd been a child. Evelyn remembered wrapping up in it when the adults were busy with dominoes or spades, laughing at jokes she didn't understand, drinking gin and tonics until they got boisterous, accusatory, angry even. That morning, it offered little support, worn thin throughout the decades, the ground hard underneath, the hay stabbing her, but she didn't complain—she just lay and breathed and stared up at the loft above her.

Her stepfather draped a sheet over her and lit four candles, placed them above her head, by her shoulders, and the last at her feet. He'd always been a mystery to her. He'd shown up in her life after she was grown, having one day materialized out of thin air, already a permanent fixture in her mother's life. She didn't even remember the first time she'd met him, really. Just one day he was at Thanksgiving, then Sunday service, and then Thursday dinner, cutting his pork chop with a knife long worn dull. He rarely spoke, prayed often, and taught her and her mother the value of being a good Christian. She didn't know much about his past. He'd spent some time in the army, served in Korea. Was once a long-haul truck driver. Just stuff she'd been able to glean from pictures he had tucked away in books and shoeboxes. He didn't speak of his life before, and she didn't ask. He just was, and that was all right by Evelyn. He stabilized her mother. She no longer took pills. She no longer burned things for no reason. And, for that, Evelyn could spare him interrogation.

The candles emitted pockets of warmth around her, but most of her body remained frigid. Goose bumps formed on her exposed arms, little hairs standing on end. He sprinkled water over her forehead, over her hands, and down her torso in the shape of a cross. It was cold and pooled on her skin, and he then began to pray. His prayer was barely audible but grew louder as he continued. His eyes rolled back into his head, and he convulsed, the words rising from him like a root out of the earth until Evelyn swore she felt the consonants vibrating her insides. It started out like a static electric charge and spread from her heart to her lungs to her womb. She could feel it vibrating, growing stronger, just like she could feel the hard wood underneath her, the smell of cow manure stinging her nostrils, the fibers of her grandmother's blanket underneath her fingernails, and then it began to burn. A fire raged inside her belly, and she panicked. The pain was immense, worse than childbirth, worse than when she'd had the miscarriage, worse even than when the doctor had told her she couldn't have any more children. It consumed her. It was eating her alive. She screamed, and she writhed, but her stepfather held her down. She pushed up against him, but he was stronger than her. A scream formed inside of her chest. It grew and bubbled and was pushing out of her throat until she didn't think she could take it anymore. She was going to die. She was sure of it.

But then it was done.

It was over faster than it had arrived, and when her stepfather was finished with his prayer, he helped her to her feet.

"Rest," he said. "You're going to need your strength."

Eleven weeks later her doctor told her she was pregnant. He called it a miracle. Evelyn didn't have the heart to tell him he was more right than he knew.

CHAPTER 2

PAPA AND GRANDMA LIVED IN WHAT HAD ONCE
been the Osage Reservation on the outskirts of Pawhuska. They'd
moved there when Caleb had been very young, the family farm having gone the way most things do when given enough time, worn de-
crepit and abandoned, and so it was the only place he ever knew his
grandparents to live. The neighborhood consisted of small homes,
all of them identical: single-car garage, ranch style with a flat roof.
Storm shelter in the backyard. No trees. Uncurbed streets. Papa and
Grandma's house was no different. Inside, it was dark, smelled of gar-
lic, chicken noodle soup, and chores. Every time Caleb visited, he had
to mow the lawn or rake the leaves or clean the gutters. He'd earned
blisters there. He'd grown muscles.

Inside it was cluttered. Caleb figured his grandmother hadn't
thrown anything away ever. She had two pianos pushed up against the
wall, old box-type things that needed to be tuned. At their legs was
stacked sheet music reaching Caleb's waist. There were broken clocks
and cookbooks and decades' worth of newspapers. Caleb liked to dig
through these when he visited, reading news stories that had happened before he'd been born—Watergate, the moon landing, the Tet

Offensive—imagining these events were happening in real time, what things would be like then.

In the corner was a cracked leather chair. Papa sat there, trails of tobacco smoke leaking out of his nostrils. He typically didn't pay too much attention to Caleb when he was around, and that was all right with him. His Papa scared him. He rarely spoke, and when he did, it was often one-word sentences. Rake, he'd command. Water. Shovel. Plant. Weed. Now. And Caleb knew better than to disobey. Out front was an oak tree, and if Caleb or his older brother, Jonah, ever misbehaved, Papa was quick to tear off a switch and lap their thighs until they bled.

"You've heard the story of Abraham?" Papa asked Caleb. Jonah sat next to them but wasn't paying attention, instead engrossed in Saturday cartoons. Batman was playing, and the caped crusader fought the Joker's henchmen, walloping them with a Bang and a Bam highlighted in cartoon bubbles. When Caleb was alone with Papa, he often questioned Caleb about the Bible. It was a test, Caleb knew, and he always grew nervous when his Papa quizzed him. It felt like an interrogation in a way, like he was being accused of something.

"Yes," Caleb said.

Caleb's mother and father were there, too, but they were off in the back of the house with Grandma. They weren't visiting for a special occasion. It wasn't Memorial Day or Thanksgiving or a birthday, just a trip, but his mother and father hadn't offered any more details. They'd been doing this more and more lately, keeping things from their kids, not telling the whole truth. Caleb knew they were hiding something by the way his mother wouldn't look him in the eye that morning when they'd told Caleb and Jonah to get in the car, the way his father wouldn't talk, jaw muscles hardened. Caleb had asked Jonah about it, but he'd just shrugged. "If something was wrong," he'd said, "we'd know about it by now."

"Abraham was a man of God," Caleb continued, "and God told him to sacrifice his son. Climb a mountain and slit his throat."

"That's right. And why would he do that?"

Caleb didn't know why. This had always bothered Caleb about the story of Abraham, and his ignorance, most of all, caused him shame.

"Think about it, Caleb. It's not enough just to know the scripture. You have to understand it. You have to live it. Do you understand what I'm saying? It's important."

Caleb looked to his older brother for help, but he didn't offer any. He munched on a banana muffin and blinked at the television. "I don't know, Papa. What about the commandment? Thou shall not kill."

Papa took a drag of his cigarette, let the smoke fill his lungs. Caleb fought the urge to cough. "What about it?"

"God tells us not to kill. It's a sin. It just doesn't make any sense why God would tell Abraham to murder his son."

"Think about the nature of it. Is it murder if God commands it?"

Caleb thought long and hard about it, but he kept coming to the same conclusion. It was. If you took another person's life, no matter the reason, it was still murder. To do otherwise contradicted everything he'd always been taught about sin, and he told his Papa this.

"No, son. The Commandments are God's law for man, not God's law for God. God commands obedience. He demands it. You would do wise to remember this."

In the back, Caleb could hear his parents with Grandma. They were talking, their voices animated and urgent, but he couldn't quite make out what they were saying over the television. He wished Jonah would turn it down so he could hear them, but he was too afraid Papa would think he was trying to change the subject. It was faint, but he thought he could hear his mother crying, and this troubled him. He'd never seen his mother cry. She'd always been strong, resolute, determined, and the thought that she too could hurt shook him.

"But God is merciful. God is love," Caleb said. "Why would he command such a thing?"

Papa coughed. It was guttural, deep, full of phlegm. He was unable to cover his mouth before the fit started, and blood splattered the front of his plaid shirt. He tried to wipe the beads away with his hand, but he just smeared them into the fabric of his shirt, staining it.

"I am but a man, Caleb. I have no idea."

A FEW WEEKS LATER, CALEB'S mother woke him and his brother. She told them to get dressed, to hurry, and so they rubbed the sleep from their eyes and got dressed. Caleb pulled on a sweatshirt and jeans but that was it. His father yelled for him and his brother to hurry their asses up, counting down from five like he'd get his belt if they weren't buckled in the car by the time he got to zero. No time for scarves or gloves. No time for socks, just sneakers, and Caleb hoped it hadn't snowed that night, or, worse yet, sleeted. That mixture of slush and ice would numb his toes and make his skin wrinkle and peel away.

Mom hadn't told them why they were being summoned, but Caleb was too tired to wonder. Caleb's head filled with sleep, the remnants of his dream still rattling his insides. In it he'd been following Moses out of the desert, and he kept questioning why they continued. He was torn between following or returning from whence they'd come. Both, he was convinced, would result in his death. Whatever or whomever waited for them at either destination would destroy him and his family and his friends and there'd be nothing he could do about it. He'd be helpless, and that frightened him more than anything. He never did come to a decision, though. He just stood in the middle of the desert, throngs of his people filing past.

Outside it was dark. Dad drove, Mom next to him. Jonah's head slumped against the window as he slept. No stars shone. Streetlights were dim. No cars drove past. There were no pedestrians, engines idling, breeze. They stopped at a red light, and his father tapped the wheel and chewed his tongue. Mom told him to go, to run the damn red light, but Dad didn't. He just waited until the light once again turned green. Caleb had never been outside at this hour. He had no idea of the time, but he guessed it had to be after midnight. The world was so still. It was like the earth itself was sleeping, resting its eyes for the turbulence of the coming day.

To Caleb's surprise, they pulled up at Jane Phillips Hospital. He'd always seen it on the way to church or school, but this was the first time he'd step foot in it since he'd been born, and this worried him— he could feel his tongue swell, lodge itself in the back of his throat. The place frightened him. People were sick here. They were in pain here. They'd had car crashes, heart attacks, strokes. He'd seen the result of that. His uncle had suffered a stroke about a year back. Now he couldn't talk, ate pureed food through a straw, and every time Caleb went to visit him, his father told him to talk to his uncle, to tell him about the recent baseball tournament in Dewey, how Caleb had smashed a double in right-center field and drove home the winning run, or how he'd come in second place in the school spelling bee, even getting the word "magnanimous" right, but Caleb just couldn't bring himself to do it. His uncle's eyes lolled in his head, never focusing on a single thing for more than a few seconds, the light of his soul having gone dim, and the only thing Caleb could think to say to him was that he hoped he never ended up like that.

After they parked, Mom and Dad herded Caleb and Jonah through the lobby and parked them in a waiting room on the fourth floor. It was cramped and smelled of McDonald's cheeseburgers. The chairs were bolted to the floor, and the carpet was worn thin. One other family shared the small room, a mom and a dad and two small children, the oldest probably a couple years younger than Caleb, pushing around a toy truck, and a toddler, his diaper wet and full. The parents looked scared, their eyes glazed over as they stared at a late-night infomercial.

"Wait here," Mom told Caleb and Jonah. "And don't touch anything."

Mom and Dad disappeared behind two swinging doors, and Caleb blinked his eyes, willing them to stay open.

"This is about Papa, isn't it?" Caleb asked Jonah.

His older brother shrugged. "Probably." He fidgeted in his seat and tried to get comfortable, resting his head against the cinderblock wall, eyes closed.

"Is he sick?"

"I heard Mom and Dad talking. He's got cancer. Had it for a while now."

Caleb's head felt heavy, his eyelids. In one moment he was back in the desert, the next he was sitting next to his brother. "Why didn't they tell us?"

Jonah shrugged. "Mom's been acting crazy. Guess they figured if she couldn't take it, we wouldn't be able to either."

"You ever know anyone who died before?"

Jonah shook his head. "A guy in my class hit a tree while skiing. Didn't really know him, though."

For a while they just sat there. Caleb fought off sleep, his head drooping toward his chest, then jerking upward. Once, he smacked his head against the wall behind him. It caused the family on the other side of the waiting room to jump, to blink at him, but then they returned to their infomercial, learning more about the weight loss miracle: The Tread Climber.

"Do you think he's scared?" Caleb asked.

Jonah shrugged. "Sure. Wouldn't you be?"

"I don't think so."

"Whatever."

"I'd be going to heaven. What's there to be scared of?"

"You really believe in all that, don't you?"

"You don't?"

Jonah grabbed the remote from the table between him and the other family and flipped through the channels. The other family looked at him in disbelief, but Jonah didn't pay them any mind. He found an old Western playing, John Wayne in *True Grit*.

"Nah," he said. "Just seems too good to be true."

An hour later, Caleb visited Papa for the last time. It wasn't anything like Caleb had expected. Tubes plugged Papa's nostrils. An IV was stuck in his arm, the tape stained red with blood. He hadn't shaved, and gray stubble spotted his chin and cheeks. His beard was sparse and thin like he was too weak to grow facial hair, the strands themselves infected with cancer. A machine beeped next to his bed. Beep. Pause. Pause. Pause. Beep. Pause. Pause. Pause. Caleb's heartbeat filled the pauses. He could feel it pounding in his ears.

"If you want to say goodbye," Mom said. "Now is the time."

Caleb tried to think of something to say—a reassurance, a prayer, a simple goodbye—but he couldn't bring himself to form the words. He couldn't bring himself to take a step closer. It took all he had to just look at Papa. He didn't appear to be in pain, which Caleb was thankful for, but he wasn't the same man. He was weaker. Debilitated. Strange. The light and fire that had once filled him had blinked out, and all that remained was a viscous shell. Papa wasn't there anymore to say goodbye to. He was already gone.

Finally, Caleb's mother told him he could go, and he breathed again. Jonah was asleep. The other family had gone home. The television had been muted. The place was quiet, the only sound the soft buzz of an ice machine at the end of the room. Caleb took a seat next to his brother and tried to sleep, but he couldn't. The sun would be up in a few hours, he'd have to go to school, and things would carry on like normal, but they weren't. The world was emptier somehow, a large balloon slowly leaking air.

THE DAY OF THE FUNERAL, the water was murky, thick with silt. A stiff breeze came over Bluestem Lake, carrying with it the stench of mud and smoke. The lake was abandoned this time of year. There weren't any boats or swimmers or wakeboarders. Nobody camped along the shoreline or grilled hamburgers next to the campgrounds.

It was cold—not quite freezing, but Caleb's nose wouldn't stop running, and he wiped the snot on his sleeve. His skin was dry, cracked, and burned. Mom carried the urn, but Grandma led the way. Dad, Jonah, and Caleb followed behind, taking careful steps over the warped boards of the dock.

On the other side of the lake, smoke billowed over the canopy. Caleb couldn't tell if it was controlled or if it was a forest fire. The smoke was thick and dark, too black to be a simple campfire. Some kids might've been setting off fireworks, maybe caught a dead oak with a Roman Candle. It had happened before. The previous summer, ten acres had burned before the fire department was able to get it under control. It was a ranch that had burned, the fields burnt brown, the ash swirling up into the sky and covering the hillside like a dense, thick fog. A couple of teenagers were found responsible, charged with arson, sent to juvenile hall. Mom had used the episode as a warning to Caleb and Jonah—if they ever did anything of the sort, the cops wouldn't get a chance to punish them. She'd bury them before anyone else could, and Caleb believed her. His mother never lied.

Caleb was surprised at how loud it was out there: the wind, the blackjack limbs rustling, the kickback of a pickup muffler, a doe and her fawn roaming through the underbrush. It was louder than the city even. Every once in a while, a hunter's rifle shot echoed over the canopy. Waves crashed against the shore. Everything seemed to accumulate into a cacophonous bubbling, humming against the backdrop.

Caleb found it odd it was just them saying goodbye to Papa. He'd been a well-liked man. Respected. It had been rare a neighbor wouldn't come visit when Caleb was at their home. They'd come by to borrow the table saw, to drop off a casserole, or just to share a pot of coffee, smoking cigarettes and swapping stories about the high-school football team or a mutual friend's big win at the casino over in Tishomingo. Caleb was sure this was his grandmother's and mother's decision, to keep this private, but it just seemed selfish.

At the end of the dock, they stopped and stood in a line overlooking the lake. The urn they'd chosen was simple. Made of cedar, it had no engravings, no stain. Mom held it tightly, pressed it against her belly as though she feared she might drop it. Or maybe she just wasn't ready to let go yet. Caleb wouldn't have been surprised either way—she had a look of disbelief about her. Seeing her cry affected Caleb more than he thought it would. His insides dissolved, and his lungs shrunk in size. He found it hard to breathe. He had to will his heart to continue beating. He had to beg his legs to keep from collapsing, and soon the world blurred and he felt dizzy.

Grandma took the urn and began her prayer. She thanked God for allowing her to know Papa. She thanked him for bringing him into her life when she'd needed him, for his strength and support over their twenty years of marriage. She said she would miss the way he brewed his coffee so strong it would make her tongue tingle, how he wouldn't wash his jeans until he wore them three times, and how he would save a rock every time they went on a road trip, down to Branson or Galveston, displaying it proudly on their mantel as the only keepsake they could afford. She prayed that he'd made it to him safely, and that he would continue to look down on her family during these troubled times. She then held the urn up to her face like she was kissing it and handed it to Caleb's father.

He didn't say anything. He just turned it in his hands, looking at it like he might be picking out produce at the supermarket, eying for imperfections. Bruises against the soft skin of a tomato, a yellow lemon turned brown. He then passed it to Jonah, who stared at it with more curiosity than anything, like it was some alien thing dropped down from a flying saucer. It then found its way to Caleb. His hands shook when he took it. He was holding his grandfather. The thought was almost too much for him to bear. A man he'd loved, a man he'd spoken to, a man who had frightened him, now reduced to a pile of ash. Caleb understood death. He did. The failure of the body, the ascension of the soul. Judgment. But before, it had always seemed like an abstraction. An idea. Now he could smell it, reeking of copper and fear.

Caleb opened the urn. Inside, the ashes were brown, packaged in a cellophane bag. It amazed him such a large man could fit in such a small place. To be reduced to ashes, it felt like a desecration. But Caleb hadn't been consulted. He hadn't been allowed to see Papa one more time after his passing, to remedy the shameful goodbye he'd had in the hospital. He'd just been told Papa was gone, and then he was handed this urn, expected to discard Papa into the lake he'd loved.

The bag was heavy, more so than Caleb had anticipated. The top opened by a zipper, and he paused before dumping the ashes. He thought he should say something, tell his Papa goodbye, that he loved him and would miss him and would pray for his soul, but nothing sounded right. It just sounded hollow and insincere, like it was something he was supposed to say rather than something that resonated in his bones. He did wish his grandfather well, he did, but he also felt the glaring absence of him, too. He'd left behind an emptiness, a gaping hole that had once been filled with granite and smoke. Even the sound of Papa's voice was starting to fade from Caleb's memory, even though he'd only been gone a few days, and this confused Caleb. But he was too afraid to ask his mother about it, and so he didn't say anything. He just turned the bag upside down. Most of the ashes landed in their destination, the murky waters of Bluestem Lake, but some of them had been captured by the wind, carried up and back, swooping and accelerating, like Papa was trying to return to the earth.

CHAPTER 3

CALEB'S MOTHER TOOK TO SLEEPING. USED TO, she'd wake before everyone else, and by the time Caleb pulled himself out of bed, she'd already have a pile of waffles cooked, coffee brewing, mopping the kitchen floor or watering the flower bed, the stream splashing against the windows. But after Papa's death all she did was sleep. Caleb would hear her alarm go off, shrill, short bursts of noise, followed by silence. After nine more minutes, it would go off again, and again she would turn it off. After the second or third time, the alarm would stop altogether, and Caleb would expect his mother to emerge from her bedroom, head wrapped in a wet towel, her bathrobe tied a bit too tightly, but she never did. When he went to wake her, she'd pull the blankets over her head and roll over to her side, and he'd grab a granola bar before running out to the school bus. Dirty dishes filled the sink. The milk spoiled. Unopened mail piled up on the dining room table. Dad worked later and later, not coming home until Jonah and Caleb were already in bed, and none of them did anything about it. It all just got pushed to the side, ignored as if it weren't growing into a problem.

On weekends Mom wouldn't get out of bed until after ten. Then she watched television: game shows and daytime soap operas. She blinked when Oprah gave away new cars, and she stifled a yawn as Judge Judy disparaged a deadbeat dad, flipping through the channels as soon as a commercial break interrupted whatever it was she was watching. After a lunch of cold ham sandwiches, she turned on the news. That's what she watched the most, the 24-hour news cycle, flipping back and forth between CNN and MSNBC and Fox News. She wrote notes in a spiral journal with a blue ball-point pen, always careful to keep whatever it was she scribbled away from him and Jonah.

At night she'd order takeout or pizza for dinner, tipping the delivery boy with a verse from Matthew rather than cash, then laughing about the kid's stunned face after she closed the door. She chewed with her mouth open and wiped her mouth with dirty towels. All they had to drink was tap water, and the ice machine had gone on the fritz. After dinner, she piled the empty boxes and bags around the trash can, circled by flies and stinking of hot garbage. The first week or so, Caleb and Jonah enjoyed the change in their mother. They stayed up later and put off homework, playing video games until they heard their father's car parking in the garage. They went days without brushing their teeth and wore the same jeans until they were crusted with mustard and the pockets lined with M&M shells. It was sort of like spending the night with a friend when their parents weren't home.

The only thing that remained constant from before was church. First Baptist was the second largest building in Bartlesville, the largest being the Frank Phillips tower. Red-bricked and white-steepled, it had a service hall the size of a basketball court, and its corridors ran deep with Sunday-school classrooms, a kitchen, gymnasium, the offices of the minister and church elders. Despite spending three evenings per week there, Caleb often found himself lost, exploring the snaking and confusing hallways, he and a few other children searching for something exciting, secret, taboo even. Once, they found some confiscated Black Cats, but other than that their searches wound up fruitless, resulting mostly in a disapproving glare from the minister. This didn't bother them, though—they were content being on the hunt, on the trail of some nameless, otherworldly thing.

Everything in it was big, too: the organ; the ornate pews; the giant, lifeless, crucified Christ upon the wall. The windows ran floor to ceiling, flooding the service hall with crisp sunlight. The nursery offered life-size dollhouses and plastic slides. Double ovens in the kitchen, a cemetery that brushed against the horizon. Even the people were big. The mayor worshiped there, the president of Phillips 66, Douglas Swenson of Swenson Chevrolet, even the elementary school principal, Mr. Owen. It was a place that towered over the city, casting its long shadow upon every street and hill, and it was a place Caleb loved. His earliest memories were set there, playing soccer out in the field with Jonah and Clifton and Russel and the rest, or rehearsing a nativity play at Christmas. He'd prayed there, worshiped there, had been baptized there. It was a second home to Caleb, wrapping around him like another skin.

Caleb's mother was a Sunday-school teacher in charge of about fifteen or so kids between the ages of seven and twelve, including Caleb and Jonah. They were kids Caleb knew well. Kids Caleb went to school with, played basketball against, shared slices of pizza at birthday parties with, and they all liked and respected Caleb's mother. They asked her questions about God, about Genesis, about Jesus and the resurrection. They even asked her stuff about home, a father who drank too much or a mother who gambled away the family's food money, about long division and late-night HBO specials, and Caleb couldn't have been prouder. His mother was an authority figure, a servant of God, and so was he—by extension.

"Revelation says the Seven Seals are only to be opened by the Lion of the tribe of Judah," Mom said.

The classroom, like everything else in the church, was large. Sharp morning light bounced across the room like it was covered in mirrors. There was a large poster of verses from Matthew and John, renditions of the Last Supper and the Sermon on the Mount. Behind his mother was a chalkboard where she'd scribbled a diagram of the Seven Seals and the description of the churches of Asia. Most of the lessons his mother taught, he'd heard repeatedly: the story of Noah, of Adam and Eve, of Lazarus, and of Moses and the Ten Commandments. She taught them about pride and sloth, about honoring their mother and father. Revelation, though, was a subject never before taught in Sunday school. He'd heard about it often at home, of course, almost daily even, but never had she broached the subject of the Seven Seals at Sunday school. Usually it was ignored both by the minister and by the other children's parents. Mom called it cowardice, the premeditated revision of God's word to placate the congregation's fear, and said she would have none of it anymore. Sooner or later these kids would be forced to learn the truth of the world.

"The First Seal opened by John the Lion will contain a white horse. 'And he that sat on him had a bow; and a crown was given unto him: and he went forth conquering, and to conquer.'"

Caleb's mother stood at the front of the classroom, the children sitting around her in a half-circle. They were much more attentive this morning than others. Most Sunday mornings they'd sit there with eyes like mirrors clouded by steam, their heads bobbing from sleep as they twirled their shoelaces. But that morning, after hearing the end of the world was coming soon, that the dead would rise, that a plague would ravage the earth, their wild-eyed gazes locked on Caleb's mother as she read from her bible. They were enthralled. They were quiet. They were, it was obvious, afraid.

"From the Second Seal will advance a red horse. 'And power was given to him that sat thereon to take peace from the earth, and that they should kill one another: and there was given unto him a great sword.'"

This might've been the first time the other kids had heard this sermon, but it was one Caleb had heard countless times, perched in bed, his mother sitting on the edge. It was one of his favorites, for his mother told him they were amongst the chosen, the 144,000 righteous and devout priest-kings who would rule with Christ over the restored paradise after the apocalypse.

"A black horse came from the Third Seal. 'And I heard a voice in the midst of the four beasts say, A measure of wheat for a denarius, and three measures of barley for a denarius; and see thou hurt not the oil and the wine.'"

Caleb's mother read from her personal bible, given to her by Papa. It was old, and it was large, bound by black leather, inscribed with golden print. Never did she allow Caleb to read from it. It was locked away in her room, and she only brought it out on special occasions: Good Friday, Easter, Thanksgiving, birthdays, and Christmas. In the margins were years of faded notes explicating certain passages, about what she'd seen and about what she expected.

"And from the Fourth Seal came the final horse, a pale horse. 'And his name that sat on him was Death, and hell followed with him. And power was given unto them over the fourth part of the earth, to kill with sword, and with hunger, and with death, and with the beasts of the earth.'"

Time was up, Sunday school over. Usually the kids would bounce from the floor, buzzing with energy to return home to play video games and basketball and ride their bikes, stalling with all of their might the sun setting on their weekend. But not that morning. Their faces looked bruised and jaundiced, as if all the blood swirling in their cheeks had drained to their feet. Caleb knew the look well. He'd felt it when his mother had first told him the story of the end of the world. They'd been accosted with the inevitability of their death and their judgment, and they feared that the accumulation of all their choices— their lies and their deceit, their theft and their destruction—might leave them unredeemed, estranged victims of the horseman Death.

The Gunters sat around the dining table eating Hamburger Helper. Caleb's father stuffed his face with bread, the corners of his mouth glistening with Blue Bonnet. The TV blared in the background. *Jeopardy!* was on, and Alex Trebek rapid-fired questions out to Mike Piazza, Donna D'Erico, and Johnny Gilbert, while Jonah blurted out wrong answers to all of them.

"William Faulkner set the name of this trilogy in fictional Yoknapatawpha County, Mississippi."

"What is the chicken pox trilogy?"

Caleb's mother was quiet, rubbing her temples with her fingertips, waiting nearly a full minute before spearing a single noodle with her fork. She didn't quite chew the food, instead mashing it with her tongue against the roof of her mouth. She was suffering from one of her headaches. Caleb could tell by the way she tried to move as little as possible, as if just lifting her hand rippled pain throughout every cell in her body. Now a few weeks since Papa's death, she'd been doing better the past couple of days. She still slept late, spent most of her time in front of the television watching the news, but she'd started to venture out of the house some, cook a meal or two a week, and started to read her bible more, which Caleb took to be a good thing. She still wasn't the same as she'd been before, still depressed his father said, but she was trying. That much Caleb was thankful for.

Mom sipped her coffee, the steam fogging her glasses, and told a story about earlier in the day when she'd been shopping at Homeland. Caleb listened intently like he always did when his mother spoke.

"She was a young mother," she said, her words even and slow, like she had to concentrate on each syllable she uttered lest one of them might break her. "Frizzy hair. Half-moon eyes. I know the look. She was exhausted, and her kid wouldn't be quiet. He hollered. He sang. He pulled boxes and bags off the shelves, and she was too tired to argue with him. She just cleaned up behind him. Didn't blame the woman. Felt sorry for her, in fact."

"This fictional character in Herman Melville's seminal work, *Moby Dick*, was obsessed with hunting and killing a sperm whale by the same name."

"Who is Pee-wee Herman?"

Dad buttered another piece of bread and jammed half of it into his mouth.

"The place was crowded, and the other customers shot her dirty looks. They mumbled underneath their breath. Another mother started yelling at her. Right there in the store."

"This American author went broke after hospitalizing his wife, Zelda, and famously asked his editor for a loan."

"Who is the Cookie Monster?"

Dad gulped down a glass of milk.

"She tells this poor girl how much of a failure she is, how her kid's a brat, how if she was the kid's mom, she would've busted his ass right then and there, and how if the mother didn't, she would have to."

"This American League slugger was the only player to hit a home run in four consecutive World Series."

"Who is—"

Dad muted the television. "Jonah," he said. "Knock it off."

"What?" Jonah feigned to be perplexed, a cheesy noodle stuck to his chin.

"The kid started crying. He screamed and balled up and reached for his mother, but they weren't within arm's reach, and so this woman grabs him and starts spanking the child."

"You know what. It's annoying," Dad said.

"Just playing the game." Jonah tined another noodle, but it slipped off his fork and landed on the carpet.

"So, what'd you do?" Caleb asked his mother.

"I did the Christianly thing. I took the kid from her. Gave the child back to his mother." Caleb's mom put her fork down, took off her glasses, and rubbed the bridge of her nose before continuing. "Then I paid for the young mother's groceries."

Dad put his fork down. "You did what?"

"I paid for the groceries. It was the least I could do."

"Jesus Christ, Evelyn."

"Don't say that," Caleb's mother said. "Do not—"

"How much were they?"

"—take the Lord's name in vain."

"Answer the question, Evelyn."

Caleb and Jonah stopped eating. A fight was coming. Caleb could feel it, the air gravid with static electricity.

"They weren't much." Mom returned to her plate, spearing a piece of venison and sticking it into her mouth.

"How much?"

"About a hundred."

"A hundred dollars?"

The doorbell rang, and Caleb jumped, dropped his fork. It banged against the wooden table and fell to the floor. When he reached down to get it, he could see his father's foot bouncing, like he was restraining himself from jumping up from his chair, doing something he might regret.

"Get the door, Jonah," his father said.

"Why do I have to—"

"Get it!"

Jonah did as he was told. Caleb couldn't see the door from where he was sitting, but he recognized the voice when Jonah opened the door. It was Minister Bly. At first, Caleb was confused. The minister had never made a house call before. He'd been a permanent fixture in Caleb's life, and he often saw Minister Bly around town attending parades or volunteering at the food bank. Once, Caleb ran into the minister at the mall while he shopped for jeans, and Caleb remembered thinking it was odd. Here was Minister Bly, the shepherd of the community's souls, doing something so ordinary, but having him in his house was even stranger. Minister Bly was a man of God. He shouldn't have time for the trivial.

"Minister," Mom said. "What a surprise. We just sat down for dinner. Are you hungry?"

"Please," he said as he came into view. "I don't want to be any trouble."

Jonah followed behind the minister, making faces as he did so, pulling his cheeks out with his fingers, turning cross-eyed, and goose-stepping. Dad, Caleb could tell, wanted to say something, but he didn't, not daring to call attention to his misbehaving son in front of the minister.

"It's no trouble at all. Really. I'll just make a small plate."

"Please, no. I couldn't."

But Mom headed to the kitchen anyway, scooping up a healthy portion of Hamburger Helper and slopping it onto a plastic plate.

"Minister Bly," Dad said. "To what do we owe the pleasure?"

Caleb couldn't help but notice his father didn't stand for the minister when he'd entered the room.

"I'm afraid my visit isn't a happy one," the minister said.

"Oh?" Mom said as she placed the minister's plate in front of him. "What would you like to drink?"

Minister Bly waved away Mom's question with a flick of his wrist. "There have been a number of complaints."

"Complaints?" Mom asked. "Is there any way we can help?"

"Well, yes," the minister said. "We've had a number of calls from concerned parents. About your last Sunday-school class."

"My Sunday-school class?"

"What'd you do, Evelyn?" Dad asked.

"You frightened a number of students, and, frankly, a number of their parents."

"What'd you do, Evelyn?" Dad asked again.

"Apparently, the kids are convinced the end of the world is coming," Minister Bly said.

"The children should be prepared," Mom said with a shrug. "They should be aware of Revelation. They should know what will happen to them if they don't repent."

"They're children, Evelyn."

"Children burn in hell, too, Minister. You of all people should know this."

Minister Bly folded his hands upon the table. They were soft hands, pale, unlike Caleb's father's. They weren't marred by thick callouses. Dried blood didn't coat the minister's cuticles. Pale scars didn't crisscross his knuckles. Caleb's father had once told him not to trust a man who didn't work with his hands, that a man who didn't work for himself wouldn't work for others, either. "Don't count on 'em," Caleb's dad had said. "They'll do nothing but disappoint you."

"For a time, I think it would be best if you didn't teach Sunday school. Let another parent take over for a few weeks. Let this whole thing blow over."

"Seems like an overreaction. Don't you think?"

Caleb's father's face turned the hue of ripe strawberries, a vein protruding from his forehead and pulsating up into his graying and receding hairline. Every day, his father looked older to Caleb, marching to the inevitability of old age, of decrepitude, of death.

"A few congregants have expressed they wouldn't return if you kept your position. I have to think of what is best for the congregation. I'm sure you understand."

"And you feel an unprepared congregation is for the best? You want your flock unrepentant upon the final judgment?"

"We don't preach hellfire and brimstone at our church, Mrs. Gunter. Revelation is more of a . . ." He waved his hand in the air, as if conjuring the right words. "A metaphor."

"A metaphor?"

"Yes, Mrs. Gunter. A metaphor."

She picked up her cup of coffee as if to take a drink, stared at the now-cool black liquid, then put it down, thinking better of it. "Sure," she said. "If you think that's best."

The next morning, Mom woke Caleb early. He rubbed the sleep from his eyes and checked the alarm clock next to his bed. 4:18. Much too early for breakfast or to do his chores. He had to mow the lawn that day, take out the trash, and sort through the recycling, but that would be much later, when the sun rose and his father headed to work. The early hour worried Caleb. Had something happened? To Grandma? To his father? To Jonah? Was there a fire burning the other side of their home, devouring in flames their family pictures, their television, their books? Memories of the last time his mother had woken him up in the middle of the night flooded him. The hospital. The late-night infomercials. Papa with tubes in his nose, in his arms, his last few moments on the earth spent in an induced coma so he couldn't feel the pain. But she didn't seem worried. She shook him harder and leaned in close. Her breath reeked of cigarette smoke and coffee, and she told him to get up, to follow her, and to not make a noise.

The house was dark. Caleb's father snored back in the master, his inhales troubled and difficult like he was gasping for breath after being submerged underwater. Sleep apnea, it was called. Caleb's mother had told him about it, that sometimes late at night his father would stop breathing altogether, and she had to lean over and place her hand on his chest to make sure he started back up again. A few months back, his father had gotten a mask to help him sleep, but he stopped wearing it shortly after. He'd said it was uncomfortable, that he'd rather take his chances.

Jonah's door was shut, the room quiet. He'd always been a deep sleeper, having on a couple of occasions dreamed straight through a late-night tornado. Caleb couldn't understand sleeping so soundly. When Caleb had been younger, he'd suffered from night terrors, dreams of creatures crawling on him, strangling him, wrapping their tentacles tight around his chest and neck, and so his parents moved him into Jonah's room thinking it would help. But it didn't. When Caleb startled awake, frightened and panicked, he'd try to wake his older brother so that he could comfort Caleb, tell him everything would be okay, but Jonah would never wake. He'd just sleep, his breaths so light Caleb feared he might be dead.

His mother led Caleb to the dining room table and turned on the lamp in the corner. The light it emitted was orange and soft, casting shadows against the walls. On the table was an ashtray, a dozen or so cigarette butts smashed and smoldering at the bottom. She motioned for him to sit. Sleep still clouded his thoughts. He had been dreaming when she'd gotten him out of bed. It was one of those dreams where he was running from something. He couldn't see it or hear it, but he knew it was something bad, something that wanted to hurt him, and it was getting closer. He was outside in the dream, someplace he didn't recognize. The terrain jagged from bluffs and stone, his path blocked by tall, spindly trees so that no matter how hard he ran, the thing chasing him just kept getting closer, and closer, and closer, and it was when it was about to wrap its fingers around his neck that his mother woke him.

"Sorry for the early hour," his mother said as she lit a cigarette, the cherry illuminating her face. "But it's about time you heard this." His mother picked a piece of stray tobacco from her tongue and flicked it to the carpet. "Things are not going to be easy for you and me. We're going to face trials and tribulations, and I have to know you're ready."

Caleb felt himself drifting back to sleep, his mind listless, incapable of differentiating between dream and reality. Whatever it was that was chasing him lurked somewhere, hiding, waiting for him.

His mother took a drag from her cigarette and exhaled the smoke in a long, billowing plume. "Your grandfather wasn't a normal man. I'm sure you were aware of this, even without me having to tell you. He was pious. Devout. A man of God. And that's why he could do things. Things other people couldn't do."

Caleb didn't know what it was chasing him, if it was beast or man. But he knew it was close, getting closer, the way he could sometimes feel a stranger staring at him from a distance, at the grocery store, or maybe at church, making his insides lose all sense of mass, turning liquid and then gaseous as if his body were a furnace. His Papa made him feel that way, too. Caleb could always feel him when he was near, and he was careful not to do anything to arouse Papa's anger. Perhaps that's what his mother meant. Papa had a way of always making his presence felt, agonizing Caleb with uneasiness until he couldn't sit still. He'd once made Caleb cry by telling him stories of working the rigs in Midland, claiming they were haunted by the ghosts of oilmen.

"The man could perform miracles," Caleb's mother continued. "He was a saint. He spoke directly with God, and God listened. A lot of people say their prayers are answered, but they're not. They ask for trivial, selfish things, for money, or for their favorite football team to win the Super Bowl, but God doesn't trouble himself with such things. If their team wins or they get a raise, they might credit God, but it's not. It's coincidence, dumb happenstance, sheer luck. Your grandfather was different, though. He understood Revelation was coming. He could feel the Seven Seals were going to be opened, and the Four Horsemen would be unleashed upon the earth, and so he asked God for a miracle."

"What did he ask for?" Caleb asked, his head still drowsy, fighting sleep.

"You."

She told him the story, of her and his father trying to have another child, of the miscarriage, of the kidney disease.

"My body was failing me. Doctors said I couldn't have any more children. I prayed and prayed and prayed, but still nothing."

She told Caleb about going to Papa, the night at the barn, how he'd laid her down and spoken the language of the Lord and prayed over her to bear a son, and it was there, she said, that an angel spoke to her. She was shrouded all in white, and she glowed and vibrated like she was made from sound rather than matter. She told Caleb's mother she'd be a vessel, and that Christ would be returning to the earth through her, and it was her son who would come for the righteous at the end of times to usher them into heaven.

"And the First Seal," she said, "has been broken."

"The white horse?" Caleb asked. "How do you know?"

"Minister Bly. You heard what he said. Calling the word of God a 'metaphor.' Your grandfather always said this would happen. The greatest trick the devil ever pulled was to convince people he didn't exist. 'Even him, whose coming is after the working of Satan with all power and signs and lying wonders, and with all deceivableness of unrighteousness in them that perish; because they received not the love of the truth, that they might be saved. And for this cause God shall send them strong delusion, that they should believe a lie.' It's all right here in the Book." She tapped her bible in front of her. "His word, son. His word."

She took another drag from her cigarette, holding the smoke in her lungs. The smell stung Caleb's nostrils and made his nose run. He kept sniffling so as not to drip snot down to his lip, but it didn't do any good. He could feel the wet, but he didn't dare get up to blow his nose or ask his mother to put her cigarette out. He just kept sniffling, and she kept talking, warning him about what was to come.

"Things are going to get tough," his mother continued as she exhaled a thick cloud of smoke. "Real tough. You're going to have to be ready. Can I count on you?"

"Yes."

"When it's time, will you be able to do what is asked of you?"

"Yes."

"Will you be able to face the devil and strike him down?"

"Yes, Mom."

She stood and stubbed her cigarette out.

"Good," she said. "For all the souls in the world are counting on you."

CHAPTER 4

CALEB AND HIS MOTHER BEGAN TO PREPARE. Spiritual inculcation, she called it. An education. An awakening of utmost vital importance for the entirety of the human race depended on them. Every day, they started before sunrise, before Jonah and Caleb's father woke, and took to reading Revelation, for "Blessed is he that readeth, and they that hear the words of this prophecy, and keep those things which are written therein: for the time is at hand."

Their focus most mornings was the Second Horseman, the red horseman, brandishing a sword to wreak anarchy and war upon the earth. He would come, Caleb's mother told him, soon. She wasn't sure how, or when, or in what form. He might come as an invading people, the call for martial law, the bombing of a building, or he might be as innocuous as a local brawl down at the Wolftrap, a bar that Caleb's father frequented. No matter how he came, though, they would have to be vigilant, unfearful, and brave. Neighbors would slaughter neighbors. They'd strike each other down with guns and with knives, even with their bare hands. It was not a time to be squeamish, she said, "for you will be faced with blood, and with gore, and with death."

"Will we have to fight?" Caleb asked.

"Yes. That's why you have to be prepared. What you will see will be like hell on earth. It may be slow at first. Things may not happen overnight. It may just be a simple act of aggression, but it will grow in intensity. It may be easy to miss. We will have to keep our eyes open, for when it comes, we will have to find someplace safe. We must keep safe the faithful to await the opening of the other Five Seals. There will be 144,000 of us, the chosen to be ushered into heaven, twelve tribes of 12,000 servants of God, and they will look to you for their salvation. I know it's a lot to ask of you, but I have faith in you. You have to be ready. The first thing you must do is ask for forgiveness for all of your sins."

"A confession?"

"Yes," she said. "A confession. Your soul must be washed clean of all transgressions against God."

They were back at the dining room table. It was dark out, but Caleb no longer felt out of place so early in the morning. The solitude didn't bother him. The quiet. It strengthened him now, as if the sleeping world fortified him against the devil himself.

"We're all sinners," his mother said. "Even you. Even Christ himself."

Caleb contemplated the Ten Commandments. Thou shalt have no other God before him. No graven images or likenesses. Thou shalt not take the Lord's name in vain. Remember the Sabbath. Honor thy mother and father. Thou shalt not kill. Thou shalt not commit adultery. Thou shalt not steal. Thou shalt not bear false witness. Thou shalt not covet.

He was, if he was honest with himself, guilty of several of these.

He'd prayed to God asking for selfish things, trivial things, things that later wracked him with guilt: a new baseball glove for Christmas, the Rawlings with the blonde leather that cracked when he caught the ball; he'd prayed to win the spelling bee so that he could stand up in front of the whole school with that trophy and be the last one standing; or, worse yet, he'd prayed for God to hurt Jonah, after he'd held Caleb down and tickled him until he peed his pants. That one he thought had even come true. Later, his brother was riding his bike, hit a crack in the pavement, and flew over the handlebars. When he popped back up, two of his teeth had been knocked out, blood gushing out onto his chin and shirt and hands.

He'd lied to his parents. He once told them he was going to Clifton's house, but instead he met up with Anthony and Margot and they shared a cigarette behind a house that was under construction down the street. He'd forged his parents' signatures on report cards when he didn't want his mother to see he'd gotten bad marks in science. Once, he'd even broken his father's antique duck call, this funny wooden thing that had been passed down through four generations, and blamed it on a neighbor kid because he hadn't been there to defend himself.

And he'd stolen. He'd stolen candy bars from the grocery store and money out of his mother's purse. He'd taken a baseball glove that wasn't his, left in the dugout after practice one day. It even had a name written on it in black Sharpie: Ankit. Yet he took it home and hid it underneath his bed, because he knew he wouldn't be able to play with it on the field—Ankit and everyone else would've known he'd taken it. Ankit's parents had called around, including the Gunter's house, asking if they'd seen it. Evelyn had asked Caleb, phone in hand, the cord dangling in a loose knot at her side, if he knew where it was at, and he'd lied. He said no, he hadn't, even though he knew exactly where it was, collecting dust. On several occasions, he'd felt enough guilt he'd gotten it out and thought about coming clean, but he feared the rebuke from his parents, the shame he'd feel when he would have to apologize to Ankit, tell him he was sorry and that he'd never do it again.

"Is that all?" his mother asked him.

Caleb nodded.

"I want you to think long and hard about this, Caleb. You have to be certain. And remember, I gave birth to you. I know you better than yourself."

"Yes," he said. "That's all."

"Don't lie to me, Caleb. I'm giving you another chance here."

"There's nothing else. I promise."

"The magazines, Caleb."

All the blood in Caleb's body rushed to his feet, to his face, to his fingertips.

"The magazines with the girls. I found them."

He'd found them in the garage, atop a refrigerator and stored in a box. There were dozens of them. The paper yellowed, edges tattered. The women in there were draped in scarves and lying in repose, legs enticingly spread, so that Caleb felt something he'd never felt before: lust. It had come at him in such a rush it surprised him, but he knew exactly what it was, and what he wanted to do with himself.

"You coveted those women, didn't you?"

Caleb didn't answer.

"Jesus never took a wife for a reason. That wasn't his purpose on this earth."

"I'm sorry."

"That's good. That's a good start. But it isn't enough."

Caleb's mother rose from the table and headed to the kitchen. When she returned, she carried a paint stirrer.

"Place your hands on the table."

Caleb hesitated.

"Do it, Caleb. God is watching."

Caleb placed his hands on the table, palms down. His mother raised the paint stirrer, and then brought it down upon Caleb's knuckles. The pain shot through his hand, up his arm, and into his neck. He flinched, but kept his hands in place. Again, his mother swung. Then again. And again. And again, until his flesh cracked and blood trickled in between his fingers. When she was done, he expected to feel different. Repentant. Conscience clear. Soul reborn. But he didn't. He felt the same, wracked with shame and guilt, coupled with an incensed throb coursing through his body.

For days they continued. He prayed. He atoned. He read scripture. They discussed the remaining Seals to be opened. The black horse would follow the red, and with the opening of the Third Seal, the meek and the poor would be stricken with famine while the wealthy and wicked would be enriched. They were besotted with greed and with lust, living their lives in sloth while the 144,000 would suffer with hunger.

"We will be tested then," his mother said. "Our faith will be tested. Our bodies will be tested. And the faithful will look to us to be their guides. We must remain strong. You must remain vigilant."

To prepare, his mother made him fast. He wasn't allowed to eat breakfast, lunch, or dinner, his mouth watering as he watched his father and brother wolf down meatloaf or waffles. The only sustenance Caleb was allowed was right before bed: a piece of dry, white bread and a glass of tepid water.

"You have to get your body used to functioning on few calories. This is important. Your very life and others will depend on it."

He lost weight. First, he noticed it in his face. His cheeks sunk in, and his flesh pulled taut against his bones. Then he noticed it in his torso and waist. His ribs protruded from his body, and he had to pull his belt in two notches tighter. He felt weaker and tired, though he couldn't sleep. Nausea kept him awake, acid burning his esophagus as his body ate itself from the inside out. When his father asked Caleb why he wasn't eating, he replied, "I'm not hungry," and left it at that. Caleb could tell his father was worried. He'd leave Caleb an extra plate in the fridge, but his mother would throw it away.

The fourth and final horseman, the white horse, would then come, and along with him, death. One-fourth of the earth's inhabitants would die, and it would be the finale of the war started by the Antichrist, who right then, Caleb's mother said, walked the earth. He walked the earth proud, and he walked the earth scornful, and he would leave behind him fields of bodies. They'd pile up on one another and be scourged with flies and maggots, and the living would become sick with the smell of death.

"You must get used to that smell. You must get used to the putrid, to the acrid, to flesh rotting."

His mother took him hunting on the weekends. She loaded up a couple of rifles in the back of the Bronco and headed west out to a friend's ranch. It was cold out, frigid actually. Despite the layers Caleb wore, he shivered. His skin cracked dry from the wind, and his joints ached and popped as he trekked through the underbrush. Soon, Caleb's hands went numb, and the rifle slipped in his grip. The cold caused cramps in his calves and thighs, and he feared he hadn't brought enough water. He just had a single canteen with him, and all he'd had to eat for weeks was bread.

He couldn't remember as harsh a winter. The previous summer, a drought had scorched most of the state. Farmers had entire crops wither away underneath the heat, turning brown, brittle, and worthless. The price of corn and soybean and wheat had skyrocketed as a result. The drought left a shortage of hay to keep cattle and hogs warm over winter, causing them to die by the hundreds, and the government was doing little in the way of subsidies to help out the farmers and ranchers. Caleb's mother, of course, called it a sign.

"The Third Seal will soon be broken. Famine and disease will follow. Mark my words."

Caleb had gone hunting before with his father, brother, and mother. Every year, they tried for three deer. The heads, his father stuffed and mounted on the walls of their home, if they were big enough, an eight point or higher. The meat, they froze and stored away in one-pound increments, some of it fileted, most of it ground. Some people, Caleb knew, didn't like venison. Either they thought it tasted gamey or had an aversion to eating a deer, as if it were the equivalent of grilling up a pet dog. Caleb enjoyed the taste, however. It was tough and chewy and salty, and he liked the way it felt to tear at a piece with his canines.

They took position atop a ridge. The gulley was long and deep, cut jagged with limestone boulders and overrun with Bluestem and Indian Grass. They sat against a couple of oak trees, rifles resting atop their laps. The wind was at their faces, so any deer moving up the ridge wouldn't catch their scent. It was peaceful out there. Quiet. It was hard to imagine the apocalypse was upon them. Caleb wondered if all of this would be awash with flame come the final war between heaven and hell, if all the trees and grass and animals would burn. It seemed unthinkable to Caleb. The world was so vast, so remote, that it almost seemed impossible it would all soon be gone. But it would. The ground would be gone and the trees would be gone, the sky would be gone and the moon would be gone, and all that would be left were the souls of all the people in the world, either anguishing in an eternity of hellfire or saved by his grace.

A doe appeared on the western end of the ridge, trotting along the edge of the tree line. It moved at a beleaguered pace, stopping at a tree, zigzagging left then right. It appeared to be wounded already, limping along the underbrush. Behind it about twenty yards approached a buck. It was young, its antlers stunted and sparse. It followed the doe intently, perhaps ready to mate with it, but kept its distance. Caleb raised his rifle and aimed down the barrel at the buck. He knew where to shoot, right behind the front shoulder so that he'd hit the heart or lungs. He clicked off the safety and moved his finger along the trigger, waiting for the buck to come to a stop so he'd have a clear shot, but before he did, his mother raised a hand.

"The doe," she said, which confused Caleb. He'd always been taught to kill the larger animal, which more often than not happened to be the buck.

"The buck has more meat," Caleb said.

"Have mercy on the suffering."

He raised his rifle again, this time centering the doe in his crosshairs. She stopped alongside a fir tree about sixty yards away, downward at about a thirty-degree angle. It was an easy shot for Caleb, and he took his time, breathing in, then out, in, then out, calming his heart rate, minimizing movement. He pulled the trigger. The buck darted north up the other side of the ridge. The doe dropped where it stood.

When they reached it, it was already dead, tongue hanging from its mouth, a splattering of blood staining the leaves. Caleb had been right—it had been wounded before. On its hind leg, an arrow stuck out of its thigh, the plastic having been broken in half, the remaining shard jutting into the flesh at an awkward angle. Some other hunter must've hit it earlier in the morning, but it had escaped without being hit with a fatal shot. Cruel fate, Caleb thought, to have lived a day perpetually stalked by predators.

Caleb pulled his hunting knife from his belt. It had been a gift from his father last Christmas, an eight-inch Kabar, the same knife Marines used. He plunged the blade into the sternum and cut down through the hide and membrane to the crotch. Once open, the smell hit him. It was warm and thick and dug deep inside of him, swimming through his nostrils and crawling down his esophagus. He thought he'd be nauseated, prone to vomiting, but he wasn't. Instead, he was filled with relief, and joy. Surprising joy. His body warmed, and the feeling returned to his fingers. It was like he could sense the doe's relief from her pain, entering a state of zero misery, forever comforted by the Lord. She thanked Caleb for this. He'd saved her, and brought an end to her suffering.

WHEN THE FIFTH SEAL OPENED, they would see under the altar

the souls of those who were slain for the word of God and for the testimony which they held. The faithful would be martyred. They would be dragged from their homes and their churches, beaten with whips and chains, stabbed and burned and stoned. There would be no mercy from the wicked. Of that much, Caleb's mother was sure. To prove her point, she taught Caleb about Polycarp, a bishop of Smyrna who was bound and burned at the stake; of Saint Pothinus, bishop of Lyon, murdered by Marcus Aurelius, the Roman Emperor, along with Alexander, Attalus, Espagathus, Maturus, and Sanctius, who were eaten by beasts in front of roaring crowds; and of Saint Euphemia, a Greek woman who refused to make sacrifices to Ares, struck down by a lion.

"Know their names," his mother told him. "Know their stories. They will become your flock's story. It will become my story. And it will become yours as well."

She told him a great earthquake would follow the opening of the Sixth Seal. "The sun will become black, and the heavenly stars will fall to the earth. A great wind will destroy the trees, and all the islands and continents will drift away from each other and out of place. And all the great men, the rich men, the wicked men, they will hide from you. This will be the time when you must be ready, for the great day of your wrath will come; and who shall be able to stand?"

And so, they proselytized. He skipped school, and they went to downtown Bartlesville, in front of Frank Phillips Tower where the rich oilmen worked, and preached the word and anger of the Lamb. They waited until lunchtime, when there would be the greatest amount of foot traffic. It was cold out, still a few weeks away from spring's thaw, and their lips chapped and their tongues dried. The men walked by in tight-fitting suits, all black or gray or blue, their shirts ironed stiff, their ties strangling their necks. Women clicked by in their high heels, faces painted, hair pulled back in tight buns. They all looked strained, concerned, riddled with anxiety, their minds polluted by the trappings of the everyday, by deadlines and mortgage payments, taxes and exhaustion.

When Caleb and his mother first started to preach, most simply ignored them. They rushed by with their purses or briefcases swinging by their sides. Some even threw change at their feet, quarters and nickels and dimes clanging against the pavement. The change piled there, untouched by Caleb and his mother. Occasionally, a passerby, one who didn't wear a suit, one who looked hungry and needed a shower and shave, would stoop to pick up the money, and Caleb and his mother would smile and encourage him to buy a sandwich, some hot coffee to warm his body. To amplify their voices, Caleb's mother brought megaphones, and they warned the men and women to repent, to confess their sins, to find Jesus and ask him to be their Savior, for the end was at hand, but no one listened. They were too busy with their lives to take a moment for their souls.

"Look at you," his mother belted out over the megaphone. "Look around you. Look how beholden you have become. Look how greedy you have become. Look how you slave for rich masters while you and your family struggle. You continue to serve them thinking you're doing good, but you're not. You're not doing good. You're serving a false master, for the only one who you should serve is Christ Lord."

Caleb listened mostly, learning from his mother. He learned her cadence and her demeanor, the way she domineered the makeshift stage. Her voice never wavered, never cracked or faltered. It was stern, resolute like rock.

"And for each second, minute, hour, day, week, and year you serve your false prophet, the one true God is watching. He is watching, and he is judging. His mercy is only reserved for the meek, for the faithful, for the truly repentant. If you do not repent, you will soon anguish in eternity in the depths of hell. You will be bound. You will be tortured. You will forever suffer for your sins."

A few would stop and listen. They'd be eating a ham sandwich and chips pulled from a brown paper bag, eying Caleb and his mother out of their periphery, leery yet intrigued. Caleb recognized many of them. Some of them were his friends' parents: Mrs. Rogers, Mr. Abernathy, Mrs. Caldwell, and Mr. Redcorn. Others attended church with them at First Baptist. He used to see them at service on Sundays, the men dressed the same in their suits, the women in more colorful sundresses, their teenage children in tow, dropping a few dollars into the collection plate for their tithe. He wondered if they were truly repentant, if they had confessed their sins or if they were actually spies for the devil, demons sent from hell to prepare for the end of times. His mother had told him they walked among them, posturing as human beings, living their lives like any normal man or woman but lying in wait, sending back reports to the rest of the fallen angels about where they were most vulnerable.

Caleb had nightmares about them. They started right after Papa had died, or at least Caleb thought that's when they'd started. It could have been much earlier than that, perhaps since birth. In his dreams, they stalked him. He was fleeing from them, and he was alone. He'd be in a strange place with a strange topography, full of rolling hills and fog, the light from the stars and moon brighter than he'd ever seen them before. Crooked, thin trees blocked his path, the limbs seemingly reaching out to him whenever he drew near. Strangest of all, though, was that instead of running, Caleb flew. He didn't have wings, but rather he floated, guided haphazardly by thought alone. Yet, he didn't have much control over it. It was like he was a sailboat amid a vast ocean, the mast having splintered in a storm, and now he wandered at the current's whim. He never did see the demons, but he knew them to be there, just out of reach, their grasp continually reaching, their fingertips grazing against his boot heel, and when they finally grabbed ahold of his ankle, he'd awake to a start, his heart threatening to burst from his chest.

He knew these dreams were omens, that he needed to stay vigilant. Lately, he could sense the demons. His skin tingled when they were around, sort of like a bat's echolocation, and he knew they were out there as he and his mother preached. One man in particular unnerved Caleb. He stood near the entrance to the skyscraper, the collar of his wool overcoat pulled high to shield his neck from the wind. He had a resolute face, dimpled chin covered in graphite stubble, and he stared at Caleb and his mother while he ate an apple. Though his eyes were soft, caring even, Caleb didn't trust him. He knew who Caleb and his mother were, and he was preparing the fallen for the final battle.

"And when the Seventh Seal is broken, there will be a great silence. The seven angels will appear with seven trumpets. An angel will stand at the altar, and the faithful will offer him incense so that he may mix the prayers of God's people. The smoke of the incense will rise up to God, and the angel will take the fire from the censer and cast it down upon the earth, unleashing lightning and thunder and earthquakes, and upon the screams of the wicked, the seven angels will sound their seven trumpets."

Eventually, a security guard came to confront them. He was short, rotund, constantly pulling on his belt to keep it around his protruding gut. Caleb recognized him from church. He was a quiet man, a good man, married with three children all younger than Caleb, and he told Caleb and his mother they needed to move on, that if they didn't, he'd be forced to call the cops. But Caleb's mother refused to listen. She continued to preach through the megaphone, becoming more urgent, her voice rising in a crescendo, and a crowd formed. A few stragglers stalling their way back to work turned into six, then ten, then a couple dozen, all watching as if a riot might erupt, features frozen in a state of shock, poised to flee if they had to. The security guard called for backup. Three more came, and again the security guard commanded that they leave, more forceful this time, hand near his belt. When Caleb's mother refused to stop, he grabbed her arm, but she jerked free. He nodded to the other security guards, and they descended upon Caleb and his mother. They knocked the megaphone from her hand, and his mother began to yell her sermon. Two of the guards grabbed her from behind and carried her, lifting her off the ground, dragging her away with her arms and legs thrashing, all the while screaming, "'And I heard a great voice out of the temple saying to the seven angels, Go your ways, and pour out the vials of the wrath of God upon the earth.' We are that wrath. My son is the wrath, and you shall repent."

CHAPTER 5

THE RUMORS SPREAD LIKE THE FLU. CALEB'S mother was crazy. She'd gone bat-shit. Cuckoo. Went off her meds or had brain damage or something. That was why she no longer taught Sunday school; that's why they no longer attended church; that's why they'd been downtown preaching Revelation like the end of times was coming as soon as next Tuesday. She'd brainwashed Caleb, started spouting off about the end of the world, that her son was the Second Coming of Christ, and the minister had to step in. Caleb could hear other students whispering about him in gym class, cracking jokes at his expense in the cafeteria. He got pelted with half-eaten grilled cheese sandwiches and snot-riddled napkins. Girls stuffed his desk with notes calling him names: retard and crazy and jackass. The teachers didn't do anything about it. They acted like they didn't see a thing when Greg tripped him in the hallway or Marcus hit his books out of his hands. They were, Caleb was convinced, complicit.

At first Caleb tried to ignore it. Turn the other cheek, he thought. Do not retaliate. Take it in the stomach no matter how much it hurt, no matter how much he wanted to tell them to just wait; hellfire was coming for them, an eternal damnation and torture they couldn't even comprehend. He fantasized about it even, how their smug faces would melt, how their cold hearts would be ripped from their chests, how demons would pull from them their limbs, over and over and over again until eternity, but he didn't. It would only make matters worse. They'd just ridicule him even more, chastise him and make him even more of a laughingstock. But it was difficult.

In first period about a week after the rumors had started, Ryan sprayed his pants with a water bottle, turned to the other kids, and announced Caleb had peed his pants. The entire class erupted in laughter, and Caleb burned in indignation. He looked to Mrs. Hall to do something, to say something, to admonish Ryan, to confiscate the water bottle, sign him up for detention, but she didn't. She just told Caleb to go to the bathroom, to use the hand dryers to clean himself up. As he walked out the door, the other kids laughed. They pointed. They called him Savior. "Oh, Savior," they said, "the Second Coming of Jesus Christ can't hold his bladder," and before he shut the door behind him, he could've sworn Mrs. Hall covered her mouth to stifle a laugh.

During lunch, the other kids cut him in line as he filled his plate with bread, the only thing he was allowed to eat. It was sloppy joe day. Waffle fries. Green beans. As always, the cafeteria smelled of grease and ketchup, echoed with laughter and the clacking of plastic food trays against linoleum. Normally, Caleb sat with his baseball teammates, Clifton, Garrett, Russell, and the rest. They'd talk about girls, Ken Griffey Jr., the new Easton C500 that had so much pop even Clifton had a shot at hitting a home run, but ever since the rumors had started, they'd shunned him. They told him to sit somewhere else. To not to talk to them. They couldn't be seen with him. So he sat by himself on a ledge near the staircase, two feet from the trashcan filled with upturned Styrofoam plates and a black liner caked with uneaten baked beans. Every time another kid went to throw something away, they'd flick a piece of trash in Caleb's direction until the ground around his feet was littered with empty milk cartons and mustard-stained forks.

He tried to let it go, to quell the anger and humiliation eating away at his stomach lining, and so he buried it deep down inside his body until it hardened and grew in mass like a tumor spreading from his small intestine to his colon. He wondered if this was the type of cancer that had killed his Papa, a mass of humiliation and hurt and angst that just grew until it made his organs shut down and his guts turn into a gelatinous sludge. It seemed likely to Caleb. He'd never known this type of pain before. These were the kids he'd been born alongside, had attended preschool with. It wasn't just emotional but physical as well, sandpapering its way throughout his body.

Last period was gym class. The boys changed in an old locker room, the tiles and grout long mildewed and smelling of sweat and unwashed shorts. That day they played dodgeball. Caleb had always enjoyed the game. Throwing those red rubber balls, ducking under-neath a toss, being the last person alive while his teammates cheered him on from the side of the gym. It was exhilarating. But not that day. That day, as soon as Coach Lyle blew the whistle, his teammates didn't run for the balls lined up in the middle of the court. Caleb took five or six strides before he realized this, the other team coming straight for him at a dead sprint, and then he stopped, alone, unprotected from the onslaught of his opponents. He got hit in the stomach, in the shoul-der, right in the face. Each pelt stung worse than the last, and after they'd thrown every last ball they had, Caleb skulked off over to the side and sat on the bench.

Every game went like that. The second. The third. His teammates selling him out to the slaughter. After the third game, Caleb tried to hide in the back, but the rest of his teammates just isolated him so that he was an easy victim. Afterward, he asked Coach Lyle if he could sit out the rest of the period.

"You want to fail gym class?" Coach asked.

"No, sir. I'm just saying—"

"It sounds like you're saying you want to fail gym class."

Caleb stayed in the games. Round after round he was pelted, until bruises formed on his shins and a black eye crawled down his cheek. He felt like crying, but he forced himself not to, choking back the tears from the shame and embarrassment. He didn't want to give them the satisfaction of knowing they'd gotten to him, that his will had been broken, that he would, if chastised long enough, recant his faith and beliefs and identity so that he could once again be a part of the group, and so he steeled himself up, took the shots to the face and to the stomach, let the mocking laughter of his peers soak into him like dirty dishwater.

Afterward, the boys were to shower. Caleb didn't want to. He only wanted to put on his clothes, run out of there before every other kid could, and climb onto the bus for the ride home, enjoy a few hours of reprieve before having to go to sleep and repeat the same day over and over until the end of the school year, but Coach wouldn't let him. If he didn't shower, he'd get detention, and so he stripped off his clothes, grabbed his soap, and headed for the first available showerhead.

He didn't even wait for the water to get warm. He lathered up, poured shampoo over his head, and was rinsing when it happened: a push. He fell forward against the tiled wall, his forehead cracking against it. He slipped a little, hands grabbed him from behind and pulled him backward. When he landed, his shoulders and the back of his skull hit so hard, pain rocketed up his neck and throbbed in his ears. Soap covered his face, so he couldn't see his attacker, but he could hear him. It was Sammie, a large Cherokee boy with cue balls for cheekbones and arms so long he could nearly touch the rim when he tried to dunk. He was just as tall as Caleb's dad and already had the shadow of a mustache above his upper lip.

"You think you're something special?" he asked.

Caleb knew better than to say anything, but he wanted to. He wanted to scream, he wanted to punch, he wanted to call on the wrath of God and banish him to hell, but he held it back, braced for what he knew was to come.

"Huh?" Sammie kicked him in the ribs. "You think you're better than us? You think you're a saint?" Caleb tried to block the assault with his arms, but he wasn't quick enough. As the kicks kept coming, Caleb swore he felt the bone inside his chest snap in two. "Get up, fucker. Get up, Jesus."

The other kids laughed.

Caleb jumped to his feet, fists balled to his sides, but he didn't know how to use them. He'd never been in a fight, never had to defend himself. It was an unfamiliar situation, and the words of his mother echoed inside his skull: turn the other cheek, but don't you ever become a victim.

"Oh, so you think you're tough, huh?"

Six kids circled him, Sammie, the biggest, in the middle. Caleb's teammates beside Sammie. "Hit him," they said. "See if he bleeds. Hold him down and see if he can walk on water." A rage built up inside Caleb. His skin vibrated. He tasted copper. He could feel the blood slam against his fingertips.

Caleb swung.

He connected with Sammie's jaw. Solid contact. Sammie's face turned to shock. Eyes wide. Jaw dropped. A slight bruise appeared on his chin, but he didn't go down. He just screamed. He balled his fists, and all Caleb could do was cover his face with his arms. The blows came from all over. Two fists. Three. Four. They hit the back of his head and his neck. His ribs. His stomach. All the air Caleb thought he owned escaped him in one, quick gasp, and they didn't stop until Caleb hit the ground, where it took all he had just to wheeze.

Caleb hobbled home and told his mother what had happened. Evelyn prayed and drove him to the same hospital his Papa had died in. When they walked into the emergency room, he was stricken with fear he was going to die. He knew it to be irrational—he was bleeding, but not badly. Mostly, it had dried up and coagulated into a soft scab on the side of his face. He touched it with his fingertips, but it hurt too bad to explore it. The doctor who saw him was young and nice. He had a short, well-manicured beard and smelled of hand sanitizer. He spoke like he was telling Caleb an inside joke, leaning forward, asking him with a sly grin what the other guy looked like. In all, Caleb had to have six stitches above his right eye, and they put a lead blanket over him and X-rayed his legs and arms and ribs, but the images came back negative. No broken bones, no hemorrhaging, just deep bruises the color of overripe plums. The doctor and nurses were nice to him, and they asked Caleb's mother if she'd like to call the police, to press charges against the other boys, but she declined. "God will take care of them," she said, and Caleb had no reason not to believe her.

The next day, the taunts lessened. Caleb wore a sling on his left arm, and he had a bandage above his eye. Kids and teachers alike avoided him altogether, not calling on him to answer questions in social studies class, not making eye contact while in the lunch line getting their tater tots and hamburgers. Coach Lyle allowed him to read a book in the gym's rafters instead of playing kickball with the other kids, all of them perhaps thinking that if they just ignored the problem, let Caleb's cuts scar over and his bruises fade to a soft, pea-green color, that it would go away on its own, that what they did hadn't really happened at all but rather was just a bad dream, a hiccup in a normal week, but that wasn't the case. After school, the principal wanted to see Caleb's parents, and so Caleb remained out in the hallway outside his office after school. It was quiet. All of the children had gone home to do their homework, eat dinner, do their chores, and play video games. The teachers were probably grading papers or walking their dogs, maybe catching a drink down at Chili's, chatting up a former student about what she was doing with her life. Caleb always felt weird when he saw a teacher outside of school. It was like seeing an animal out in the wild, a deer or mountain lion, not confined to a cage in a zoo.

Caleb had never seen the school so empty. There wasn't anybody there to berate him, to tease him, to throw crumpled pieces of paper at him. There was no one to laugh at him, call him the Savior, asking him in a mocking manner to pray for them and to save their souls. Instead, it was quiet. It was peaceful. It was like he could hear every noise echo against the cinderblock walls. Somewhere around the corner, wheels squeaked against the linoleum floor, followed by rhythmic, quick foot-steps. He wondered who the person might be, if it was a teacher or a janitor, someone he knew, someone he could still trust.

"You told him that? You told Caleb he is Jesus Christ?" Caleb's father's voice boomed from inside the principal's office. Caleb couldn't see him, of course, but he knew the expression he wore on his face, full of incredulity, full of shame. He'd never been a believer like Caleb and his mother. He went to church, sure, but there was always a soft monotony to his voice when he prayed, so that even Caleb knew it wasn't genuine.

"This isn't a conversation we should be having here," Caleb's mother said.

"Mrs. Gunter," Mr. Owen, the principal, said, "you and your son are telling everyone the end of the world is coming and that you and Caleb are to usher them into heaven. The other parents, they are worried. And rightfully so. Especially after what happened at the church and the disturbance downtown."

Caleb had always liked Mr. Owen. Usually a quiet man, he often had bits of his lunch left in his mustache. Potato chips, mostly. Plain, salted, greasy. The occasional breadcrumb from a turkey sandwich. Never did he raise his voice or talk down to a student. He treated them like he treated his teachers, with respect. It had made Caleb always feel like an adult around him, the only time he ever felt that way other than when he was with his mother.

"I can't even believe this," Caleb's father said. "How am I going to be able to show my face anymore? How am I going to be able to go to work? Face our neighbors? Our friends? They're all going to think we're crazy."

"Maybe you should stop worrying about what others think of you. You don't have to answer their questions. You don't have to be ashamed."

"You're going to have to answer some questions, Evelyn. That's for goddamn sure."

Caleb had heard his parents argue before. They'd fought over pedestrian things: the mortgage payment, the credit card bill, his and Jonah's eating habits, the friends they were hanging out with, voicemails left on their answering machine Caleb didn't understand. But never had it been this bad. Never had their tones been so accusatory. So pointed.

"I think it would be best if we all just calmed down a bit," Mr. Owen said.

"Please," Caleb's mom said, "do not take the Lord's name in vain."

"Oh? You mean our son? Is Caleb going to come in here and smite me, Evelyn? Is he going to damn me to hell?"

"Don't be melodramatic, Earl. It's not a good look on you."

"I can't even believe this is happening."

"What exactly is happening?" Caleb's mother asked. "I still don't quite understand what we're being accused of."

"You're not being accused of anything," Mr. Owen said. "We're just trying to find out what is going on. That's all."

"Okay, sure. How can I help?"

"Yes. Fine. Please, enlighten us, Evelyn. Where did Caleb get this idea?"

"What idea?"

"My god, Evelyn. Don't act dumb. Ever since your stepfather died, you've been acting crazier and crazier, and now you're telling people our son is Jesus Christ. What isn't there to understand?"

Caleb wanted to sink into his chair. Grow smaller until he was as tiny as a molecule, slip into a crack in the floor and disappear forever.

"What I want to know is why we're here but the kids who assault-ed our son are not," Caleb's mom said. "Why is Caleb being punished when they are not? Why aren't their parents being questioned? Ac-cused of something? I know who they are. I've known them for years. Even have their phone numbers if you don't. Why aren't they here, Mr. Owen? That is the question that needs to be answered."

"We will be talking to their parents as well, Mrs. Gunter. We'll get to the bottom of all of this, I can assure you."

"Assured I am not."

" 'Assured I am not?' Who talks like that, Evelyn? Are you Yoda now? Do you not hear just how bat-shit crazy you sound?"

"I think everyone just needs to calm down," Mr. Owen said.

"Calm down? Calm down?"

"Why don't we call Caleb in here?" Evelyn said.

"Sure! Fine! Grand!"

"Earl, you're causing a scene."

"Shut up, Evelyn."

"I don't think that's a good idea," Mr. Owen said. "Not until every-one agrees to calm down."

The door opened. Caleb's mother stood there with eyes that told him to get up, and Caleb felt he was on one of those amusement-park rides that used centrifugal force to pin him against the wall, spinning around and around and around right before the floor gave way be-neath him. His vision narrowed. He had the sudden urge to run. But he had no idea where. Home? To the bus station? Hitch a ride south to Tulsa, find some place safe where he could start anew? A church or fire station. God, he wanted to, but he knew he didn't have that type of courage.

"Caleb," his mother said. "will you join us?"

It was the first time Caleb had ever been inside the principal's office. He'd always imagined it a mysterious place, a bunker in which Mr. Owen hid, pulling levers and ropes like the Wizard of Oz, controlling the mechanisms of the school through some intricate contraption Caleb could never understand. Instead, though, it was bland. Simple upholstered chairs. Plain, gray carpet. Undecorated cinderblock walls. Pictures of the principal's wife, of a pet lizard, of a ranch at dusk awash in orange and purple light. The fluorescent bulbs buzzing overhead gave the place a hospital-like quality, and all of a sudden Caleb felt like he was visiting Papa again, wheezing upon his deathbed.

Mr. Owen looked uncomfortable. He sat behind his desk with his palms on the table, hunched forward. He had the look of someone about to deliver bad news. "First of all," Mr. Owen said to Caleb, "I want you to know you're not in trouble. Do you understand that?"

Caleb's parents stared at him, his father with a laser focus Caleb had grown accustomed to when he'd scuffed a wall in the house or broken a chair while mimicking the wrestlers he'd seen on TV. Caleb's mother, on the other hand, seemed to be trying to say something to him without actually uttering a word—she looked like a spy, signaling from across the room that he was in danger.

"Can you tell us where you got the idea that you're Jesus Christ?" Mr. Owen asked.

Caleb didn't know what he was expected to say. Should he lie? Should he tell the truth? For one, he didn't believe Mr. Owen. Whatever he said, he was sure he was going to be in trouble. If he told the truth, his father would be angry at his mother. His mother would be mad at him. If he lied, Mr. Owen would be angry, and he was sure he'd get detention, or, worse yet, suspended.

"I didn't say I was. The other kids did."

"So where did the other kids hear it?"

Caleb shrugged.

"You don't know?"

Shrugged again.

"There's no right or wrong answer here. We just want the truth. That's all."

"And I won't get in trouble?"

"Just answer the goddamn question, son," Caleb's father said.

Mr. Owen raised his hand to quiet Caleb's father and peered down at Caleb with the softest gaze Caleb had ever seen. "I promise. You won't be in any trouble," he said. Though Caleb didn't believe him, he wanted to. He did, and so he did the only thing he could think of. He pointed at his mother.

Later, on the drive home, everyone was quiet. His father driving the Bronco, his mother in the passenger seat, smoking. Caleb sat in the back, his school stuff on the seat next to him. When he got home, he'd do his English and math homework, learning vocabulary words like "sever" and "oasis," solving for x in simple algebraic expressions. When they parked in the garage at home, Caleb's mother opened the door and got out, and Caleb followed, his backpack perched high on his shoulders, his chin buried in his chest. Before Caleb made it into the house, however, his mother grabbed him by the shirt.

"Don't you ever," she said, "do that to me again."

THINGS TURNED COLD AFTER THAT. Not physically. Outside, it

started to warm. A little anyway. Spring thunderstorms hadn't quite started yet, nor the humidity, the landscape still brown and brittle, trees not yet bloomed, but the temperatures were slowly rising, promising the beginning of spring. When not in school, kids stayed inside to play video games, and if they did venture outside, it was to play pickup games of football, their winter coats serving as their pads. Except for Caleb. He was no longer invited to play with his neighbors. They didn't invite him to ride bikes or head up to Braum's for a milkshake. Instead, they acted like he didn't exist, avoiding eye contact if they happened to see him outside helping his mother unclog the gutters of fallen leaves. They'd ride on by, quiet as if in church, acting like they didn't even know him, and then, as soon as they thought they were out of earshot, they'd start laughing, their demeanor changing quickly, like spring's first thaw after winter.

Despite this, Caleb tried to return to normalcy. Once his wounds healed some, he went to Clifton's house to see if he wanted to play *Mike Tyson's Punch Out!!* or maybe go rent *Nightmare on Elm Street*, but when Clifton's mother answered, she told him Clifton wasn't able to play. Same with Garrett. Same with Russell. Same with Ankit. No one was allowed to see him. At first Caleb tried to rationalize it. It was an anomaly—all of the kids just had prior engagements, dinner with family members, a trip to the movies, a punishment for some unnamed crime. But then it continued to happen. The next day and the next day and the next. A pattern formed. When he rang the doorbell, a parent peeked through the curtains or blinds to the front porch, and when they noticed it was Caleb, they told him the same story: their child was busy. Every single time Caleb asked if one of his friends could come out, they were inexplicably unavailable.

He still saw them, though. He saw them at school, of course, and although the taunting and beatings had stopped after their meeting with Mr. Owen, Caleb continued to be marginalized. He couldn't eat at their lunch table or join their reading groups, and he was the last to be picked for teams in gym class. At home he thought it might be different. He could play with them one at a time, away from the judgmental aspersions cast by the mob that was elementary school. But it wasn't. He'd look out his window to find Garrett and Russell riding past on their bikes twenty minutes after he'd been told they had chores to do, and, excited, Caleb would grab his bike out of the garage and pedal after them. When he caught up with them, though, they told him they weren't allowed to hang out with him anymore, and that they didn't want to anyway.

"Their parents won't let them play with you," Jonah said when Caleb asked his older brother. He was playing *Legend of Zelda* on their Nintendo. Jonah had declined when Caleb asked if they could play a multi-player game like *Double Dribble* or *Super Mario Brothers 3*, and so he sat there watching his brother navigate his way through the digital world, the screen reflecting in his brother's glasses.

"But why?"

"You don't know?"

Caleb did know. He just couldn't bring himself to say it aloud. He and his family hadn't really talked about it after the meeting in Mr. Owen's office, instead letting it fester until the whole subject turned sour, their mother and father ignoring each other, even so far as going into the other room when the other entered. Jonah just seemed angry all the time. Angry at their mother, at their father, and especially at Caleb. Before, it hadn't been like they were best friends, but at least he acknowledged Caleb. He'd pick on Caleb mostly, smacking him in the back of the head when he was eating his dinner or crumpling up his homework into a folded, crinkled mess. Other times he was nice. He'd invite him to play a pickup game of basketball if they needed one more player or take him out to shoot off some extra Black Cats after July 4th, but now he just glared at Caleb. He glared at him in the morning before school, as soon as they got home afterward, or when they were forced to do their chores together, taking out the trash or folding the laundry. He hated Caleb, couldn't stand his very presence, and Caleb had to admit this hurt even worse than the kids at school taunting him or beating him up—Jonah was his older brother, after all.

"I don't understand, though. They all go to church. They believe in the Bible."

"You're not this stupid, Caleb. Think about it."

"They believe in good and evil and sin and prayer."

"That's not the point, Caleb, and you know it. Just say it."

"They believe in heaven and hell. They believe in God."

"Believing in God is one thing. Believing the Second Coming of Jesus Christ is the neighbor kid is something totally different."

"But you believe it. Don't you?"

Jonah didn't answer. He maneuvered Link into a cave where a couple of blinking goblins waited for him. They shot orbs of light at Link, but Jonah was able to dodge them, get into position, and stab them to death with his sword.

"Answer me, Jonah. You believe Mom, don't you?"

"I'm trying to play a game here."

"I'm serious, Jonah."

"I am, too. Just drop it, okay?"

Caleb reached for the controller, but Jonah was too quick for him. He jerked the controller out of the way, paused the game, and pushed Caleb over in one swift movement.

"What the hell's your problem?" Jonah stood over him, and though he was only a few years older than Caleb, for the first time in his life, Jonah looked like a grown man, towering over his brother. "You want to know the truth? Do you? You really want to know?"

"Yes," Caleb said. "Yes."

"Mom's crazy!" Jonah sat back down and un-paused his game, and he navigated Link to the back of the cave where he opened a treasure chest that yielded a shiny, golden shield. "And you're crazy too, if you believe her."

CHAPTER 6

FOR A WHILE, CALEB'S FATHER TRIED TO GET things to return to normal. He took Jonah and Caleb to get donuts before school on Tuesday and Thursday mornings, saved a little cash during the weekday by bringing his lunch from home so that he could take the family out to the movies on Saturday night, careful to keep his head high and his eyes straight ahead so as to avoid the sideways glances from their neighbors, coworkers, and fellow members of their congregation. It was difficult, though. Caleb could feel them crawling all over him like ants, itching around the hemline of his shirt as he waited in line for popcorn, and he was thankful when the lights dimmed and the previews started so he could sink low into his chair and return to the relief of anonymity. On Sundays his father had them attend church again, finding a place in the back, near the aisle just in case they needed to leave in a hurry. But it wasn't the same. Even Caleb could tell that much. The air in the church felt different. It was heavier. It vibrated. It was like walking underwater, Caleb having to will his legs to move forward amid the leering gazes and whispers when he and his family entered.

It wasn't like they hadn't expected it. "Keep your heads held high," his mother had told them before they exited their car. "Remember, they can't judge you. Only God can."

Jonah had rolled his eyes.

His father had no reaction.

But once inside, their reactions were hard to miss. Jonah kept his eyes on the floor, dragging along his feet, hands stuffed into his pockets. His father turned the color of a stop sign, his brow beaded in sweat, a vein protruding from his forehead in some mixture of shame and anger. But his mother looked proud. She smiled a smile that comes only when a person knows something others don't, awash in certitude and strength. Caleb found hope in this. He found courage, and so he tried to do the same, making eye contact with the very people who judged them and shunned them and called them crazy behind their backs. He wanted them to see the still-healing black eye that their sons had caused, the way he still walked with a limp from their kicks when he was helpless on the ground. He wanted them to see what they had done and have to face their own failings and transgressions. He felt bad about this impulse—for judge not lest ye be judged—but he couldn't help but garner a little pleasure from it as well.

It wasn't long after they found a seat near the back that Minister Bly took the pulpit. A small man, Caleb had known him his entire life. He'd baptized Caleb. He'd counseled Caleb. He'd attended birthday parties and basketball games and school functions. He was ever-present, there during Caleb's triumphs and during his failures, commending him and consoling him like his own father, his own mother. Caleb had even grown to love Minister Bly over the years. He'd been a mainstay his entire life, but he now knew this to have been a ruse. The man was a pawn of the devil, purveying the false and wicked teachings of the Antichrist, claiming Revelation to be a mere metaphor, not the direct and incontrovertible teachings of the Lord, and if he were not to repent, he'd spend eternity in hell.

"I want to thank all of you for showing up this morning," Minister Bly began. "I know you lead busy lives. Fulfilling lives. Stressful lives. It's no small thing to come here every Sunday, during some of the only free time you may have available. This very act shows your devotion to God and to your community. And that's important. It is."

Minister Bly was a quiet man by nature, soft-spoken and gentle. He seemed to touch everything with only his fingertips. The pages of his sermon, the Bible, even an ice cream cone enjoyed in the church's gymnasium, cheering on a volleyball match after service, and Caleb had always felt comforted by this, like he was wrapped in a warm blanket, his cheek resting against its soft cotton.

"That's really what I want to focus on this morning: community. It's a strange word, isn't it? Community. It could mean any number of things, really. It could mean the physical neighborhood in which you live. The square grid mile of houses. The kids who play together, and the parents who raise them. It could mean a group of people who are committed to a common endeavor: a workplace, say, or even a book club. And then there is, of course, the church community."

Several of the other congregants nodded their heads—the women mostly, their hair coiffed and sprayed into place. The men stared straight ahead, heads slightly tilted upwards, eying the world down their long noses. It was weird for Caleb, not being able to see their faces, their expressions. Being in the back of the church, he could only guess, but he imagined they carried expressions of affirmation, dutifully accepting all that their minister told them, just like a congregation should.

"As you're all aware, I'm sure, communities often come with peculiar characteristics. They don't form through happenstance. They are molded. Groomed. Selected and excised through constant and immaculate precision. Not by just one person either, but by the entire group. Their collective choices form the community, bind it together, keep it strong and healthy."

The children, on the other hand, seemed to be in their own little worlds. They drummed on the pews in front of them or twirled their hair in their fingers, popping gum and yawning audibly. It wasn't that they weren't hearing what the minister was preaching; it was just that they were incapable of holding only one thing in their heads at a time. It had to be full, jumping and rolling and plodding along in a jumbled and chaotic mess.

"Community is something to protect. It's precious. Valuable. Immensely so. You have to fight for it. Love it. Cherish it. And when something comes along that threatens that community," the minister said, motioning in the air like he wielded an imaginary knife, "you have to cut it out."

He didn't make eye contact with Caleb and his family, but Caleb was aware he was talking about them. Everyone was: the women with their hair, the men with their long gazes, even the children, their minds torn between the cherished lyrics of their favorite song and their spiritual leader, telling them to estrange one of their own.

"We don't do this with carelessness or capriciousness. No, it is with grave forethought we have to make this choice. It is with compassion and empathy we make this choice, because think about it—we could take the approach to be more accepting of their behavior. Turn the other cheek. Write their behavior off as eccentric and politely discuss our differing views. But what does that accomplish?"

Minister Bly paused to have the congregation answer him, and a few did, shouting out that they'd be condoning sin, blasphemy, heresy, and Minister Bly nodded and pointed and smiled.

"Yes," he said. "Yes. We'd be condoning it. Encouraging it. Normalizing it. And we can't have that, can we? We are to shepherd people to the light, not excuse sacrilege. We are to save souls, not accept the workings of evil."

Caleb's mother stood. As soon as she did, Caleb's father reached for her hand, but she pulled it away. She didn't say anything. She stood on her tiptoes like she wished to propel herself up into the air, and she shook. She shook with anger. She shook with hatred. She shook with all the might God granted her, and the minister stopped his sermon. He looked right at her, and soon the congregation followed suit, turning in their pews to find Evelyn Gunter standing near the back.

"'I know your reputation as a live and active church, but you are dead. Now wake up. Strengthen what little remains, for even what is left is at the point of death. Your deeds are far from right in the sight of God. Go back to what you heard and believed at first; hold to it firmly and turn to me again. Unless you do, I will come suddenly upon you, unexpected as a thief, and punish you.'"

Caleb knew the quote. It was from Revelation Chapter 3. He'd learned it well over the past few weeks, studied it, contemplated it, and when Caleb's mother was finished speaking, she grabbed Caleb's hand and motioned for his father and brother to follow them. They didn't rise at first, instead sitting there, Jonah's head buried in his chest, Caleb's father trembling. But she didn't wait for them. She pulled Caleb out into the aisle, the church quiet as if all members of the congregation held their collective breath, waiting for what was to come next, and Caleb and his mother strode out into the bright morning sunlight, the heavy wooden doors shutting quietly behind them.

AT HOME, CUPS WERE THROWN. Cupboards slammed. Butter knives pointed. Accusations slung. Caleb's parents had never been a loving couple. They'd never held hands in public or called each other pet names such as Honey or Dear. They'd always addressed each other by their first names, Evelyn and Earl, as if they were business associates rather than husband and wife. That wasn't to say they were cold to each other either. They often did small things for the other, Evelyn sometimes picking up a six-pack of Earl's favorite beer when she knew he'd had a stressful week at work, or Earl might out of the blue get Evelyn a bible, screen-printed with her name. There was love. There were disagreements. Sometimes, they fought.

This, however, was different.

This was something guttural.

This was full of rage.

Caleb watched his parents through a crack in his bedroom door. Their movements were erratic and quick. They jerked and spasmed, spittle flying from their mouths as they accused one another of ruining their lives, brainwashing their children, sabotaging everything they had worked so hard to build.

"You've ostracized us, Evelyn. You see that, don't you? We're no longer welcome at church. At work I'm treated like a leper. People cross the street when they see us out in public. Our kids don't have friends anymore. They're bullied and beaten. Do you not realize this? Do you not see what you've done?"

They stood in the kitchen, his father's chest heaving, his mother's hands waving. His dad still wore an Oxford shirt and khakis, what he'd worn to church week in and week out for as long as Caleb could remember, the only difference being his shirts were getting tighter, his hair growing thinner. In the past six weeks, it was like his father had aged six years. He now seemed ancient. He seemed like a grandfather. His mother, on the other hand, busied herself. Usually, she spent Sundays preparing for the week, making lunches for Caleb and Jonah, prepping their lesson plans for school, outlining bible studies to prepare for the end of the world. At that moment, she made peanut butter and jelly sandwiches for Caleb, one of his favorites even though he felt he was getting too old to enjoy them, and she scooped a dollop of creamy Jif onto a butter knife like she was using it as a weapon. Every time Caleb's father tried to make a point, she'd sling the peanut butter across the room in the direction of her husband.

It was the first time Caleb had ever seen his parents argue like this, and it made him feel heavy, bloated, like he'd eaten to the point his stomach might burst. He felt the air weigh down upon him like a thousand pounds of water. He could feel himself choking. He could feel all his organs collapsing in on themselves.

"You've always been too concerned with what others think of you," Caleb's mother said. "The only one who can judge us is God, Earl. God. Not man. And this is a family of God."

"You're nuts. You are. You need to go see somebody. A shrink. A doctor. Hell, a chiropractor. Whatever. I don't care."

"You're tearing this family apart. You've brought blasphemy and sin into this house. You've turned Jonah into a skeptic, and don't even act like I haven't seen it. He is turning his back on God. You've put his soul in jeopardy. You need to pray. That's what you need to do."

"Oh god, Evelyn. Do you really think any of this is my fault?"

"If you turn your back on God, he will turn his back on you."

"Are you even listening to yourself anymore?"

"I will not tolerate wickedness in this house. Do you understand me?"

Caleb's father screamed. Head thrown back, body convulsing. It was something animalistic, out of his control, birthed from rage and frustration and shame. He jumped up and down. He grabbed a drawer and ripped it from the cabinetry, spoons and forks slinging across the kitchen. Afterward he stood there with the drawer hanging from his fingers, and Caleb's mother smiled, vindicated, standing amid all the cutlery. Caleb just wanted it to stop. He prayed for their anger to quell, for them to soften, for their rigid muscles to relax. He willed it to be so. He asked God directly, as his Son, as the Second Coming of Christ, for his will to materialize, and it did. His mother grabbed a broom and swept the tiled floor, and his father picked up the cutlery, their demeanors changed. They were quieter now, still cold to each other, the wounds still festering, but they were exhausted and unable to fight even if they wanted to. Caleb was at least happy for that. His prayer had been answered.

THAT NIGHT, HIS FATHER SLEPT on the couch. He could tell without even seeing him, his snores rattling close. Caleb's father had always been a deep sleeper, oftentimes sleeping straight through a spring thunderstorm, the plains wracked with thunder and lightning and wind that could send a piece of hay straight through a century-old oak. Sometimes he'd crack a joke that if anyone ever broke into the house, he'd sleep through it, and he'd wake up the next morning with their TV and DVD player and their video games all gone. The family might've even been tied up, put in their closets, duct tape stuck over their mouths, and he wouldn't even have a clue, dreaming away about winning the Super Bowl and smoking the perfect ribs. Caleb had never found the joke funny, but he imagined his father dreaming away right then, all six feet, two inches and 200 pounds of him curled up, a blanket much too small for him pulled to his chin, and couldn't help but get a little pleasure out of him being so uncomfortable.

Caleb's door opened. It was his mother. She was dressed and had her car keys in her hand.

"Pack a bag," she said.

"What?"

"Get up. Get your suitcase out of your closet. Grab enough clothes to last awhile."

"Where are we going? We going on a trip?"

"Don't ask questions. Just pack."

And so he did. He went to his closet, and he grabbed a duffel bag he usually used for gym class and packed a few long-sleeved T-shirts, a couple pairs of jeans, some underwear. He packed enough for three days, like maybe they were going on a trip to Kansas City or something, like they had a few years back to go see a Royals game.

"Grab your heavy coat. Some shorts. Your other shoes, too," his mother said. She had a backpack slung over her shoulders, another bag strapped across her chest. "Hurry. Before your father and brother

72

wake."

"Where are we going?"

"You'll see," she said. "Just meet me in the truck." She pulled the straps tighter around her shoulders and readjusted the bag. The weight was so heavy she slouched and strained to hold her bags up. "Hurry."

"But what about Dad? What about Jonah?"

"There's no time."

Caleb started to cry. He didn't want to. He was embarrassed, but he couldn't help it. He was scared and confused, and it felt like his stomach might crawl right up his throat. His mother knelt down to him and grabbed him by the shoulders.

"The Second Seal. It's been opened."

"It has?"

She nodded. "The physical attack against you. Our banishment from the community. From the Second Seal will advance a red horse, 'and power was given to him that sat thereon to take peace from the earth, and that they should kill one another: and there was given unto him a great sword.' People will begin to die soon. There will be anarchy. Violence. We must go someplace safe."

Caleb stopped crying. He was still scared, but he felt calmer for some reason. He felt all his organs return to their original places.

"When?" he asked.

"Now."

"And Dad and Jonah can't come?"

She shook her head.

"Why not?"

"You know the answer to that."

He did, but he didn't want to admit it. "They've lost their faith."

She nodded. "There's nothing we can do to save them now."

When they pulled out of the driveway, Mom headed for Frank Phillips Boulevard and then east toward the edge of town. Even though he hadn't been out much that winter, the town looked the same. The moon was high in the sky, the night clear, thousands of tiny stars shining down upon them from light-years away. They passed the two water towers in the middle of town, one branded Hot, the other Cold. They passed Swanson Chevrolet, new Z-71s looking ominous, their metallic paint jobs brilliant underneath the sharp white security lights. Tomorrow, Caleb knew, the entire town would wake up. They'd stretch and have their morning coffees and take their morning showers and everything to them would be like it was yesterday, their unmuted lives transposing themselves against the world in a recurrent time loop. They would go about their business without regard to Caleb's and his mother's actions, and Caleb felt sorry for them—no matter what he said and did, he wouldn't be able to save them all.

THE BOOK OF JUDGES

CHAPTER 1

THEY HEADED EAST ON HIGHWAY 60. THIS PART of the state was called Green Country, but now it was all brown and gray. They drove through rolling hills, the plains brittle with dead Indian grass, hardened fields cracked dry from the harsh winter. Woods sprawled in every direction, spread out for miles and miles, farther than Caleb could see when they peaked the apex of a hill, and then everything would turn dark as they bottomed out in the trough, towering oaks blocking out the sun. He'd left Bartlesville before, but he never really took time to look at the landscape. It truly was breathtaking. The world was just so large, in every direction, the highway stretching out for miles in front of them. It was a two-lane road. Eighteen wheelers, F-250 super diesels, and decades-old minivans all rumbled past them heading back the way they'd come. Old men in trucks zoomed by, cowboy hats shadowing their features, their cattle and horse trailers stinking of hay and manure. Caleb had no idea where they were going, or why, but he was excited. They had an infinite amount of choices. Head north, head south, continue east. It didn't even matter. It was like they were on an adventure, just the two of them, and anything could happen when they got there. They were explorers on a mission to discover new worlds. He was Columbus, or Magellan, or Juan Ponce de León, searching for riches and the secret of never-ending youth in distant lands.

When they reached Grand Lake, they stopped. They parked at a scenic outlook off the highway that overlooked the lake, and got out of the car. The lake was dark, murky, and whitecapping from the wind barreling in from the north. There were no boats this time of year, though he could see some bobbing in the marina, their hulls covered in thick tarpaulin. Caleb couldn't see the shore on the other side, only had to have faith it was out there. It was the biggest thing Caleb had ever seen in his life. To him, it was as big as the ocean he'd only read about. As big as any city he'd ever been to. As big as all the heavens and the earth. He was convinced if he were to go swimming in that lake, it would just swallow him up whole, and he'd never be seen or heard from again.

"Here," his mother said. "This is where we're supposed to be."

Caleb didn't argue. He felt it too, deep down. This place was their new home.

The first couple of nights, Caleb and his mother slept in the Bronco. They found an old dirt road outside of town, parked in the ditch, and kept the windows rolled up. It was so cold out Caleb had a hard time breathing, and the sounds kept him from sleeping. It was probably the wind, rustling the tree branches, whistling as it bounced off the lake, but Caleb couldn't help his imagination from running wild. He thought it might be werewolves out there, hunting for a bloody meal before the sun rose, or maybe it was a demon sent from hell to take him and his mother down to the devil for execution. He knew he had to keep vigilant, and so he didn't sleep. He didn't sleep for two days, until his head felt heavy and his eyes burned and everything smelled of trouble.

In the morning they ate donuts from a truck stop, and his mom traded cigarettes for shower tickets. The fourth morning was the first time Caleb ever tasted coffee. His mom took it black, and she got a large cup along with her bear claw. Because he hadn't really slept the night before, he asked if he could have a drink. She stared at him for a bit like she was considering the notion, but then handed him the cup. It scalded his tongue and tasted bitter and he wanted to spit it out, but he didn't dare. He didn't want to ever show his mom he was weak.

"Good, right?" she asked, and he nodded because he didn't know what else to do.

He tried and failed to hide the aftertaste with a bite of his maple bar, then wiped his mouth of the crumbs, watching them fall to his lap. They were in the Bronco outside the truck stop watching a few big, denim-clad men checking out their rigs before taking off for their morning jaunt. It wasn't quite yet 7:00 a.m., and it was still below freezing. It was late February. Soon the winds would change direction, and the southern jet stream would bring warmer weather. Thunderstorms would drench the earth, flowers would bloom, and the lake would be filled with sunburnt teenagers riding Jet Skis and sneaking beers out on the water, but for now Caleb wrapped his coat tighter around himself and tried to steady his shivering body.

"First thing we got to do is find me a job," she said before taking another sip of her coffee, the steam from her Styrofoam cup fogging her glasses. "Then we got to find a place to live. Then we need to find Sam."

"What about school?" Caleb asked.

His mom took a bite of her donut. It was the last one, and glaze stuck to her fingertips.

"Never mind that."

Caleb wanted to ask what she meant, but he didn't know how.

"Things are going to be good," his mom said, nodding her head as if answering a question nobody asked. "From here on out, things are going to be tough, but they'll be good in the end."

That whole day was spent filling out applications at bait shops and souvenir shops and convenience stores. His mom filled them out, left the address and phone number line blank, and handed them to assistant managers who didn't even glance at them. They said they'd call, but even Caleb knew they were lying. There wasn't a phone number they could call. They did this for three days, and each time, she asked if they knew a man by the name of Sam Jenkins. Caleb had never heard the name before, but he didn't dare ask who he was. He figured his mother would tell him when he was ready to know, and it was at a gas station on the edge of town where they caught a break. The guy behind the counter knew Sam Jenkins, said he worked at a retirement village down the road called Sunset Acres.

They drove straight there. It was a long, gray cinderblock building with a warped roof and dead ivy snaking across its windows. The concrete was littered with last summer's mulch, and old men in wheelchairs waited outside, smoking, blankets wrapped around their legs, not talking to anyone, not even acknowledging the others' presence. Inside, the receptionist called Sam over the intercom, and he sauntered up a few minutes later, wiping his hands with a red handkerchief, a look of incredulity plastered on his face. He was a large guy. Pear shaped. Balding. Had breath that smelled of onions and thousand is-land dressing. He was the head of maintenance, and it was his job to make sure the HVAC was working, the halls were clear of spilled Dr Pepper, and the toilets weren't overflowing. This was Sam, and he took to Caleb right away.

"Praise God," he said when he saw Caleb's mother. "How long has it been? Twenty years?"

"It's been a long time, Sam."

They hugged for a while, Caleb's mother somehow melting into Sam, her body relaxed, her whole weight bearing down in his warmth.

"It's good to see you," he said.

"You have no idea," Caleb's mother said.

They broke away, still holding each other's hands. Caleb hadn't seen his mother this happy in months, perhaps even years.

"This is Caleb," she said. "My son."

"Caleb," the man said. His voice was a warm pillow. "I've heard of you. Knew I'd get to meet you one of these days."

His presence comforted Caleb. It was like he'd known Sam for years, a permanent fixture in his life like an old baseball glove that formed perfectly to his hand.

"You like peanut butter cups?" he asked.

"Yeah," Caleb said. "Of course."

Sam winked at Caleb's mother. "Think I might have a couple in my office if you want one. If that's okay?" he asked Caleb's mom.

His office wasn't really an office. It was a closet, full of bleach bottles and Ajax cleaner. An old mop and basin cluttered the corner, and a television and VCR rested on a wire shelf. Beside it were movies Caleb had never heard of: *Clegg, After Dark My Sweet,* and *Swingtown.*

Off to one side was a metal chair next to a folding table. There wasn't much there, no pictures of family, no computer, just a couple of pieces of paper, order forms for more cleaning products.

Caleb stuck the whole peanut butter cup in his mouth. He wished he had a glass of milk, but he didn't complain. The taste of milk chocolate tickled his taste buds—he hadn't had anything this good since leaving home.

"You two just visiting?" Sam asked Caleb's mom.

"No, no," Caleb's mother said. "Not just visiting."

"Thought as much."

"Oh yeah?"

"You don't have that look." He gestured toward the tiled ceiling. "Lake town and such. The tourists. They always have this look about them. Carefree. Careless."

"And what do we look like?"

"Careworn."

Caleb's mother smiled, cocked her head as if unsurprised.

"No trouble at home, I hope."

"There's always trouble, Sam. You know that."

"Your husband?"

"Out of the picture."

"Your oldest?"

She shook her head.

"Shame," Sam said. "Terrible shame."

Caleb's mother picked up a picture frame from a wire shelf. It was a black-and-white picture of a younger man, head buzzed, goofy grin, head cocked to the side in adolescent cocksureness. Caleb figured it must be Sam as a teenager, probably taken when he was in high school, before he embarked on the tribulations of adulthood, stress and worry etching itself into his muscles and bones and face like dirt and grease from a hard day's work.

"Heard about your father," Sam said.

Caleb's mom didn't say a word. She didn't move. Didn't flinch. Just stood there frozen like she was trying not to exert any energy whatsoever.

"He was a good man. I wanted to pay my respects, but I didn't want to be in the way. I'm sorry for that."

"You knew Papa?" Caleb asked.

"Years ago."

"They fought in the war together," his mother said.

"Korea. Your Papa always had my back."

"I didn't know he was in the war."

"He didn't speak of it much," his mother said.

"But you knew him?"

"Sure did," Sam said.

"What was he like back then? What was it like to be in the war?"

"Caleb," his mother said, shushing him.

"It's okay," Sam continued. "Let's just say I felt a lot better with your Papa there with me. Let's just say that."

Sam picked up a rag from a shelf and wiped his hands before unwrapping a peanut butter cup. He studied the chocolate before taking a bite, turning it over, running his dirt lined fingernails along the grooves, then plopping it into his mouth. He chewed quickly, his jaw audibly clicking.

"What are you doing for work these days?" he asked Caleb's mother. "I take it you're sticking around here for a while."

Caleb's mother shrugged. "I'm figuring it out. Not much in the way of work around here it seems."

Sam stuck out his bottom lip like he wasn't surprised. "I could use a little hand around here. That is if you don't mind getting dirty."

"Not at all. Prefer it, actually."

"Doesn't pay much."

"Doesn't need to."

"Good. Glad to hear."

Sam had her fill out an application. Formality, he called it. Caleb helped her with her answers. For previous work experience she put down volunteering at First Baptist in Bartlesville, organizing canned food drives and Christmas toy fundraisers. Much of the rest was blank. Address. Phone number. Education. References. Nobody back in Bartlesville even knew where they were.

"When will you be able to start?"

"Right away. Today if you need me to."

"And does"—he pointed to Caleb—"he have a place to go?"

Caleb's mom hesitated. Just for a moment. Her lips puckered, eyebrows arched. It was like she was, for the first time, fully considering the consequences of her actions.

"I know of a place, and I hope I'm not crossing a line here," Sam said, "but if you need a place to stay, I got a trailer for rent. It's not the nicest place in the world, but it's a roof."

Caleb's mom smiled at Sam. It was a forced smile. No teeth showing. Glazed-over eyes. Pupils narrowed. She looked embarrassed she had to ask. He'd just given her a job and now a home, but that didn't mean her smile wasn't genuine. If anything, Caleb's mother had always been a grateful person. Grateful to others who gave. Grateful to

God for his blessings. And this certainly was a blessing. Finding Sam. His generosity. They had been looking for him, but they didn't have a number. Didn't have his address. Just God looking out for them, and they found him within a week. That had to be it. His mom always said miracles happened when you least expected them. They could come out and bite you in the ass if you weren't careful.

The rest of the day Caleb, watched old black-and-white movies in Sam's office while his mother cleaned toilets, mopped floors, and disposed of bedpans, coming back every couple of hours or so to check on him, make sure he was okay. And he was. He ate a bologna sandwich with mustard and drank a cold Dr Pepper. He read a magazine he'd found, an old *Sports Illustrated* with Michael Jordan on the cover, and despite the dust and the weird chemical smell, he felt at home for the first time in a few days, like he could relax and leave his guard down.

After work they followed Sam down a two-lane highway until they found a dirt road heading toward the lake. The terrain was rocky and overgrown, the road walled in by thick woods. Squirrels darted through the underbrush, and long-abandoned homes crumbled inside the tree line, oaks sprouting forth from what once had been a bedroom. It was a wild place, full of energy and tasting like smoke. The road went on like this for about a half mile before giving way to a trailer park. It was a large place, much larger than what Caleb was used to, twenty acres surrounded by overgrown woods filled with blackjack oak and maple. The trailers weren't much to look at, but were well-kept. Simple metal exteriors painted yellow or green or indigo blue. Out front, the tenants had smokers and lawn chairs. A few people were home, grilling dinner on charcoal grills. Near the back of the property was a long, muddy beach and a dock butting up against Grand Lake, a few fishing boats bobbing in the water. Sam owned all of it, he said, passed down from generation to generation. Large blocks of limestone littered the area, and hiking trails zigzagged through the woods. A large family of whitetail lived back there, nesting along the tree line.

Sam parked in front of a trailer near the back of the park. It was small and silver, the screen door rusting along the edges. Inside was a narrow kitchen with a sink, a stovetop, and a fridge. To his left was a laminate table with a couple of benches, and to his right a bedroom with two twin beds in it, the mattresses stripped bare and stained brown. It wasn't anything like their old home in Bartlesville, which seemed like a mansion compared to this place, but it had four walls and a roof and insulation, and that was enough for now.

Caleb dropped his bags in the bedroom. On the wall, someone had drawn a picture with crayons. There was a snake in the middle, surrounded by women dancing. They had their hands above their heads and their tongues hung from their mouths. It was an odd picture, drawn by a child, the proportions all wrong, hands and heads way too large for their bodies, their eyes mere dots, but Caleb liked it nonetheless. He took it as an omen. This was a place where people could defeat serpents.

CHAPTER 2

THAT FIRST MORNING AT THE TRAILER PARK, his mother had already left for work when he awoke, the trailer smelling of coffee and toast. The sun had just broken the horizon, and faint light trickled in between the blinds, which wouldn't quite close all the way. The place looked disheveled. The Bible lay open on the table, his mother's notes left next to it. Last night's dinner of SpaghettiOs hardened inside a saucepan on the stove, and he became overwhelmed with a debilitating loneliness. It wasn't so much an abstract feeling. It gutted him. It weighed down his bones. He could feel it in his throat, a lump impeding his airways that was just as palpable and real as the old blanket on top of him, the threadbare pillow barely propping up his head.

He needed to get up. Idleness, he knew, bred sin. His mother had told him this his entire life, and so he got up and took a shower. The pressure was weak and the water was cold, dripping from the cracked showerhead, and so he made it quick, washing quickly as he shivered. Once dried and with his teeth brushed, he didn't quite know what to do with himself. He could read the Bible; that would be what his mother would want him to do, but he wasn't really in the mood. He felt guilty about this, the taste of shame now latching onto the ball of loneliness in his throat, but his mother wasn't around to chastise him. He'd save the Bible for later. Maybe in the afternoon.

Their new home was a mess, not just from the previous night but from years of neglect. Dirt lined the crevices of the cupboards, and the sink drain was oxidized with rust. The windows were opaque with dust and cobwebs, and water damage had warped the linoleum tile near the door. Wallpaper curled away from the sheetrock, and the carpet was worn thin, pockmarked with burn holes. He checked underneath the sink for cleaning supplies. A couple of rags, a half-empty bottle of Ajax. He found an old broom in the closet, its handle wedged between a couple of coats, but no dustpan. He started with the kitchen. He wetted a rag and wiped down the laminate, using his nails to dislodge what he thought was crusted cheese and mashed potatoes from the stove, knocking the crumbs onto the floor. He washed dishes the previous tenant had left behind the best he could, scrubbing at coffee stains with Ajax since he couldn't find any dish soap. He then filled the sink with water and poured in more Ajax. Not much, but just enough for the water to bubble and turn chalky, and he started to feel a little better. It was good to be moving, to keep his hands busy.

Next, he focused on the floors. He swept first, opening up the screen door and brushing dust out the front door. The sun had risen, and birds chirped in the distance. It was still cold, but getting warmer. It was the first day of March, and soon he wouldn't need his jacket anymore. Back inside, he got down on hands and knees and scrubbed the linoleum with a damp rag. It didn't make much difference in the appearance. The lime tiles were still scuffed black from the soles of sneakers and work boots, both from him and his mother and from countless other residents over the years, the men and women and children who once called this place home. He wondered where they were now, what they were doing, why they left. He imagined one family: a mom, dad, and two sons. In his fantasy they didn't have names. The father was a rancher. Wore plaid shirts and denim jeans every day, knuckles perpetually cut and bruised, never able to fully heal. The mother spent her days reading science fiction and fantasy novels and making decorative crafts to earn a little extra grocery money. She'd look back longingly over her teenage years, questioning the decisions she'd made throughout her life that had brought her there, but never for too long, for her own mother had always scolded her not to live in the past. The older brother would be ornery, constantly dirty, hands caked with soil, knees scuffed raw, staining his jeans in blood. Lips always curled into a mischievous smile. The younger brother envied him this, but didn't want to be a burden on his overworked parents. Instead, he was studious, obedient, almost to a fault. Caleb figured they'd moved on to a place not unlike this one, Arkansas or Texas probably, doing the same things the same way, a life filled with routine and monotony, no chance of escape, either out of fear or lack of choice—Caleb wasn't sure.

When Caleb was finished, he stood in the middle of the trailer, stretching his arms to see if he could touch both sides at once. It didn't feel like home, but it was getting there, and so, satisfied with his work, he decided he'd explore the lake. Around the bank on the north side, the woods gave way to a clearing, and it was easy to traverse. For the first time in a long while, he didn't shiver when he was outside. The air had a chill in it, but as he got moving, his body warmed and he was comfortable. Sweat even damped his forehead. There wasn't a breeze to speak of, and so the lake was still. Across the lake, mansions towered over the forest canopy. Large windows reflected the morning sun, and the homes were built from stone and brick. In the distance he could make out Monkey Bridge crossing the lake. It was the only sign of life as far as Caleb could tell, cars and semis trundling past, people going to and from work and school, leading their lives in ignorance of what was to come. Caleb was jealous of that. Sometimes he wished he didn't know the end of the world was near. That way he'd be able to lead a normal life with normal friends at a normal school, his only worries his upcoming math exam and if a girl maybe liked him in the same way he liked her. But he brushed these thoughts aside as quickly as they had come—no use pining for what wasn't, his Mom always told him. He could only prepare for what was to come.

About a quarter mile from the trailer, Caleb came to a clearing. There was a sandy beach dotted with pebbles and trash and a large boulder near the back. In front of him rose a limestone bluff. It must've been sixty feet high. A lone pine grew out of its crest, jagged and bent, roots sticking out into the air without anything to latch onto. A path led to the top of the bluff. It wound around haphazardly, jagged with rocks, uneven and steep. As soon as he saw it, he knew he would climb it. An impulse that surprised him. Usually, he avoided heights. Anything dangerous, really. But this was a compulsion he couldn't ignore, like trying not to eat a piece of pie on Thanksgiving.

The climb at the beginning wasn't that difficult. Not too steep. Very few obstacles. But as he made his way higher, the grade grew steeper, and soon he had to use his arms to pull himself up, his hands searching for tenuous holds onto crevices and grips jutting out of the rock face. About halfway up, though, he got stuck. He couldn't find a hold within his reach. He was cornered into the side of the vertical bluff at about a sixty-degree angle. To his right was a place he could grip, but it was three inches out of reach. The only place he could go was down. Unless he let his feet go and swung himself to it. The thought frightened him. Though he wouldn't fall straight down the thirty feet below him, it'd be difficult for him to find his footing if he slipped. He'd tumble back down the stone trail, battered and bruised, most likely breaking a bone as he did. No one knew he was out there. He hadn't told anyone. If he did fall, he could be there for hours before someone found him. Days even. He could die.

Then Caleb heard laughter. A girl and a boy. It came from above him, and at first Caleb was confused. School had started a few hours ago. There shouldn't be any kids out there, and he worried he was hearing things. Maybe he was going crazy. After the exile, the desertion of his father and brother, after coming here, he'd somehow lost his mind and had started hallucinating. Then it came again. Laughter.

"You stuck?"

Above him Caleb spotted the source of the voice. It was a large boy, probably thirteen or fourteen, broad-shouldered, his cheeks still pudgy like a child's, but the size of his neck like a grown man's. Just his head peeked out from the side of the ledge. Next to him was a girl and a smaller boy.

"Can you reach that crack to the right?" the larger boy asked.

"No," Caleb said. He reached again, but his fingertips fell just short.

"Wait right there."

The larger boy's head disappeared, and after a few seconds he reappeared at the top of the trail. He made his way down with ease, like he'd traversed this bluff countless times. His feet knew every stronghold, his hands bouncing off the limestone until he made his way down to Caleb. He braced himself with his feet and then grabbed Caleb's hand, taking on his entire weight so that Caleb could grab the crack just to his right. He then helped Caleb all the way to the top.

The view wasn't as grand as he'd thought it would be. In fact, it was disappointing. He could see for miles in each direction, every nook and cranny of the lake, the little alcoves and embankments. A few boats buzzed by. Fishermen probably, older men enjoying retirement. What struck Caleb, however, was the land surrounding the lake. In almost every direction he looked, the houses were in disrepair. Older, paint chipped, landscape overgrown. Crumbled chimneys. Fire-damaged roofs. There were a few nice homes, replete with glimmering pools and cabanas, but they were outnumbered at least fifty to one. It was the first time Caleb had ever been confronted with his own poverty. If he moved his and his mother's trailer next to one of these mansions, it would look unseemly. It would be embarrassing. The rich neighbors would complain, their judgmental gazes locked upon their eyesore of a home, and for a moment Caleb was gripped with shame.

"You're the new kid, aren't you?" the larger boy asked. "You and your mom just arrived yesterday?"

Caleb nodded.

"Name's Scoot." He reached out a large paw to shake Caleb's hand.

Caleb introduced himself.

"This is Brandon." Scoot pointed a thumb to the smaller boy. "And this is Catherine."

Catherine curtsied like in those old movies his mother sometimes made him watch, and Caleb couldn't help but find the gesture a little amusing. When done, she stood up as straight as she could and let out a loud, echoing belch, causing everyone to laugh.

"Why aren't you in school?" Caleb asked.

"Why aren't you?" Scoot asked back.

"I asked you first."

Scoot smiled. "I like you."

"We're homeschooled," Catherine said.

"All of you?"

They nodded in unison. "All of the kids here are," Scoot said.

Turned out, Scoot and Catherine were twins, though they looked nothing alike, and Brandon was their stepbrother. Their parents had married about ten years earlier, after both their previous marriages had failed. Brandon never saw his real mother, who he said was addicted to meth, and Scoot and Catherine never saw their real father, who had a flair for blackjack and Tennessee whiskey.

"Don't really miss him much," Scoot said. "Don't even remember what he looks like, actually."

"So, what about you?" Catherine asked. "What's your story?"

Caleb wasn't sure how much to tell them. He had a desire to purge everything, his immaculate conception, the death of his Papa, his mother's prophesizing the end of the world, the estrangement from church, the desertion of his father and brother. He had fears, was sometimes crippled with self-doubt about his ability to survive what his mother warned him was to come, but he also feared her reprimands, her disappointment in him. After what had happened in Bartlesville, he worried she blamed him. She told him she didn't, but he didn't quite believe her, her tone laced with insincerity. Instead, she told him to remain vigilant, to make better decisions going forward. She warned him of demons in human form come to stop them for the final fight between good and evil, but he wanted to trust Scoot. He wanted to trust Catherine and

Brandon. They were kids just like him, and Caleb longed for someone to confide in besides his mother, to make a connection, some friends, telling them everything, it all pouring out in a rush while they nodded their heads and agreed that the world was weird and unfair and run by adults. Instead, though, he remained quiet.

An awkward silence followed. A horn blared in the distance. The water washed against the limestone below them, and then, without warning, Catherine took off running. Caleb was confused at first. What could she be doing? But this was soon replaced with terror. She was heading straight for the edge of the cliff. Deep inside him, he could feel the genesis of a cry, a plea for her to stop, but it somehow got buried before it could reach his lips, and soon she was midair, arms spread wide. It seemed like she hovered right at the apex of her jump, like gravity had ceased to function just as she'd leapt, but then she fell and disappeared behind the ledge. Caleb, Scoot, and Brandon raced over to the side and got there just before she hit the water, feet first.

When she submerged, Caleb held his breath. He was sure she was dead. He counted to five, to ten, to fifteen, but then she broke the surface. She whipped back her hair and had the biggest grin on her face. Scoot and Brandon erupted into cheers, whooping and hollering and spurring her on, and Caleb couldn't believe it. She could've died. Didn't they realize that?

"Come on!" she yelled from below.

Scoot and Brandon didn't hesitate. They stepped back, ran, and jumped at the same time, flanking Caleb as they did so, splashing next to their sister, and emerging to more laughter and cheers. That left Caleb standing atop the bluff alone, and all of a sudden, the cliff seemed to rise another hundred, two hundred, even three hundred feet into the air. Scoot, Catherine, and Brandon shrunk until they were just dots amid the dark, choppy waters, and they screamed up at him to jump, telling him he'd be fine, there was nothing to worry about, but fear clenched his chest. All his organs seemed to shut down, and the world turned dim, his footing unsure. He thought he might pass out.

"You can do it!" they yelled. "Trust us!"

Caleb took deep breaths until he regained control. The blood flow returned to his extremities. He found comfort in their encouragement. He found a semblance of strength and courage. Without thinking about it, he started to run. His arms pumped, knees high, straining for just a little more speed, and when he reached the ledge, he jumped as far as he could. Once in the air, he felt as high as the clouds, and for a second there, he thought he might float right through the atmosphere to heaven itself, angels reaching down and lifting him up into the air until all turned white and his fear and anxiety simmered away like steam, but then gravity took over and he began his descent. He wasn't afraid like he'd thought he would be. Instead, he was euphoric. He'd never before felt so much joy. Adrenaline coursed through him until his skin vibrated and his teeth tingled, and when he hit the lake, it washed over him like baptismal waters.

THE TRAILER PARK WAS FILLED with noise and life. Several dozen families lived on the property. They were younger mostly, men and women with calloused hands and grimy hair, two or three or even five children in tow, but they were happy, not haggard or worn, wracked with exhaustion and despair. The teenagers rode four-wheelers and hunted, coming back with dead-eyed bucks. Their parents hung the meat on clotheslines, salted it, and dried it to make jerky. When it was ready, they invited Caleb and his mother to try some, and it was absolutely delicious. It was salty and chewy, and it warmed his belly. Everyone was just so nice and welcoming and gracious, so much different than Bartlesville. They didn't eye Caleb suspiciously or call him names. None of the children went to school. They tilled the fields, readying the soil to plant soybean and corn along the western side of the property as the weather warmed; they hauled trash and burned it down by the lake, and hacked down firewood with short axes. Everyone pitched in and shared the fruits of their labor. They shared their meals and their clothes and their bibles and their water, passing their belongings back and forth but never asking for anything in return. It was strange yet exhilarating, a community in and of itself, somehow connected but at the same time removed from the worries of the outside world.

On Sunday mornings, Sam hosted the property's church service. It was a lot different than First Baptist. Instead of a large building, service was held outside, the congregants sitting on aluminum folding chairs, their only shade from a tarp pulled taut over a PVC pipe structure. They didn't wear trendy outfits, suits and ties and the latest dresses offered down at the JC Penney. Instead they wore plain cotton dresses and denim overalls, mud-covered work boots and off-brand sneakers. Their faces were creased and puckered and beaded in sweat. Caleb thought he would be uncomfortable around them, viewed as an outsider, but he wasn't—once he got to know them, they turned out to be the friendliest people he'd ever met. They shook his hand and patted him on the back and fed him potato chips and Dr Pepper.

All of them lived on the property or close to it. Ranchers, sharecroppers from nearby farms, janitors and plumbers, Walmart cashiers, and blackjack dealers from the casino. They lived paycheck to pay-check and had no use for a savings account. They wore what they could afford, old denim from Goodwill mostly, and they ate what they could buy off their SNAP benefits or grow or hunt. But unlike the church Caleb and his mother had attended in Bartlesville, there wasn't judgment for this, the smug pride of those who were better off giving charity to the less fortunate. Instead, there was acceptance and warmth. Attendees always greeted each other with firm handshakes and genuine smiles, never once susceptible to the human follies of greed or avarice. Didn't matter their name or position in life, they were welcome, loved even.

There wasn't an ordained minister wearing an ill-fitting suit, hair slicked back, bearing down upon them from an elevated pulpit. Instead, it was just Sam. He wore a pair of faded overalls, a simple white shirt underneath. On his head sat an old ball cap for the '89ers, the former Triple-A baseball team in Oklahoma City. He took his time as he made his way up to the makeshift pulpit, which wasn't much: a few wooden pallets stacked three high and a long particleboard floor. There wasn't a microphone to amplify his voice, and when he stood atop the stage, Caleb had a hard time seeing him. Caleb and his mother sat near the back and off to the side, and large men obstructed their view.

Sam cleared his throat and began the sermon. "Good morning," he said. "I want to first thank everyone for coming out and spending some time with us. We realize you're busy. You have jobs and responsibilities and bills, and I know how life can be eaten up a minute or two at a time until all you got left are just a few minutes to rest, recharge, and start the whole process over again. For you to show up and show thanks to God and to find communion with your neighbor—it's a glorious thing. A glorious thing."

His voice was comforting. It was deep and smooth, the consonants and vowels draping over the audience in waves the way a concerned parent lulls their sick child to sleep.

"I just want to ponder on that for a moment if we could, how busy life has become for all of us. We toil and we work. We work ten, twelve, fourteen-hour days. We have to answer to managers and supervisors and owners. We cater to angry customers and tolerate ungrateful vendors. We head to work, dreading it most days, slog through it, and then try to savor every moment out of it despite the nagging anxiety it brings, even when we're not there. And for what? To provide what? Food for our family? To be able to feed them and clothe them and pay the banker his money? Sustenance, right? We strive to provide sustenance for our family. And that is a noble undertaking. It is. It's the right thing to do."

As he spoke, Sam didn't look at his audience. Instead, he looked everywhere else: the fields in the distance, the lake, the tent, and the table of orange juice and donuts. He stared at his feet and at his hands, at the cattle in the distance. He looked everywhere but at his congregation. Not once. Caleb found this bizarre but mesmerizing. It was like he could enrapture his audience without even trying, placing them under his spell with his voice alone.

"But remember," Sam continued, "sustenance isn't just the material. It isn't just the bread. It isn't just the house. It isn't just the new sneakers and video game. In your pursuit to provide these things, keep in mind a deeper kind of providing, of support and acceptance and inclusion and love. We must create safe harbors of learning for our children. We must teach them to do right and help their neighbors and friends and strangers. We must place in them a sense of community, and every single waking day, we must strive to make our lives and the lives of those around us better. We must build homes and give to the needy. We must feed the hungry and warm the cold. We must write books and make art and help a neighbor in need. It should amaze us what we're all capable of doing. We're the makers of our own world. We are. It's simply amazing. We're all architects of our own reality. And when we cease to exist, that reality also ceases to exist."

The congregation nodded their heads and spouted impromptu amens. Grandmothers held their hands above their heads, and grand-children snacked on cookies. Sam took a sip of water, used a handker-chief to wipe his lip dry.

"We often speak of God's grand design and plan for us, and he has one, that is irrefutable, but a part of that design is our ability to make our own fate. It's a complicated matter, this conflict between free will and omniscient creator, and it often isn't evident to us. We sometimes feel lost and isolated, and it's difficult for us to imagine a benefactor looking out for our best interests both in this life and the next, and at other times we have a hard time seeing how we can affect our own lives for the better, bemoaning the fact nothing we do seems to go right. Still other times, we're often confused about whether a turn of events, whether a promotion at work or the loss of a loved one, was the culmination of human choices or divine fate. To me, I would say they're both. They are humanly constructs made possible by heavenly divination. We are the creators of our own world. And when we cease to exist, these worlds will cease to exist along with us. And, really, what it comes down to is that we have to make our own choices. We have to take responsibility for our actions. We have to do good and strive to be better. We have to find acceptance. We have to face the consequences of our choices, whether good or bad, whether grand or mundane, whether divine or evil, and if we do that, then God will take care of us. He will lay out a divine fate both in this world and in the next, but if we deflect blame, if we no longer try to do what is right, then God will lay out a different plan for us, a plan that will splinter our lives, splinter our families, and splinter the very world we make. We will have forced God's hand. We will have forced God to create a hell on earth and a hell for us in the afterlife."

Sam stopped to grab a pitcher of water, pour a glass, and take the whole thing down in five or six gulps. He stared at the glass when he was done like he was surprised it had gone dry. He then placed the glass back at his feet and clasped his hands in front of him.

"That's why we're here today," he continued. "We're here to challenge ourselves. God has a plan for us, but we must choose to follow that plan, to trust in the Lord, to love and to be kind and to help our neighbors. That is what life is about, taking care of people, friends, family, strangers, doesn't matter. Each and every one of God's children deserves our love and compassion and forgiveness. He demands it of us. And we will not let him down."

Sam raised his right hand above his head and began to utter a strange sound, his speech a smattering of unintelligible syllables rising and undulating in tone and intensity. It surprised Caleb at first. He'd never before heard such a thing, and he looked to his mother for guidance, but like him, she was enthralled. Sam's words sparked with electricity. They spread like contagion. Soon, the rest of the congregation raised their hands, upturned their faces, eyes closed in rapture, and Caleb could feel this stirring inside of him. A building anxiety turned warm in his belly. He wanted to join in. He wanted to stand up and speak the language of God and share this experience with everyone else. It was a wonderful feeling, something he'd never experienced before. It was like he levitated. It was like he was an astral projection, witnessing all this from high above the tent. That was when he stood. He stood, and he began to speak. It was slow at first, and it felt strange on his tongue. The syllables he uttered were indecipherable, just a long stretch of vowels and consonants that didn't form any discernible words, but they seemed to. Despite not being any language Caleb had ever heard in his life, they made sense. They communicated perfectly the message he wanted to convey, his love for God, his devotion, his indissoluble and unwavering faith that what he was doing was right and good and no language or words could ever even come close to that.

Caleb moved out into the aisle, and the congregation spurred him on. They reached out and touched his arm and patted him on his back. He felt so many hands, dozens of hands. They were hands of brothers and sisters and fathers and mothers in Christ, and they grabbed ahold of him and lifted him into the air, and Caleb felt overcome. He burst from the inside out, filled with vibrating energy. His skin trembled, and he could smell the sweat and dirt and love emanating from everyone around him. It was transcendent. He no longer had control of his appendages, his legs and arms held firmly in place, his tongue moving across his gums and teeth, all of it controlled by some other being than him. It was God. It had to be. He was sure of it.

CHAPTER 3

ON MONDAYS EVELYN HAD THE DAY OFF, HER work week every Tuesday through Saturday, and they filled their time reading the Bible and talking about things to come, the opening of the Seven Seals and the final battle between good and evil. They sat at the dining-room table, which was just a fold-down table bolted to the wall and a couple of benches crammed in between the kitchen nook and the small living area, and Caleb's mom was diagramming the signs she'd already deciphered, the things that had prompted them to move in the first place.

"You see this here," his mother said, pointing to a news article she'd clipped out of a *USA Today*, its text marked with circled words and scribbled notes in the margin. "This was the first sign I noticed."

It was a story about an earthquake in the middle of the Pacific, which had caused multiple tsunamis in eastern Asia. Approximately a hundred thousand had died, and another million were left displaced. Most had zero resources with which to rebuild, so they migrated to urban centers such as Hong Kong, Beijing, and Tokyo. The pictures next to the story made Caleb's stomach fold up like a fitted sheet. Cities ruined. Buildings demolished. Concrete crumbled and cars bent. People stood by with heads buried deep into their chests. They held onto one another loosely, arms draped over shoulders, fingers scraping another's wrist. The pictures were black and white, but the streets were stained dark. Caleb hoped it was just water not yet dry after the tsunami had hit, but he feared it was blood.

"They're happening all over the world," his mother said as she opened up a cigarette case, picked out a one hundred, and lit it with a flick of her wrist. She inhaled deeply and spit out a thick plume of smoke. "Look at this one here."

She showed him another story clipped out of a *National Geographic* magazine. On the front page was Mount Everest. Caleb had never seen anything so big in his life. It was like it scraped the bottom of heaven.

"Avalanche hit a camp in the middle of the night. Killed about ninety people."

She picked out another story.

"Hurricane hits Haiti. Thousands are dead."

Caleb read the first paragraph. Winds topped two hundred miles per hour, powerful enough to pick up an eighteen-wheeler and take out an entire resort. Floods six feet deep. Survivors starving and stuck on rooftops, unable to be helped.

"You don't think all these are coincidences, do you?" she asked.

Caleb knew better. "No, ma'am."

"God's angry," she said. "Mankind has forsaken him, and he isn't pleased."

"Like Sodom and Gomorrah?" he asked.

She ashed her cigarette. Some of it landed in the ashtray, some on the table. She wiped it away with the side of her hand, the heel smudged black.

"That's right," she said. "And you know what happened to them, correct?"

"Fire and brimstone."

She nodded, took another drag. "The people out there," she said, waving her hand above her head, "they're living a life of sin. They steal. They covet. They murder, and they lie. Worst of all, they don't repent."

"Like Dad and Jonah?" Caleb asked.

"Exactly like Dad and Jonah."

"They still could, though, right? They could still ask God's forgiveness."

"They could, but they're running out of time. I fear the Third Seal has already been broken. These catastrophes, every time they occur, famine follows. Poverty. Destitution. Every single time. People lose their homes, their jobs, their very livelihoods, and who do you think benefits?"

"The greedy."

"That's right. The wealthy. The powerful. The follower of the white horse, the Antichrist. They're the ones who profit. They hike up prices. They rebuild cities the poor can't afford. They displace them, move them out, leave them with crumbs if anything." She pointed out the window. "Look out there," she said. "Look at those mansions. If something ever happened to us, do you think they'd be lining up to help us?"

"No."

"No. And you know why?"

"Because they're slaves to the devil."

"That's right. They'll burn the world before helping their fellow man."

A knock came at their door. Caleb's mom jumped, eyes turned metal. She'd been nervous since arriving at the community a week before. The community had been welcoming and gracious, but she feared Caleb's father would track them down, get the law involved, force her to return with him where Caleb would be subjected to his blasphemous ways. Caleb feared this, too. He still loved his father and his brother, but he understood they were lost now, pawns under the will of the Antichrist whether they realized it or not, and there was nothing Caleb could do to save them.

"You know who that is?" his mom whispered.

"No," Caleb said so softly he couldn't even hear it.

Another knock.

Caleb's mother went to the door. It didn't have a peephole, so she couldn't see who was on the other side. Caleb couldn't help but think it might be his father and brother. He imagined that after he and his mother had left, his father hired a private investigator to find them. Caleb had no idea how the PI could've tracked them down. They paid cash wherever they went. All the utilities and phone and everything were in Sam's name, not his mother's. He hadn't enrolled in school. Like his mother had said, they were living off the grid, but Caleb still worried, and he hoped. He hoped even though he knew he shouldn't, but he still desperately wanted it to be them, standing there on the doorstep, realizing they'd forsworn God and pleading for forgiveness, but it wasn't. Standing on the other side of the screen was a young couple, two kids in tow. The man held a hat in front of him. It was new looking, emblazoned on the front with the University of Oklahoma's familiar logo. The woman held a pan wrapped in a tea towel. It had a plastic cover, and Caleb couldn't tell what was inside. All he knew was that it was warm, and his mouth filled with saliva. The two kids hung back. They were younger than Caleb, maybe four or five years old. They looked to be twins, and they busied themselves with a couple of rocks they found at their feet.

"We hope we aren't intruding," the man said after an uncomfortable silence. He had a slender build, but he looked strong. Big hands, tan despite the weather just now turning warm, fingernails lined with dirt.

Caleb's mom didn't say anything.

"We've meant to come sooner," the man said, scratching his head. "Well, Pat and I saw you at church the other day, and we thought it was just the Christianly thing to do."

Pat, presumably the man's wife, held up the pan for Caleb's mom to take, which she did almost as if by instinct.

"Thank you," she said. "Would you like to come in?"

Both the man and his wife smiled, corralled the two kids with a touch on their shoulders, and headed inside. Caleb's mom put the dish on the makeshift table. It was a casserole. Noodles, hamburger, onions, green pepper, and it smelled delicious. It smelled as good as a miracle, and even though it was breakfast time, his mother grabbed plastic forks and paper plates and made a plate for everyone. Caleb dug in. It was the first really good meal he'd had in weeks, and he devoured it.

The man's name was Frank Goldsby. He'd been a banker in another life, living in Oklahoma City with his wife, Pat, who'd been in medical billing.

"But the world just seemed so empty, you know?" he said, taking a sip from his coffee—black, as there was no sugar or cream to offer him. "There was just this feeling. It's hard to explain. We had good jobs, and the kids were healthy. Doing all right in school, but there was just something missing. It's like when you were a kid and the teachers kept telling you not to stare at the sun, but you did anyway and when you looked back at the world there was this black hole where the sun had once been. That's how we lived. There was just this black hole in the middle of everything, sucking up all the joy and happiness until we just felt numb. Does that make sense?"

"Yes," Caleb's mother said.

"We sold everything," Pat said, laughing. "The house. My car. All of our stuff. Our books and TVs, most of our clothes. It was a crazy thing to do. Quit our jobs. Pulled Devon and Luke out of school." The kids were playing on the floor. They didn't have any toys, so they'd brought the rocks inside with them, pretending they were cars, smashing them into one another and making explosion noises when they collided. "Then we just hit the road."

"Bounced around a few places," Frank said. "Kansas City. Omaha. Chicago."

"Never found anything that stuck, though," Pat said. "It was the same everywhere. Same people. Same problems. Same monotonous life. Everything was rushed. Everything in motion. Work never done. Anxieties never quelled. The whole world stunk of desperation and despair. There was no joy in anything."

"So, we decided to come back. When I was a kid, my family used to go to Grand Lake in the summers. We'd rent a boat and a cabin and have a long weekend fishing and tubing. It was the last time I ever remembered being carefree."

"I took a job at a marina," Pat said. "Didn't pay much, but we had enough in savings to last us. I filled up boats with gas and sold beer and ice. It wasn't a bad job, but there was still something missing."

"That's when we met Sam."

"Yes. Sam. He took us into his home, and he taught us how to love. He taught us about God."

"Sam tells us he knew you as a kid," Frank said.

"Yes, he did," Caleb's mother said. "He was friends with my step-father."

"William, yes," Pat said. "He's told us a lot about William. He saved Sam's life."

"You know about Papa?" Caleb asked.

Pat smiled. She had eyes like emeralds. "Of course. He told us about you, too."

"What did he say about me?"

Pat smiled at Caleb, and Frank took the last bite of his casserole, his plate and coffee cup empty in front of him.

"That was delicious, Pat," Frank said.

"Yes," Caleb's mother agreed. "Delicious."

"Well, we'll leave you to your day. Again, welcome to the neighborhood."

"If you two need anything, anything at all," Pat said. "Don't hesitate."

Pat grabbed one of the twins, Frank the other. They bid Caleb and his mother goodbye, promised they'd be by again soon, and then they were gone just as quickly as they'd arrived.

CALEB FOUND A HOME IN the community. If a family had an extra loaf of cornbread, they shared it with their neighbor. If they noticed a stranded motorist, they stopped to give her a ride into town, or offered to change a flat tire, or even helped push a stuck sedan out of the mud. They were gracious and grateful, quick to give thanks for what they did have, even quicker to lend a helping hand to a stranger in need. Caleb found this heartening. Despite his mother's dire warnings of the end of the world, he found hope in this congregation—there were still good people out there, leading good lives, and he was lucky enough to be among them.

Sam owned the land and worked at the retirement home and led the church. He spoke softly and touched his listener when he did, a reassuring hand on a shoulder or a knee, his voice the sound of warm fudge melting over ice cream. He had the habit of eating sunflower seeds, and often Caleb could hear the crack of the shell, followed by a satisfying spit. When Caleb was in his presence, he felt at ease, welcomed, appreciated for all his virtues, forgiven for all his faults. It was something Caleb had never felt before—complete acceptance—and he couldn't help but smile until his cheeks hurt.

Weeks passed, and Caleb and his mother continued to attend Sunday service. Each time, Caleb spoke in tongues, and the congregation grew riled and energetic. They'd lift him up on their shoulders and carry him around the tent, each of them reaching their hands out toward him, and Sam and his mother would look on proudly, and Caleb felt so strong, so good, so big, filled up like a balloon ready to take flight. Soon, Caleb garnered attention. The congregation smiled when they saw him and shook his hand and asked how he was doing. After service, Sam often retired to his home, opting for the cool of a window air conditioning unit instead of convening with the families for lunch and juice. No one seemed to mind Sam's reclusiveness—it was something accepted and understood, and so Caleb and his mother didn't question it. He was, after all, the pastor. One morning after service, though, Sam didn't automatically retire, instead sticking around to ask after sick relatives and growing nephews, and it was while Caleb was drinking an ice-cold Coca-Cola that Sam first approached him, a packet of David sunflower seeds outstretched.

"Want some?" he asked.

Caleb thanked him and chucked a handful into his mouth. The salt soon dried out his cheeks and tongue.

"I've always thought sunflower seeds a superior snack," Sam said. "Don't have the fat of potato chips. Don't have the sugar of cookies. They're good for your heart. Doctor says I need to cut down on my sodium intake, but they're just so the salt of the earth. Know what I mean?"

Caleb nodded even though he hadn't any idea.

"I've always wanted to roast my own. Plant a field full of sunflowers and harvest them. I could sell them at football games and such. Give them out before service. I daydream about it. Being out in the field. I have this fantasy where a group of people are out there. Families. Great-grandparents and grandparents and moms and dads and brothers and sisters and babies. A whole legion of people. They're lost and confused and hungry. And so I feed them. I feed them the salt of the earth and then they lay down their things and take root right then and there. And it's like they sprout. They sprout and they grow and it's like I can watch them thrive as I nurture them. I am the nurturer of lost souls. You understand?"

Caleb did. It made sense. It wasn't so much the words Sam said, but how he said them. The way he made Caleb fill up with warmth and dirt and kind thoughts.

"Your mom still here?" He looked around the gathering.

"Yes, sir."

"She tells me your father is out of the picture. Is that so?"

Caleb didn't respond.

"No reason to be embarrassed, son," he said. "Speak."

"We don't live with them anymore. My father and my brother."

"You still talk to them?"

"No, sir. We're separated."

"Separated, huh?"

"Yes, sir."

"That's a funny way of putting it, isn't it?"

"I'm sorry, sir?"

"Separated. It's like there was some sort of inhuman fissure that broke your family apart. Something no one had control of. Not your mom. Not your dad. Not you or your brother."

"I suppose that's right."

"Is it?"

Caleb didn't say anything, tried not to have any reaction at all.

"They believe in God?" Sam asked.

"Yes, sir."

"They belong to a church?"

"Yes, sir. First Baptist in Bartlesville. At least they did."

"You don't know now?"

"No, sir."

He nodded as if he had thought as much.

"We don't seem to fit in most places," Caleb said, thinking back to when they'd been exiled from First Baptist. "My mother, actually. They asked us not to come back. Said we caused problems."

"I hear that more than you would believe," he said. "It's a shame every time I do."

"But we like it here. My mom and me."

"We like having you."

Sam spat and palmed another handful of sunflower seeds. On his teeth were the dark remnants of shells.

"I've been watching you," Sam said. "You have a way about you. It's hard to put my finger on it."

Caleb smiled.

"It's something special, I think. An old soul. Natural leader. I believe God has something very special in store for you."

"You think?"

He shrugged. "I do."

"My mom thinks so, too."

"Is that right?" Sam asked, now peering over Caleb's head at his mother. "You know, she's told me an awful lot about you. So did your Papa."

Caleb didn't say anything, his mother's warnings coming back to him not to say too much, that the devil could send demons to hunt them. He trusted Sam, he did, but he also couldn't trust himself sometimes. His mother had always told him he too often wanted people to be good, to be faithful, to be loving and warm and trustworthy, but oftentimes that wasn't the case. In reality, most people would leave him to die rather than raise a helping hand.

"She tells me you're special. She tells me you have a very important task ahead of you."

Caleb's stomach turned, and his chest constricted. He found it hard to breathe, and Sam leaned in close.

"Don't worry. Your secret is safe with me."

Caleb's mother approached, and she had an eager look about her, wide eyes bouncing from Sam to Caleb.

"And what are you two talking about?" she asked. She smiled a smile Caleb had never seen on her before. Used to, when they'd be at church in Bartlesville, his mom would smile, but it was a practiced smile. It was a smile full of pretense—like she was merely revealing her teeth rather than showing genuine warmth to her fellow congregants. This, however, was different. She glowed like a lightning bug. The act itself seemed spontaneous, the result of a subconscious yearning she couldn't—even if she wanted to—help.

"Caleb tells me you think him special."

"Of course," she said, wrapping her arm around Caleb's shoulders. She pulled him in tight, so tight it almost hurt. "He's my son."

"I think you're right. You have a magnificent child here in Caleb. I've been watching him during our sermons. He's wondrous. Enrapturing even. Spellbinding. Truly. You must be so proud."

"He's my golden child."

"I can tell," Sam said. "Tell me, Caleb, what do you think about what your mother has told you?"

Caleb turned to his mother, expecting her to have a pensive look, casting a warning glance over the rim of her glasses, but she didn't. Instead, she looked expectant, prodding him on.

"I don't know."

"It's okay, Caleb. You're among friends. Tell me why you think you're here."

"We're waiting for something."

"Good. What are you waiting for?"

"The end of the world?" Caleb didn't mean for it to sound so much like a question, but it did, his voice wavering and inflecting up as if in doubt.

Sam smiled, and he nodded, pleased and resolute. He paused for a moment and then quoted from Revelation, "I was on the island of Patmos, exiled there for preaching the Word of God, and for telling what I knew about Jesus Christ. It was the Lord's Day and I was worshiping when suddenly I heard a loud voice behind me, a voice that sounded like a trumpet blast saying 'I am A and Z, the First and Last' and then I heard him say 'Write down everything you see and send your letter to the seven churches in Turkey: to the church in Ephesus, the one in Smyrna, and those in Pergamos, Thyatira, Sardis, Philadelphia, and Laodicea.' When I turned to see who was speaking, there behind me were seven candlesticks of gold. And standing among them was one who looked like Jesus who called himself the Son of Man, wearing a long robe circled with a golden band across his chest. His hair was white as wool or snow, and his eyes penetrated like flames of fire. His feet gleamed like burnished bronze, and his voice thundered like waves against the shore. He held seven stars in his right hand and a sharp, double-bladed sword in his mouth, and his face shone like the power of the sun in unclouded brilliance. When I saw him, I fell at his feet as dead; but he laid his right hand on me and said, 'Don't be afraid. Though I am the First and Last, the Living One who died, who is now alive forevermore, who has the keys of hell and death—don't be afraid.'"

Sam cracked a sunflower shell in his teeth and spit out the remnants. Behind him, a few children erupted into laughter, running around in a game of frenzied tag, their parents looking on, sipping from plastic cups, their faces pink from the sun. They all looked so happy. Caleb felt himself embracing it, his whole body wrapped up in the warmest of blankets and the softest of pillows, the whole place enveloping him in rapturous joy.

"You are the First and the Last, Caleb," Sam continued. "And for the first time in a long time, I'm no longer afraid."

CHAPTER 4

CALEB SPENT MOST OF HIS TIME WITH SCOOT, Brandon, and Catherine. They fished and swam and played *The Legend of Zelda* at their place. Their parents, Buster and Ruth, would make them pizza rolls and Sunny D and tell them about the time Buster had raced cars back in the seventies all through Alabama and Georgia and Arkansas, winning enough cash for gas and beer money to make it to the next race. Ruth showed them how to spot the constellations in the night sky, Orion and the Big Dipper and the signs of the zodiac, and told them how people long ago used the constellations as their calendars so that they knew when to plant crops and to harvest them, even used them as navigation tools when they ventured far from home.

"You see that there," she said, "that's Virgo." She pointed it out with her fingers, tracing the stars in the shape of a woman extending her hand as if reaching for God himself. "A lot of people think it's just a woman holding a spike of grain, but I don't think so."

"It's the Virgin Mary," Catherine said.

They lay on their backs in the middle of the park, near a communal fire pit the congregation would gather around on the weekends. They'd grill cheeseburgers and drink iced tea. Some would play guitars and sing. Everyone would be there. Sam and the Goldsbys, Mr. and Mrs. Atler, Barbara Eggleston, and Peyton Wouk, all of them. They'd gather around and laugh and sing hymnals and pray. It was a party, really, something Caleb looked forward to every single week.

"That's right. And over there?" Ruth pointed a little to the left and down.

"That's Libra," Scoot said. "The scales. Sins that must be paid for."

"Correct," Ruth said.

"How do you guys know all this stuff?" Caleb asked.

"Sam, of course," Ruth said. "How else?"

Caleb sat next to them in church, riding out the heat and the humidity, keeping cool with fans as they listened to Sam preach the gospel. Underneath the revival tent, the place vibrated with energy. It reminded Caleb of a spring thunderstorm, the way the temperature would drop fifteen degrees in a matter of moments, how the wind would whip from all directions, how the sky would burn a mixture of mint and algae. At first, the thunder would rumble in the distance, the lightning muted by dark, heavy clouds, but soon it would drift overhead, and the sun would be blotted out, and all he'd be able to hear would be the thunder and the howling winds and the rain and hail pelting whatever structure it smashed. The difference, though, was Sam. Amid all the energy, he stood in front of the congregation like he knew what God knew, that they would, if they just believed hard enough, survive the storm together.

"In the first Epistle of St. Paul to the Thessalonians, it says 'Pray without ceasing,'" Sam said. He sat on a solitary chair and spoke without a microphone. Caleb sat in the front row, attentive, his body leaning toward Sam as if being pulled by a magnet. "I was very young when I first read these words. I wasn't a child, but still, I wasn't a man, and I suppose perhaps this was one of the many reasons why I was lost at this time. I'd thought I'd welcomed Christ into my heart. I'd been baptized. I attended church. I sinned, and I asked for forgiveness, but even I knew this wasn't enough. I felt an emptiness inside me. It was something palpable, tangible, like hunger. I felt hungry, not for nutritional sustenance. Not for a sandwich. Not for ham. But something more. A spiritual hunger is what I felt, and that's when I came across these words, 'Pray without ceasing.' I'd heard sermons throughout my life about the value of prayer. I had a friend at the time, William, a young man I served with in the war. Evelyn's stepfather, actually. Caleb's Papa."

Caleb's mother grabbed his hand and squeezed.

"For hours, he'd go on about prayer. Why we do it. Why it's important, and I listened and agreed and prayed in the morning and at night, but still, the hunger persisted. That's when I came across these words. Pray ceaselessly. No one had ever preached about praying ceaselessly to me before, and it baffled me. The very notion of it seemed to fly in the face of logic. We're human, of course. We have needs. We must eat and drink and work and provide for our families. We sleep, and we toil. We play with our children. It would be impossible to pray ceaselessly. Our minds wander, and we're bothered by worldly things. Things necessary for survival. For emotional wellbeing. For making connections and fulfilling life's goals. These are not fruitless things. Necessary, in fact, for both our physical and emotional survival. So how would one pray ceaselessly?

"This question haunted me, and it gave me pause, for I felt as though I was not fulfilling my promise to God. It was in the Bible, after all, and as we know, the scripture is a covenant between God and his subjects. We are to abide, not question, not make excuses, not abdicate our duties to him, so I asked William about it, but he at first seemed stumped. He'd read that passage before, of course, but he'd never given it much thought, this idea of praying ceaselessly. Being a thoughtful man, he said he'd have to think about this for a while, and so he did. For weeks and weeks, I waited for an answer until finally, after a couple months of my first inquiry, he told me that to pray ceaselessly, my mind, body, and spirit must always be acting in service of God. In waking and in sleep, I must remain wholly and irrevocably devoted to him. I could not equivocate. I could not waver. All my thoughts, all my energy, everything I had must be completely and wholly and absolutely devoted to him.

"I replied that this is what I feared because I didn't understand how to achieve this. How could this be possible? How could we devote all of ourselves all the time to God? Was God not asking the impossible? Was he not setting us up for failure from the outset? If so, what kind of god would do this? William thought about this for a moment, vexed himself, but then he told me to go home, to quiet my thoughts, and to repeat the following prayer three thousand times: 'Please, Jesus, have mercy on me.' And so I went home and I repeated this prayer. When I awoke in the morning, I recited it, and I wouldn't leave or begin my day's work until I finished all three thousand. The first few days, it was difficult. My mind wandered, and I worried over the troubles I faced, how my crop was coming in and prices for bushels of corn and soybean. My back ached after sitting in the same position for an hour or two on end, and I rubbed it with my hands, wondering if I had any Tylenol remaining. Eventually, though, it became easier. I was able to recite the prayer all three thousand times within an hour, and I was able to begin my day refreshed. After the three weeks were up, I visited William once again, and he told me I had done well, but now to go back and repeat my prayer six thousand times. And so I did, and again I found it difficult at first. Once I got to three thousand recitations, my tongue hurt and my mouth turned dry. I worried about rising interest rates and if I'd make enough money to pay the bank back for the cost of seed and labor. I worried what would happen if I couldn't. If I'd be cast out on the street, homeless and jobless, and what would I do then? What would I become then? How would I be able to feed myself? But after about a week, the prayers became easier. It was then I started to notice a change. My mood was better, and I treated others with more kindness. I looked forward to my day's work. It was a good thing, and so when I went back to William, I told him I thought I was beginning to understand, and he told me good, good, that's good, now go home and repeat your prayer twelve thousand times. With purpose, I went home and began right away, and, of course, I found it difficult at first. I found myself tiring and suffering from vertigo. My gums bled, and I felt faint from lack of food. I became dehydrated and suffered from fever. I even thought I was hallucinating at times from sleep deprivation and lack of nourishment, but, like the other times, as the weeks went by, it got easier, and I found that when I completed my twelve thousand required prayers for the day, I'd continue to chant them silently as I worked, when I went to the bank or grocery shopping, often using the prayer as a farewell; 'May Jesus have mercy on us,' I'd say, and others would smile and shake my hand and sometimes even thank me. When I slept, I even dreamt of the prayer. In my dreams, an angel would appear before me, and I'd recite the prayer for her. For several weeks, she wouldn't speak. She just sat there silently, smiling as I chanted the prayer for her. 'Please Jesus, have mercy on me.' It was like I was telling her the most compelling story, she was so attentive. I felt comforted by this. It was exactly what I needed, for someone just to listen to me. When I told William about the angel, he told me good. He told me to pay attention. He told me to keep praying. This is important, he said. She is here for a reason.

"This went on for several more weeks, and soon I found I no longer needed to count my prayers; it just happened naturally. I recited the prayer when I woke until the moment I laid down for rest. I chanted the prayer while waiting in line at the bank or ordering coffee at the diner. I chanted the prayer while herding my cattle and while I went shopping for my children's Christmas gifts. It became like ambient noise to me, always there, always on repeat, and I could hear it, I could, and it comforted me, but it didn't impede my day-to-day activities like I feared. It helped them even, and I relied upon the prayer, both in waking and in sleeping, and all the while I continued to dream of the angel who listened to me pray. She just sat there, smiling, smiling, always smiling, and I continued to pray to her patiently, knowing that when she was ready, when I was ready, when God was ready, I'd know why she'd come to me.

"It took about a year before the angel spoke. And what she told me took me by surprise. It was so unbelievable I had a hard time accepting what she told me. 'Sam,' she said, 'a group of people will soon come into your life. Good-hearted people. A people full of compassion and good intentions. A people in need of guidance. They will be a special people. The chosen people. God's children. And you are to guide them. To lead them. For God will test them, and they will need your hand to cling to.'"

Sam took a long drink of water. Caleb felt as though he levitated.

"This shocked me. It did. God's people. The chosen people. And I, lowly old me, would have to lead them. For years I struggled with this. I have to admit, it tested my faith. But here you are."

He extended his arms as if to envelop the congregation in a hug.

"And you will follow me, yes?"

"Yes."

"Amen."

"Hallelujah."

"You will never abandon me?"

"No."

"Thank you, Jesus."

"You will walk with me into the kingdom of heaven?"

The congregation erupted into cheers and exclamations, testifying their allegiance, all washed up into a single organism, and Sam began to speak in tongues, his head thrown back, what hair remained on the top of his head dangling like curtains. Several of the congregation followed suit, Caleb included, the words spewing from his lips the language of God. Soon, he couldn't distinguish between where his body ended and the person next to him began. The entire congregation melted into one body. One mind. One soul. He was sure of it. As sure as the cracked earth underneath his feet, the wind whipping against his face, as God up above, he'd found his place.

THE STORM HIT RIGHT AFTER service, intensifying as the hours bore on, the worst of it hitting around dusk. Caleb and his mom were outside pulling down the laundry from the clothesline when the temperature dropped. The wind picked up, and to the west over the lake the clouds turned dark. They coagulated over the water, turning broad and brimming up toward the heavens in the shape of an anvil. The color of it was a mixture of charcoal and bluegrass, swirling up and down, bubbling as it neared the earth. It didn't scare Caleb. Having grown up in Oklahoma, he'd grown accustomed to thunderstorms.

His mother yelled something over to him, but Caleb couldn't quite make it out over the storm. Sheets and her hair whipped around her head, and he could see her mouth moving, hear bits of syllables over the wind, but the sounds were indecipherable, just the cacophonous cries of urgency. The wind blew harder. Caleb struggled to grab ahold of a T-shirt, but as soon as he unclipped the clothespins, it took flight. He jumped after it, but he knew it to be futile. It was gone, hundreds of yards out in front by the time he took just a few steps.

Lightning illuminated the sky. Thunder rumbled. The first crack made Caleb jump. The storm was behind him as he watched a pillowcase float away. It jerked up, down, to the side, ballooning and collapsing in on itself. It careened through the air, almost as if it were conscious. The pillowcase seemed frightened. It was trying to flee, to find refuge, turning this way and that, but it had no idea where to go. Caleb almost felt sorry for the pillowcase. He did, even though he knew it to be ridiculous—it was, after all, just an inanimate object— but he wanted to keep it safe.

His mother grabbed him by the shoulders just as the rain unleashed. It pelted him, stinging his face, his shoulders, and his back. The drops were hard, charged with ice.

"Forget it!" his mother yelled.

"What?"

She pointed. He followed her finger to the pillowcase. It had to be forty feet in the air by then.

"It's gone."

She pulled him toward the trailer. It was hard moving against the wind. It clawed at them. Pushed at them. Grabbed them by the hair and the shoulders and pressed them back down toward the earth, but they kept moving. Inside, the trailer rocked, like the ground itself was unsteady. Mom grabbed an old AM/FM radio and turned it on. First, there was only static as she dialed through the stations until she found a man's voice. Caleb had grown up listening to weather reports. Usually, the meteorologists had steady voices, reassuring. They'd seen this before. They knew what to do. It was just another day at the office. Take cover, they'd say. Get on the ground floor in a center room. Place mattresses over you. Pillows. Stay safe. That day, however, the man's voice was laced with panic. Vowels soft, unsure of themselves. Consonants fumbling off his tongue. He lost his train of thought on multiple occasions, confusing the cardinal directions, saying there was a hook on the east side of the lake, no the west, heading east, right for Grove. It would be there within the hour. Please, everyone, get underground if you can.

Caleb pulled back the blinds. The storm had blocked out the sun. Lightning flashed every second or two. It reminded Caleb of a strobe light. Hail battered the trailer. They sounded like gunshots, and each time a larger stone crashed against the metal shell of their home, Caleb clenched despite knowing they'd keep coming for quite some time still. The wind whistled. It sounded otherworldly. High-pitched, ear puncturing, like the earth was a large teakettle about to boil over. Over the lake, Caleb thought he could see a funnel cloud spinning, but he wasn't quite sure. It only became visible when lightning flashed, but then winked out without warning. It hung low, though. He could tell that much. And it was broad.

Usually, Caleb enjoyed storms. He looked forward to them. The heat building up to them, the short burst of chaos, followed by the cool, cleansing smell of rain and wet soil. He'd always felt reborn afterward. Every time it stormed, it seemed to signify a demarcation between past and present. Whatever had happened lost its importance, and possibilities opened up before him like a supercontinent. This storm, however, was different. An electricity buzzed through the air. The violence of it didn't wane and ebb and come at him in waves. Instead, it thrashed. It only grew stronger, and it was coming right for them.

"Maybe we should head to Sam's house," Caleb said. He didn't mean to sound so frightened when he said it, but he couldn't help it, his words leaping from his tongue as if fleeing a burning building.

"We'll be okay," his mother said. "Just have faith."

The man's voice on the radio broke up. Static punctuated his warnings, and his description of who was in the path of the storm disintegrated into unintelligible gibberish. Vinita, Jay, Afton, Grove, all of it within the next few minutes. It was big, the man said. Wide, bigger than anything he'd ever seen before. Caleb couldn't make out any more. He peeked back outside. He thought he could make out debris flying over the lake: paper bags, insulation, tree limbs, and newspaper. A dog barked nearby. Its yelps seemed to come from every direction, west, east, south, even from right above him. The wind was so strong even soundwaves were being altered.

Caleb's mother grabbed his hand, and they pushed through the door. Sam's house was close, about fifty or so yards away, and they sprinted. Hailstones battered them, striking their backs and shoulders and their heads. The pain rocked Caleb. It entered him everywhere and shook him down at a cellular level, but he pushed through. He willed his legs to keep moving across the field, and his mother pounded on Sam's door. They pounded and pounded and pounded but nobody came. They tried the door, but it was locked. Caleb looked behind him, and the tornado sirens sounded. They blared over the storm, loud and clear. Caleb's mom turned toward him, her skin turning pale like he could see the blood draining to her feet. Over the lake, he could see it, or he thought he could. It was a large, oscillating wall. Dark, bulbous, veined with lightning. The sound it made churned. It groaned. It growled. It was a deep and cavernous frothing. He heard metal grinding, trees uprooting, the ground vibrating like the earth was being ripped asunder, but then the door opened. It was Sam. He grabbed them, and he led them downstairs to the basement. The entire congregation was there, huddled near the floor, the children wearing bike helmets and holding their parents' legs, their parents holding on to one another so as not to be torn apart.

Then it hit. Everything went dark. Then white. He couldn't make out any detail, just an endless luminescence. And peace. Surprisingly, he wasn't afraid. In reality, there was violence. Outside, trailers crumpled. Trees were uprooted. Cars tossed. Hail shattered windows and rain flooded homes. It only lasted about a minute, though. Eventually, the roar subsided to a growl, then a hum. Thunder dissipated. Rains let up. For a while, they all sat there in stunned silence, everyone just blinking, but then they reemerged one by one. It took awhile for Caleb's eyes to adjust, but when they did, he saw the devastation. It looked like a bomb had been dropped. He heard crying and a dog barking. He moved his hands and his legs and his arms, testing them for the first time since being pelted with hail. There didn't seem to be any serious injury. Some bruises, deep into the muscle. He tasted blood on his lip. A gash throbbed on his forehead. But he'd live. He'd carry on. He and his mother and Sam and all the rest, they'd tend to the injured, mend their bones, then pick up where they'd left off, hardening themselves for an even greater storm to come.

CHAPTER 5

LATER THEY LEARNED THE TORNADO HAD BEEN over a mile wide, with winds exceeding three hundred miles per hour. An F5, they called it, the largest ever recorded in the state. Four hundred eighteen homes were destroyed. The elementary school. The sheriff's station. The hospital. Fourteen marinas. Two hundred fourteen boats. All of it gone. A complete loss. The entire town had been razed, and sixty-seven had lost their lives. Many of them were elderly; even more were children. Caleb mourned for each one of them, and for their families. The only person he'd ever known who had died was his Papa, and he remembered the emptiness when he'd passed. It had been like a vacuum, void of air and friction and gravity, like Caleb levitated without anchor to the rest of the world. Eventually, this subsided. But it took time, and it took prayer.

At the trailer park, ninety percent of their homes were destroyed, shattered and strewn across the field in a jumbled mess. All of them soaked, bent, jagged, and dangerous. Gas lines spewed noxious fumes into the air. Broken glass littered driveways, and muddy waters flooded the drainage ditches and what had once been people's front yards. Only three still stood, in addition to Sam's house. It had taken damage. Windows busted, the roof a complete loss from hail damage. The detached garage smashed his '92 F-150, but on the whole, the house was still standing, and it still provided refuge from the elements.

Over the next few days, there wasn't much else to do but clean up. Most businesses were either destroyed or shut down, and so the residents meandered about, collecting what they could, clothes and stuffed animals and refrigerators, piling what couldn't be salvaged on the edge of the property. Sam directed people. Older folks wandered around passing out coffee, water, and bread. Men dragged away tree limbs. Caleb and his mother tended to the injured. There were several. Bruises and lacerations mostly. A few broken bones. They made splints out of fence posts and tied them to arms and legs. But, thankfully, no one in the community had perished. Everyone was accounted for. It was a miracle, Caleb's mother said.

"We were right," she said. "We are the chosen people."

And Caleb believed her. There was no other explanation. The rest of the area had been devastated with death, but here in the community not a single person had died. Not a single person with serious injuries. They would have to look after one another and help one another, but they were lucky. They had been spared.

Caleb cleaned wounds with hydrogen peroxide, bandaged them with gauze. Victims had to remember to blink, to breathe, to brush a fly away from their face. Conversations were clipped short, words fumbling off the tongue, sound losing all meaning. They wore an expression Caleb would never be able to forget. It was one of complete and utter despair. Loss. Confusion. Anger. Everything they'd known was now gone, wiped from the earth in a matter of seconds by a monstrous wind. They couldn't be grateful at this point. They couldn't bring themselves to thank God for being alive after losing so much. It would've been unconscionable, and Caleb understood.

Over the next few days, they waited. They waited for the mayor to come, the National Guard, FEMA, but no one did. They carried water in buckets from the lake, boiled it over the communal fire pit in order to drink. They slept outside, many of them in tents, underneath lean-tos, a tarp pulled over a couple logs, anything to escape the sun, to find some shade. Mosquitos plagued them. Fires helped some, the smoke keeping the insects away, but after a few minutes the heat would become unbearable, and Caleb would have to jump into the lake to cool off. When they weren't helping clean up, he, Scoot, Brandon, and Catherine killed time by playing games: hide-and-go-seek, tag, football, Marco Polo. They talked about what they missed most from what was lost, their N64 video game system or their televisions.

"I miss having ice," Scoot said.

They were sitting next to the lake, feet dangling in the water, skipping rocks. Catherine was the best at it. She'd pick up the smoothest stone she could find and then whip it across her body. It would glide from her fingertips and skim the water, bouncing across the surface for what seemed like a mile until it lost all its energy and skittered to a stop, floating for a second before it disappeared.

"I know what you mean," Brandon said. "I'd kill for a cold Dr Pepper right now."

"A cherry Dr Pepper," Catherine added. "Or a SONIC Cheeseburger."

"No tomato, though," Scoot said.

"You're going to be picky?" Caleb said. "Right now? With everything gone, you're going to be picky?"

"Hey, it's not like we're starving," Scoot said.

Not yet, Caleb wanted to say, but he didn't.

Across the water Caleb noticed the mansions still stood. Didn't even look like they'd been damaged. Three of them stood high atop a rockface bluff, their windows letting in the morning light as if it were just like any other spring day. They might've lost some shingles, or maybe some guttering hung loose, but nothing like the poor folk it seemed, their trailers and trucks a complete loss. In fact, just to the east of them a mile-long swath of trees had been wiped clean like a giant lawnmower had barreled through, but the mansions remained unscathed like they'd been protected.

"Do you think help's going to come?" Catherine asked. She picked up another rock and let it go, and it bounced six or seven times before submerging.

"Sure," Scoot said. "Why wouldn't it?"

"It's been two days," Brandon said. "We're running out of food. Have you heard anything?"

"God will take care of us," Caleb said. "He always does."

"Yeah," Catherine said. "You're probably right."

Caleb picked up a stone and tried to mimic Catherine's form, the way she held the stone between thumb and pointer finger, how she whipped her arm back and slung it forward in one smooth motion, but it released from his fingers at an odd angle, wobbling upon an axis, and didn't even skip once before falling below the surface.

"You know what I miss," Scoot said. "My freaking bike."

The third morning after the storm, a few of them decided to go into town to talk to the mayor. Sam went. Scoot's dad. Evelyn. She allowed Caleb to tag along, but he was to keep quiet, stay out of the way.

Scoot's father's pickup still ran, and so they all piled into that and set off on the highway toward town. It was the first time Caleb had seen the extent of the destruction. A few of the others had already ventured into town and brought back reports of what little still stood, but it was nothing like seeing it firsthand. The trees were what got to Caleb the most. What seemed like a thousand of them had been splintered and thrown across the landscape, left fractured and jagged and piled atop one another. There had once been so many, the forest large, unyielding, and deep. It had seemed something impenetrable, forged by God himself. But now it lay in ruin, a miles-long bed of kindling.

Town wasn't any better. Most of it lay in rubble. Brick, cinderblocks, stone, and pipe scattered everywhere. Electrical poles were down, the wires crisscrossing the streets. The roads were blocked, and so they had to park the truck at the edge of town and walk from there. Firefighters, police officers, and first responders took to the streets to clean up, perhaps looking for survivors, the dozen or so who still hadn't been accounted for. The rest of the townsfolk just seemed to wander. They'd pick something up, a tattered book or a store's door signage or a bent stop sign, and just look at it. They'd look at it like they were studying it, and then they would place it back down on the street like it wasn't what they were searching for. A few men with beards and plaid shirts and blue jeans bulldozed much of the rubble with heavy equipment, their engines loud, puffing, deep, and guttural. They made neat piles of the wreckage on street corners, waiting, Caleb supposed, on a better idea of what to do with all of it.

City Hall, like much of town, had been destroyed. The only thing left standing were the concrete stairs leading up to the once grand building. Caleb had seen it when they'd moved to Grove and his mother needed a new driver's license. Inside its halls were large murals painted by local artists. Landscapes mostly, they depicted the lake, sailboats, cattle ranches, and loggers. Now, of course, they were gone, and so too was the mayor. In his stead they found Sheriff Whetsel.

"Gone to Oklahoma City," he said, "to talk to the Governor."

The sheriff was a bulbous man. Round belly, square shoulders, a trailer-hitch jaw, he had the build of an ex-football player. On his face was a bandage, a long strand of gauze that ran from his ear down his cheek and onto his neck, a streak of red staining the middle. A wound, Caleb figured, he'd sustained in the storm. He looked like he hadn't slept in days, his complexion the color of olives, his lips chapped and dry. He showed them to where the Red Cross was handing out supplies. People from all over Oklahoma, Missouri, and Arkansas had come together to donate food, blankets, sunscreen, bug repellent, and water.

"You can take three packages of water," the sheriff said. "We got some bread in there, too. Some dry cereal. Canned corn, beans. Take what you need. We don't have much, but hopefully more will be on the way. Mayor's talking to the Governor and FEMA about declaring a natural disaster, a state of emergency. Bring in trailers. Food. Medical supplies. It's slow going, but we're doing what we can."

They thanked the sheriff, and each of them gathered as much as they could carry from overworked volunteers, strangers who had come from all over to give their time, their resources, and their labor to help those who were in need. Caleb felt comforted by this. Despite so much destruction, good could still be found.

That night they had a feast. Sam baked cornbread, and Caleb's mom cooked a stew. Scoot's family whipped up some sweet tea. They were all over at Sam's house. It was large, but with all thirty-six of the congregation in the first floor, it was a tight fit. The place smelled funny to Caleb, a bit like a wet sponge. The carpet stunk of dust, its fibers worn thin where Sam often traversed, from the kitchen to the den to his master suite on the ground floor. In the kitchen, the appliances were outdated, the color of wilting limes. The toilet downstairs constantly ran, the tank in the back squealing a perpetual, high-pitched whine, but despite this Caleb felt comfortable here, at home.

Caleb sat with Scoot, Brandon, and Catherine. They were quiet, had been since the storm. Their home had been destroyed, along with most others in the community. The vast majority of their possessions had been blown away by the winds, their *Spawn* and *Team 7* comic books, their twelve-gauge shotgun, and their Pog collection, all of it vanished. But Caleb didn't think that was what really bothered them. They were just things, after all. Their sense of security had been shattered, this feeling they were safe and invincible. For the first time in their lives, they had to face the fact they weren't indestructible. Quite the contrary, actually—they were fleeting, vulnerable, and soft.

"I know it doesn't seem like it," Caleb said, "but everything is going to be okay."

They chewed their cornbread, slurped on their stew. They hadn't had a proper shower since the storm, and so their faces were dirty, their hair ratty, tangled into knots. Clothes hadn't been washed, worn for a few days straight. They weren't in the mood to be reassured, and Caleb didn't blame them for this. Sometimes it was okay to be angry.

"Were you guys afraid?" Caleb asked. "During the storm, I mean."

"No," Scoot said. "We were underground."

"Don't lie," Brandon said. "I heard you. You were crying."

Scoot backhanded Brandon in the shoulder. "Like you weren't."

"It's okay," Caleb said. "I was scared, too."

He took a bite of cornbread. It tasted good. A bit hard, the crumbs scratching the roof of his mouth, but despite that it tasted better than any cornbread he'd ever had, filling his stomach, returning his energy, making him feel human again for the first time in days.

"You saw it, didn't you?" Cathcrine asked Caleb.

"Sorry?"

"The tornado. Did you see it?"

Caleb nodded.

"What did it look like?"

He told them. He told them it was the biggest thing he'd ever seen. It didn't look like any tornado he'd seen on TV, twisting violently, throwing up debris, dark in the center, wispy like smoke on the edges. It was just a wall. A black wall, rumbling forth, stampeding across the woods, throwing up trees like matchsticks. It didn't twist, but barreled at him. In that moment, he'd been sure it was the end. He braced for it. He came to terms with it. He said a prayer and repented for his sins, welcomed the moment he would be transported from this world to the next, but it didn't happen. He was spared. They were all spared, and now he was no longer afraid, for he knew God would always take care of them.

"You think this is God taking care of us?" Scoot asked.

"Of course. We're still here, aren't we? Dozens of people died in town, but no one here. Why do you think that is?"

"Luck. Coincidence. I don't know."

"You really believe in luck?"

"You really believe in a god that would do this to us?" He spread his arms and looked about him. The park was in ruins, homes twisted and crumpled, debris strewn about. Wood splintered. Aluminum jagged.

"I do," Caleb said. "I really do."

Scoot took the last bite of his cornbread, washed it down with the last of his tea, then wiped his mouth with the back of his wrist. He didn't say a word. He just stood, picked up his plate, and left.

"Don't mind him," Catherine said when Scoot was out of earshot. "He's just mad. That's all."

DAYS PASSED. A WEEK. BUT help didn't come. The food they'd received the first day in town didn't last long. They tried to ration it, but they had thirty-six mouths to feed and only a few loaves of bread, a dozen or so cans of corn. Even at one meal a day, a ladle full of green beans, one slice of bread, a six-ounce glass of water, it didn't last. Caleb lost weight, just like he had when his mother made him fast. It started out in his face. His cheeks felt sunken. His eyes heavy. His tongue sandpapered. Then he could see his ribs. He'd lie at night on the ground, a fire burning next to him, and count them. One, two, three, four. His stomach growled. It rumbled. But then it started to ache. He felt sick. He dry-heaved even though he didn't have anything in his stomach except phlegm. They waited for word from Oklahoma City and Washington, DC that more help would be coming, huddled around radios and Sam's television, but it never came. A billion-dollar budget deficit had already depleted the state's rainy-day fund, and it couldn't afford to help out at all. FEMA's administration was mired in bureaucratic ineptitude. Insurance companies were delaying payment, stalling through weeks of adjustments and evaluations, trying anything they could to keep from paying out on policies. They were on their own.

Supplies in town ran short. First it was the bottled water. Then soap. Gas. FEMA brought some food but no shelter. Not enough antibiotics. Pharmacies from surrounding communities sent what they could, but it wasn't enough. Victims' wounds got infected. They smelled like pennies and turned the color of mold. People got sick because of it. Kids and the elderly mostly. The infection had seeped into their bloodstream. That was all it took. One moment they were fine, and the next they weren't, the middle occupied by days of painful agony.

Sam sent another contingent into town: Caleb, his mother, Scoot, Brandon, their father, and Sam. Very little had been accomplished since their last visit. Debris still piled up on the roadside. Power lines still hung low, dragged across the streets. Buildings still lay in rubble. The townsfolk took to sitting more than anything. They sat on front stoops that still stood, on lawn chairs bent from the storm, on the ground even, just anywhere they could. More than anything, what struck Caleb was what was absent. Kids no longer played. They didn't ride their bikes down the street or get into fights over pickup games of basketball. Neighbors didn't greet each other or help to take out the trash. Families weren't attending barbecues or birthday parties. Industry stopped. The retirement village where Sam and Caleb's mother worked had been destroyed. Many of the residents had perished. Tourism halted. Summer homes that hadn't been razed went vacant. Hotels and cabins went unoccupied, bait shops closed. And they were out of supplies.

"We don't have anything," the sheriff said. He wasn't defiant about it, or confrontational. He just seemed disappointed in the fact, his bulldog cheeks hanging lower than before.

"You have nothing to spare?" Sam asked. "We need medicine. Rice. Flour. Anything."

"We're all dry. Both FEMA and the Red Cross said they'd bring more food. More medicine. But that was days ago."

"We got kids out there, Sheriff. Old folks. We need help."

"I understand, Sam. I do. We got them here, too."

But it was no use. The sheriff couldn't give what he didn't have, and so they decided to head back to the trailer park. On the way, they passed Pickleman's, a little convenience store still standing. It wasn't much, just a brick building on the edge of town selling bait, soda, beer, cigarettes, and souvenirs: I Love Grand Lake T-shirts and earrings shaped like fishing hooks. A window was broken, and through it, Caleb could see some of the items were missing, others strewn across the floor. Cereal had spilled, and the cash register had been smashed, its drawer open and empty. The sign on the door said "closed," and the lights were out. Sam tried the knob. Locked.

A rifle fired above them. They all jumped. Dread gripped Caleb. He'd heard gunshots before, out hunting with his father and brother and mother, down at the gun range, even just sitting on the steps of his trailer back at the park, the blast echoing over the forest canopy, but it was nothing like this, so close, so unexpected. He didn't know where it was coming from, where it was being aimed, if he himself may be the target. He had the sudden urge to flee, didn't even matter in which direction, but it was like his thighs had filled with concrete. He couldn't move, so he did the only thing he could—he covered his ears. It did no good, though. They still rang a high-pitched hum, so loud Caleb feared they might bleed.

"Get out of here!" a man yelled. It was Mr. Pickleman. He was on the roof of his store, a .30-06 in hand. He'd fired a warning shot when they'd tried to enter his store. Evelyn grabbed Caleb by the shoulder and dragged him back toward the truck, but the message was clear: the people were starting to turn on each other. The clues sprouted all around them. Boarded-up windows, deserted streets, rubble that hadn't been cleared. The people were afraid of each other, so desperate they'd steal from their neighbors, the very friends and confidantes they'd known for years.

And it was, Caleb's mom said, just the beginning.

"There's a war coming," she said, now back at the trailer park, her voice carrying over the congregation without aid from microphone or speaker. For everyone to hear her, she yelled, her face red from strain and drenched in sweat. "It will be a grand war. The final war. The ultimate battle between heaven and hell. You can see the beginnings of it all around us. God has noticed our pride and greed and sloth. He has seen our envy and our wrath. The way we turn our backs on our neighbors, our family, and our friends. And so he has sent us this storm."

The congregation sat outside on the ground. They were all hungry, tired, faces and shoulders sagging, dirty. None had been able to bathe since the storm or eat a proper meal. They were weak and disillusioned. They were searching for help and for answers, wherever they could find them.

"You can see it in our homes even. The godlessness of the youth, of adults possessed by work and toil. They are slaves to the bottle and to the capitalist and to the nightly sitcom. They don't live by the teachings of Jesus. They don't heed the warnings of his apostles. They don't honor their father and their mother. They put other idols before the Lord God."

"Amen."

"Praise Jesus."

Caleb's mom paced, pointing as she spoke, so animated spit flew from her lips. She didn't blink. She didn't stop to take a breath. She was spitfire and exhaust fumes, and she wouldn't stop for anyone.

"A long time ago, the Lord spoke to me. Going on fifteen years now. God came to me when I was wide awake. I wasn't dreaming. I wasn't hallucinating. I wasn't drunk or on drugs. I was at my parents' house. My doctors had told me I was unable to have children, and so I was heartbroken. I didn't see life as worth living anymore. And so, I went to the most pious man I knew, my stepfather, William. He was praying over me when my vision went white. It was strange. I panicked at first, thinking I might be going blind. I wasn't dehydrated or seeing stars or about to pass out. I felt fine. Energetic even, with that rush of adrenaline prayer can bring, but I stopped moving. I stopped where I was at, and I was afraid. I was afraid to speak out, thinking if I said it aloud, that I was going blind, I might somehow make it true, but then I heard a voice. It was clear and crystalline and comforting. He said, 'You will have a son. You will have a special son. You will have my son.'"

"Hallelujah."

"Thank you, Jesus."

"God bless you."

"He said, 'A time will come when you will meet a man. A godly man. A saintly man. This man you will know as Sam, and he will be John the Lamb, and the Seven Seals will be opened and unleash upon the world the end of times.' And that time has come. The Third Seal has been broken. The storm has come, and the people are destitute, but the rich don't come to help. They hide behind their worldly altars, debating the merits of sending aid, of helping their neighbor, lest it hurt their bottom line. 'But fear not,' God said, 'for this will be a blessed event as you, the Lamb, and the Son of God will usher the chosen people from the worldly to unending and infinite bliss.'"

Evelyn's hands were raised above her head, and the congregation hummed feverish dreams. Every single member of the congregation stood on their feet, clapping, stomping, praying, a complete, vibrating organism, and Caleb rose to his feet and he writhed, and his eyes rolled back into his head and he spoke the tongue of the Lord. It came forth from his core. It spewed. It propelled out of him without forethought. It was out of his control. Hands clasped him around his legs and his torso, the congregation lifting him into the air, and he smelled dust. Dust and sweat and the choking, vast humidity, and they carried him as he seized and spoke in tongues, and there were just so many hands touching him, so many hands, so many hands.

CHAPTER 6

THE TOWN TRIED TO PULL TOGETHER. THEY SO-
licited donations from family living elsewhere, Enid and El Reno and
even out of state, wiring in money from cousins in California and old
friends from Kansas. The Southern Baptist Convention sent water, food,
and books for the kids. The Red Cross shipped in volunteers to clear
the roadways, and construction companies from Little Rock and Tulsa
brought in heavy machinery to disperse the debris. Habitat for Humanity sent volunteers from Tulsa and Oklahoma City, and they hauled
with them concrete, shingles, wood, and brick. It wasn't much, the town
was still in ruins, but it gave the people hope, something to cling to.

When news reached the congregation of the donations, the church
volunteered to help. They sent in a contingent of fifteen: Sam, Caleb,
his mother, Scoot, Brandon, and their father, as well as a few more
able-bodied men. The houses weren't much, one-room tiny homes with
a kitchen nook, two beds, and a single toilet. Their only luxuries a few
fans and a wood-burning stove. FEMA still dragged its feet. The state
still hadn't sent help. The electric grid was still down, and the water still
didn't run, but it was enough for the time being. The people needed to
get out of the elements. They needed someplace they could call home.

Caleb, Evelyn, and Sam worked on a home for the Fourkillers, a family whose father had lost his job when the Shangri-La Resort ran into money troubles, so he'd made ends meet by doing odd jobs around town, painting and fixing lawnmowers, basically anything he could. That had meant cuts had to be made, and insurance was one of those things, a luxury poor people often did without, a safety net many took for granted. Then, when the storm had hit, they lost everything, house blown away in the winds, what belongings hadn't disappeared soaked beyond repair by the rains.

It felt good to help, to be outside, stretching underneath the long spring sun, working their muscles and getting exercise. To be a part of something good after so much had gone wrong. Caleb welcomed the change in routine, and he could see it was helping the other members of the congregation. People smiled again. They laughed. They shared stories over a bottle of water, Scoot teasing Brandon about only being able to carry a single two-by-four at a time. It filled Caleb with hope. Maybe more of the chosen were out there. Maybe it wasn't just the congregation who would be saved. Good still permeated the world, its fissures filled with life-giving water, but that was when it started. It wasn't much at first, just whispers and furtive glances from the other volunteers' peripheral. They were from other churches and organizations throughout the community: The Bank of Grand Lake and Warming Dove Baptist and the local PTA. It was the latter who Caleb first noticed staring, like they were hoping the congregation had decided not to show. It was the look that came over their faces, something akin to disappointment but mixed with a certain degree of disgust.

At first Caleb was confused. What had they done to them? But the realization seeped in slowly: news had travelled fast about his mother's warnings. Her sermons to the congregation. They'd heard rumors his mother had preached the end of the world, that her son was the Second Coming of Christ. Caleb knew those looks well, laced with fear and confusion and distrust. He tried to ignore them, but they were ever-present. North, south, east, west, no matter the direction Caleb looked, sideways glances greeted him, whispers, the slight point from a child.

Other members of the congregation soon noticed. Scoot, Brandon, and Catherine were helping unload two-by-fours for the frame, and the other teenagers would go out of their way to avoid them, scared as if the congregation had leprosy. There was no telling what lies their parents had told them. They'd probably called the congregation crazy, whackos, some cult out in the woods who performed animal sacrifice and devil worship. It ate away at Caleb's friends, Brandon especially. He walked with his head buried in his chest, his shoulders sunken, face red not just from the blazing sun. Catherine appeared confused more than anything, trying to strike up conversations with kids she'd known since diapers, but they only offered one-word answers—yes, no, maybe, thanks—before walking away. Scoot, more than anything, was angry. He threw down the lumber with a bang, stomped back to the truck to carry more, picking up two, three, even four two-by-fours at a time, the parents whisking away small children lest he come near.

The adults were aware, too. Sam helped some other men nail the frame together, a long bead of sweat running down his forehead. While the other men chatted away, complaining about the governor and the legislature for their lack of response, FEMA for its bureaucratic mess, Sam was ostracized. They didn't ask for his opinion, and Sam didn't offer one. Instead, he seemed content to toil away. Caleb's mother, of course, wasn't surprised. She smiled a pugnacious smile, making eye contact with anyone who dared come near her, hoping they'd make a snide remark, show their true, sinful selves.

"See how scared they are of the truth," she told Caleb while they were eating lunch. "See how they won't open their eyes to see what's around them."

She and Caleb handed out bottles of water to the volunteers, Caleb carrying the box, his mother grabbing one or two at a time, giving them away to the thirsty, each time with the prayer, "May God have mercy on your soul." No one said anything in return. They just stared at her, confused, or avoided eye contact, not even muttering thanks, and his mother would get closer to the next person, then closer still, to the point she got right in their faces, her eyes mere inches from theirs. "Pray," she said, "or you will regret it."

Eventually, Dr. Cox stopped them. He was a tall man, long-faced, smelling of soil and sweat. Caleb knew who he was—he'd come to the park a couple times during the winter on house calls, checking on elderly patients who had a hard time coming into town. Caleb had liked him then—he'd given Caleb a Capri Sun and asked about him and his mother, if he liked it in their little community so far. He also served in the state legislature, working on behalf of the people to get further aid from the state and the federal government, struggling against powers greater than himself, and when he stopped Caleb's mother, he did so with a warm smile, a reassuring hand on her forearm.

"You're scaring people, Evelyn."

"They should be scared, Doctor."

"This isn't the time or the place."

"It's always the right time. It's always the right place. Tell me, Doctor. Do you believe in God?"

"These people are tired. They're scared. They've been through a lot. They don't need this on top of it."

"Then this is the best time for them to hear the word of God. It's coming soon. Whether you believe or not. God doesn't care."

"I think it might be best if you leave now."

"The devil is coming. He will come for you. He will come for you all. When the final war is fought, you will all be doomed."

"Please, Evelyn. I must insist."

When he ordered them to leave, Caleb was hurt, but he wasn't surprised. Neither were his mother or Sam. It was like they'd been expecting this, waiting for the inevitability, their banishment from the regular goings-on of the community. But their hurt wasn't because of the banishment itself, of being marginalized as outcasts. They'd grown accustomed to that. They hurt because they knew the others didn't realize what they were doing. There'd be the chosen, and then there'd be everyone else. The congregation would be ushered into heaven, and the rest would be destined for an eternity in hellfire. It was just a matter of time. His mother and Sam weren't hurt because the townsfolk didn't accept them. They were hurt because there was nothing they could do to save them.

THE CONGREGATION SECLUDED THEMSELVES FROM the rest of town. They spent more time at home, at the church. When they were forced to go into town, they pooled together their resources, went in groups of ten or twelve to ask for food for the entire congregation.

Whatever they had to do in the community, whether it was get medicine or supplies, tools or clothing, they always did it in groups. No one was ever alone, not man, woman, or child, until they could determine their members were safely at home in their beds, deadbolts locked in place and lights turned dark. It was easier that way. They weren't so exposed.

The community didn't react with violence. Most of the time they were cordial enough, shaking hands and having a friendly chat about the latest from the capitol or FEMA, how they kept dragging their feet, how things were getting worse as opposed to better. A few townsfolk were getting sick. They coughed and hacked up phlegm, ran a fever. Their appetites had deteriorated, and they were growing weaker. Doctor Cox did what he could, but they weren't getting better, and the congregation would offer their thoughts and their prayers. What Caleb noticed more, though, was that the conversations were stilted, their gazes no longer teeming with the intimacy of communion and knowledge but rather replaced with suspicion and judgment. The town didn't trust the congregation. They feared them, not understanding their convictions. If they were crazy, what, exactly, were they capable of? And that's what worried the congregation the most—this fear. A man gripped with fear was capable of many a monstrous thing.

Other things returned to a semblance of normalcy. After a few weeks, the children of the congregation resumed their schoolwork. They met at Sam's house in the mornings, and Caleb's mom and a few of the other parents would teach subjects they were most learned in, Caleb's mother tackling math and science, and Sam history and English. The curriculum was the same as before the storm. In English, they read the classics, *Great Expectations* by Charles Dickens and *Lord of the*

Flies. What books Sam had the children shared, taking turns to read by firelight at dusk. They discussed themes such as mob rule, anarchy, affection, loyalty, and conscience. They related it to the community at large and their smaller church family. They wrote essays and debated the merits of democracy, republicanism, oligarchy, and monarchy in social studies. In biology, they touched on the subject of evolution.

Slowly but surely, the congregation rebuilt. They built new homes, small ones that went up one or two at a time, never really with an overreaching goal in mind. Caleb's and his mom's was nice. A simple one-room home featuring two beds, a sink and shower, a little stovetop to cook. It didn't have luxuries such as a TV, but Caleb didn't mind. Really, he only went there to sleep. The rest of his days he filled studying, working with the community, hunting with Sam and Scoot and Brandon, and attending service. They built a large fence around the community, the gate at the entrance perpetually locked. They built a worship hall, large and unadorned, out of simple oak. It didn't have windows or a large, towering steeple, but it was enough. What they built served a purpose, and Caleb enjoyed their new homes. They would provide shade during the heat of the summer and warmth in the cold of winter. The elderly and the young could better brave the elements, the sun and the wind and the rain. The worship hall was a place they could all congregate, support one another, and worship together. It was a practical thing. That was all, more or less.

Next came a small one-room schoolhouse. It also wasn't anything grand or special. It had a fireplace, and desks bolted to the ground. Sam opted for a regular green chalkboard instead of a whiteboard. It worked well enough, but the problem, they soon realized, was the students were of all different ages, some in middle school, a few high-schoolers, and several small children, anywhere between kindergarten and fifth grade. They used sheets to separate the grades as best they could and tried to keep their lessons quiet lest they disturbed their neighbors.

They built a barn and planted a garden. They built sheds to store tools: rakes and saws and tillers, hammers and wood screws and drills. They built several outhouses and dug a well. More and more they spent their time there, and though needs arose that took them to town, they mostly stayed home, happy with their few belongings. Each day that passed, they became more self-sufficient, having to travel out less and less. They had water. They had food. They had rifles to hunt and tackle to fish. Before Caleb even realized it, spring spilled into summer, and it had been weeks since he'd been to town. News of the townsfolks' well-being became scant. He knew it couldn't be good. On the highway leading to town, he never saw National Guard or FEMA trucks going in to help, bringing in large supplies. The sky was devoid of airplanes or helicopters. They, like the congregation, had been mostly left to fend for themselves. At first, he worried about them. He prayed for them. But after a while it got easier not to.

But then the townsfolk came to them. It was late when it occurred, the last week of June. That particular night was just like any other. Caleb couldn't get cool, and so he couldn't sleep. He tried to shut off his mind, but he couldn't. He thought about hunting with Scoot earlier in the day, the doe he'd had in his crosshairs but missed. He thought about what they'd learned in school that afternoon, lessons on Nehemiah and the Seven Seals. He stared up at the ceiling, counting his mother's breaths in the dark like a bomb counting down, ten, nine, eight, seven, six, when he first heard something off in the distance. It was just a low murmur, like a dog's growl, which wasn't all that unusual in the day, but this was about two in the morning. Despite the howl of the wind and the distant sounds of waves crashing against the lakeshore, the night typically was calm.

At first, he just ignored the noise. It could be any number of things. It could've been a coyote, growling at his shadow, or even the GRDA, patrolling the lake because of an anonymous tip of some teenagers partying on a dock somewhere. It could've even been a crazy neighbor, revving up his chainsaw in order to cut down another neighbor's tree in the middle of the night because the limbs hung over his property line. For a while, it just stayed at the same level, this low hum, so Caleb ignored it, but then it grew louder until he could make out what it was: a truck.

This was about as strange a noise as could be heard at this time of night. They lived off a seldom-used county road. To make it this far out, they had to have a reason. It was doubtful someone who was lost would wind up at their property. When the road narrowed and the pavement turned to gravel and then to dirt, most people turned around, knowing they'd taken a wrong turn somewhere. If they made it out this far, whoever they were had to know where they were going.

Caleb sat up in bed, careful not to wake his mom, and made his way to the window. Outside, it was dark. There were no streetlights or lampposts on their land. The moonlight wasn't strong enough for him to see anything with any type of definition. It just looked black out there, the landscape dotted with shadows and the strange, rhythmic movement of the forest canopy. Despite willing himself not to be, he was still, if he was honest with himself, scared of the dark. It petrified him. He was ashamed of this fact and fought it with as much courage as he could muster, but the gnawing fear something lurked out there, monster or demon, perpetually grated his good sense. Soon, the truck's headlights came into view, illuminating a narrow swath of land. The truck approached the gate, but the lights were too bright for Caleb to make out the make or model. He checked to see if the sound of the truck had woken his mother, but it hadn't.

As the truck got closer, the driver killed the lights, and soon it was close enough Caleb could somewhat make it out. It was a smaller truck, boxy, with a rail of KC lights on top of the cabin. In the bed appeared to be a couple figures, men, women, he couldn't tell, and they were moving. The engine idled, so Caleb couldn't tell if they were talking or not, but then he saw something that alarmed him: the flickering of what appeared to be a cigarette lighter.

He shook his mother, and she stirred.

"What?" she mumbled. "What do you want?" She pulled the blanket tighter around her shoulders and kept her eyes shut tight.

"I think you should see this."

"What is it, Caleb? I'm exhausted."

"Seriously, Mom." He shook her shoulder again, harder this time. "You need to see this."

The light took, and a small flame burned in the back of the truck. Caleb could make out the features of a man. He was young looking with a shaved head. He had on a white T-shirt that was too big for him, the sleeves flapping in the breeze around his smaller arms, but then Caleb couldn't see him anymore. He threw the item burning in his hand, and it collided with the side of their home. That's when Mom bolted upright and pushed Caleb aside. A second collision banged against the side of the wall, and Caleb could smell grass and rubber burning.

"Run," Caleb's mom said. She didn't scream it. She didn't seem panicked. It was just an order, like she was telling Caleb to wash the dishes or take out the trash. "Run," she said, and Caleb obeyed.

When he swung open the door, the truck tore out of there, its tires squealing and kicking up dirt. By the time Caleb and his mother were a safe distance from the trailer, the truck was already speeding down the dirt road, too far to make out any identifying characteristics. They'd never know for sure who it was, but the damage they'd done was clear. Their home was engulfed in flames. Caleb and his mother had no phone to call for help. No hose to quench the flames. There wasn't even a fire department close enough to help in time. Soon, all their belongings burned, and Caleb and his mother just stood there watching, not knowing what else they could do.

Others woke. They came to help, dousing the flames the best they could with buckets of water, forming a line back to the lake, sending bucket after bucket after bucket, but there was nothing to be saved. In a matter of weeks, Caleb and his mother had watched their home be destroyed twice. It wasn't until around dusk that they were able to extinguish the blaze. What remained was a black, smoldering pit, full of ash and stinking of sulfur. There wasn't anything else to do but rebuild, but that would wait until later. They instead washed up the best they could, enjoyed a small breakfast of biscuits and water, and then convened for their morning sermon.

"The end is upon us," Caleb's mother said. She stood at the pulpit in the newly built church. She stood alone, tired and worn, but as she spoke, she shook with passion and with fury. "And the seventh angel poured out his vial into the air; and there came a great voice out of the temple of heaven, from the throne, saying, it is done. And there were voices, and thunders, and lightnings; and there was a great earthquake, such as was not since men were upon the earth, so mighty an earthquake, and so great.'"

As his mother spoke, Caleb felt a burning inside of him. It started out in his stomach, a slight tremble, but it grew in intensity, catching fire and raging through his muscles and bones.

"'And the great city was divided into three parts, and the cities of the nations fell: and great Babylon came in remembrance before God, to give unto her the cup of the wine of the fierceness of his wrath. And every island fled away, and the mountains were not found. And there fell upon men a great hail out of heaven, every stone about the weight of a talent: and men blasphemed God because of the plague of the hail; for the plague thereof was exceeding great.'"

"Amen," Sam said. "Praise Jesus."

"I know you can see it," Caleb's mother continued. "The seventh plague is upon us. It is here. We are living it now. The earth is being destroyed. Our leaders are allowing it to happen. And our neighbors have turned against us."

Caleb's entire body stirred. The energy cascaded through him, his mother's words spurring him on.

"The final battle between heaven and hell is being fought right here, in our very own community. The tornado. The destruction. The violence. It is time for us, the chosen, to stand up, and it is time for us to fight."

Caleb erupted into tongues, the Lord's words flowing through him. They filled him up. They heated and expanded his body until he felt ten times his normal size. He felt indestructible. He felt immortal, and Scoot and Brandon lifted Caleb above their heads and raised him above the congregation, carrying him across the loving arms of his brothers and sisters in Christ, warriors of God.

CHAPTER 7

SCOOT GOT SICK ON JULY 4TH. AT FIRST, HE JUST lost a bit of weight. He was a big kid, muscular and lean, and so he helped the men with construction projects and manual labor around the community, mending fences and digging ditches and building furniture. He was strong and tough and good with a hammer, and Caleb was, he hated to admit, jealous of him. Jesus had been a carpenter after all, and though Caleb could help out with simple tasks, measuring the lumber, hammering nails, Scoot could build a dining-room table from scratch. He'd go out and chop down the trees. He'd cut the wood. He'd sand it down. He'd fashion it together. It was just something he could do, an inherent trait buried deep down in his bones.

But then he changed. His muscle mass deteriorated. His complexion turned wan. It was slow at first, hardly noticeable. Caleb noted something strange the morning of the fourth. They were preparing for a communal feast where all the members of the congregation could eat and gather together, give thanks for all they had, break bread and pray together as one voice. To help prepare for the feast, Brandon, Scoot, and Caleb set up tables. There were about a dozen of them in all shapes and sizes. Scoot often liked to show off, but this morning was different. He got winded. He seemed lethargic, like he hadn't slept in days. Before, he'd have been able to pick up the tables from the bed of Sam's pickup and hoist them above his head, carrying them into the worship hall almost effortlessly, but that morning he breathed heavily, bent over at the waist. His normal smile gave way to a pained grimace, his normal Herculean self worn down to something average, soft even.

"Sure you're okay?" Brandon asked.

"Yeah," Scoot said. "Yeah, of course. Just tired. That's all."

Scoot turned quiet. He sweated until his shirt was soaked, and he breathed through his mouth. But he didn't stop. He tried to pick up his pace, straining to lift and willing his feet to move forward, one after the other, dragging just above the ground. Caleb worried. He'd never seen Scoot like this. Usually a ball of kinetic energy, Scoot was an electron in an excited state. He never tired. He never struggled. He never fell ill. It was almost against the laws of physics how he worked. But when he went back to the truck the final time, Caleb knew he was hurting. He bent at his waist and leaned against Sam's truck, taking deep breaths with his face turned toward the ground like he might vomit.

"You're not," Caleb said. He put his hand on Scoot's forehead, but he jerked away. "You're burning up. Let me get your parents. Sam. My mom. Somebody."

"I'm fine," Scoot said. "Really. Let's just keep working."

"Just take it easy. Sit over there. We'll get the rest of the chairs."

"You two wimps?" Scoot tried to laugh but coughed instead. It was deep and raspy, choked with phlegm.

Caleb found Sam inside the worship hall, pushing pews against the walls so as to make room for the tables, and asked him to come. By the time they returned, Scoot sat against Sam's truck, trembling. He'd vomited since Caleb had left, and he moaned and rocked back and forth, his arms crossed in front of him. He'd deteriorated quickly, and it scared Caleb. He'd seen people sick before, with bronchitis, pneumonia, even cancer, but he'd never witnessed someone turn so pale, so fragile, so hot to the touch within minutes. He wondered when and if it would stop. At this pace, it seemed Scoot might die within the day.

They got Scoot to his feet and took him to his home, where they found his parents. They put Scoot in bed and got him a washrag to put over his forehead and a glass of water to drink. They didn't have anything else to help him. No Tylenol or Aspirin to curb the fever, nothing to numb the pain. All they could do was give him fluids, a bed to rest, and prayers for his quick recovery. Caleb's mother soon arrived, and they deliberated what to do next.

"He needs to see a doctor," Scoot's father said. He was a tall man, soft-spoken, with a gangly build. When he walked, his joints appeared to move in opposite directions, his shoulders up, his knees forward, his elbows back. It was as if he were always moments away from falling over, but Caleb admired him—he was a good man, a godly man, giving and kind.

"How?" Caleb's mother asked. "He's too weak to make it into town. And we have no idea what it's like there now. We haven't been there in weeks. It could be chaos for all we know."

"We have to do something," Sam said. "The boy is suffering."

"I know he's suffering. I saw him, Sam. That's not the point."

"I'm going whether you give your permission or not," Scoot's father said.

"It's dangerous. You saw what they're capable of. They tried to kill us. They burned down our home."

"He's my child, Evelyn. My child. If it were Caleb, you'd do the same."

"He needs you here. With him. What will happen if they hurt you? If they won't let you leave? If, God forbid, they kill you?"

"I have to take that chance."

"We're in a war here."

"Stop," Sam said. "Stop." He had a pained expression on his face, one of great consternation, like he had to command his blood to continue to flow through his veins. "The child is sick. We have to go. Period."

Caleb's mother looked at him. "Okay," she said, her face toward the ground, hands raised in resignation. "Fine."

Sam and Scoot's father climbed into Sam's truck, and Sam turned the engine. A plume of black smoke kicked back out of the exhaust pipe, and as they inched down the drive toward the gate, Caleb took off running and jumped into the bed of the truck. He didn't even think about it. It was just instinct. His friend was in trouble, and he had to do what he could to help. Find medicine. Find a doctor. It didn't even matter what. He had to do something. His mother yelled for him to stop, for Sam to stop, but they didn't listen, instead heading out on the gravel drive toward the highway to town.

Grove was deserted. There were a few people. Men, mostly, still rummaging through the destroyed buildings, picking at trash that had been scattered by the breeze—empty cans, mud-covered shopping bags, shredded blankets—looking for anything that might be useful. It was obvious help hadn't come, the state, the feds, nobody. Most of the people had abandoned their homes, hit the road if they had a running car, staying with relatives in nearby towns or just finding what they could where they could, maybe a motel in Joplin, a job bussing tables at a roadside diner. What was left in Grove could hardly be described as livable any longer. A tent city had sprung up in the middle of a park that had once been filled with the laughter of children playing on swings, slides, and seesaws. Now it teemed with people cooking over open flames, five or six per fire, wrapped in dingy shirts and shorts, their conversations hushed and clipped. Several hacked and coughed as Sam, Scoot's father, and Caleb passed by, covering their mouths with dirty handkerchiefs or the inside of their elbow. None appeared to have eaten a decent meal in weeks. Cheeks sunken. Complexions the color of pea soup.

To Caleb's surprise, nobody paid them much mind as they searched for help. He'd expected a visceral reaction, one of disdain and scorn for their foretelling of the coming apocalypse, their very damnation. Rocks to be thrown. Curses spat. But that wasn't the case. They didn't cast aspersions to Caleb or Sam or Scoot's father. No sideways glances. No judgment. Instead, they kept to themselves, wrapped up in blankets to fend off the mosquitos. Caleb didn't blame them, though. He'd learned before about the five stages of grief: denial, anger, bargaining, depression, and finally, acceptance. Caleb had seen their denial, and he'd seen their anger. Now they'd reached acceptance. Or maybe it was depression. Caleb wasn't sure.

Near the back of the park they found a larger tent. It looked like something from out of a carnival, though it was made of simple blue tarp instead of the red-and-white candy stripes. A smell creeped from there, something nauseating, debilitating, a stench that seeped inside of Caleb, wrenched his insides, making him gag. It reminded him of his uncle's pig farm. He raised about 150,000 pigs per year in forty low-slung, warehouse-like barns. Caleb had visited it once when he'd been about six or seven, and his uncle let him go into one of the barns. Inside he found about fifteen hundred sows locked up in small cages, unable to turn around. They spent their whole lives like that, his uncle explained, eating there, sleeping there, even going to the bathroom there. Their waste was vacuumed out through large vats, but despite the tubes Caleb couldn't get over the smell. It was a mixture of ammonia and hydrogen sulfide, poisonous gases that could, if breathed in for a time, kill him.

Inside the tent, Caleb, Sam, and Scoot's father found rows of men, women, and children lying on makeshift cots. They coughed. They wheezed. They moaned. A woman near Caleb squirmed in pain. She was a younger woman, perhaps mid-twenties. Red hair. Freckles covered her face. A complexion like she suffered from jaundice. She sweated, her dingy blanket soaked with perspiration around the hem. To his shame, Caleb had the immediate impulse to run. Not to help. Not to grab water and a cool rag and try to comfort her. Instead, he wished to flee, his fight-or-flight instinct kicking in so strongly he had a hard time catching his breath, his inhales raspy, quick, and urgent, his exhales clogged in his throat. The place frightened him, and he couldn't help but cover his mouth and nose with his shirt lest he should breathe in whatever these people were ailing from. They looked like they were dying, and for the first time in his life Caleb feared death.

He wondered what this said about him. He was to usher the chosen into the kingdom of heaven; he was a virgin birth, the Second

Coming of Christ, but his reaction to those suffering was nothing Christ-like. It was pedestrian. Common. Cowardly. He wasn't any better than the rest who had fled town, who had burned their home to the ground. Or perhaps, he thought, Jesus could have been afraid, too. Maybe when he'd healed the leper, the soldier, the sick in Peter's house, he'd been afraid, but he acted anyway. Afraid he'd catch the skin disease, that he, too, would become feverish. But it didn't stop him from acting. That was what separated Jesus from man—the ability to help despite his dread, and so Caleb went to comfort the woman in spite of his misgivings, his fears of what would happen if he became sick like her. But before he could reach her, Sam grabbed him by the shoulder to stop him.

Near the center of the tent was Dr. Cox. He looked exhausted. Hair disheveled, eyes bloodshot. He had a stethoscope on and was listening to a teenage boy's heartbeat. He had a pained expression on his face, one mixed with deep concentration and thinly masked despair. He didn't wear latex gloves or a doctor's lab coat but instead had on a plaid button-down, and blue jeans stained dark with mud. When he noticed Caleb, Sam, and Scoot's father near the entrance to the tent, he didn't acknowledge them. He just stared at them as if determining whether or not they were real.

"Dr. Cox," Sam said.

The doctor took out the earbuds to the stethoscope. He didn't offer a hand to shake or a greeting.

"There's a boy sick at the park," Sam continued. "Scoot Finch. Fever. Nausea. Pain. He's delirious and needs help."

"Dysentery more than likely."

"Is that what everyone has?" Caleb asked.

The doctor nodded. "There's been an outbreak. No IVs. Little clean water or antibiotics. We've had two die already."

"Where is everybody?" Scoot's father asked. "Why isn't the government helping?"

"We've asked," the doctor said. "We've been made promises. They told us there would be doctors and medicine and food and water and shelter, but it hasn't come. They've done nothing."

"Can you come see my boy?" Scoot's father asked.

The doctor swallowed like his throat hurt but was trying not to complain. "How long has he been sick?"

"Today. That's when the fever started."

"He's been weaker than normal," Caleb said, "Not quite Scoot for about two or three days. Sluggish. Fatigues easy. Stomach pain."

The doctor nodded. A patient moaned. Another coughed. The tent filled with raspy breathing, a man hacking up phlegm, the gags of a child. Caleb wondered if it was safe for them to be in there, if the bacteria was seeping down into their lungs with every inhale, infecting them, embedding right down into their cells. The doctor's words rang in his ears: two had died already.

"Is there blood in his stool?" the doctor asked.

"No," Scoot's father said. "Not that I know of."

"Is he responsive?"

"Yeah."

"Can he hold a conversation? Lost his appetite? A lot of weight?"

"A little, I guess. Yeah."

The doctor walked to the other side of the tent. Sam, Caleb, and Scoot's father followed.

"He'll need plenty of rest. Clean water, if you have it. Lots of it.

Try to keep the fever down as best you can. Cool washrag on the forehead. If you have any medicine left, use it. Tylenol. Aspirin. Anything that can break the fever. Keep him away from the elderly and the young. Quarantine him as much as possible if you can. Implement strict sanitation protocols."

"Are you not going to come?"

"I wish I had some antibiotics to give you. I wish I had anything. But I don't."

"Are you not going to come?" Scoot's father asked again.

"I have so many patients here."

"You're not going to come?" he asked again.

The doctor sighed. It wasn't one of exasperation but of dismay. He wanted to help. Caleb could tell by the way his shoulders slumped, the look of defeat etched into his face. He'd taken an oath, after all, but he was just one man.

"I'll try," the doctor said. "In a few days, I'll try."

When they returned to the community, they found Scoot's mother sitting by his bedside. She wetted a washcloth and read from the Bible.

" 'So do not fear, for I am with you; do not be dismayed, for I am your God. I will strengthen you and help you; I will uphold you with my righteous hand.' "

It was from Isaiah, the Helper of Israel.

"'All who rage against you will surely be ashamed and disgraced; those who oppose you will be as nothing and perish. Though you search for your enemies, you will not find them. Those who wage war against you will be as nothing at all. For I am the Lord your God who takes hold of your right hand and says to you, Do not fear; I will help you.'"

They tried to go about their lives as usual. In the morning, the children went to school. Caleb struggled to pay attention during social studies class, and so did all the other kids, too. Sam lectured, but there was a noticeable change in his demeanor, his voice timid, his gaze lingering above the classroom full of children, daring not fixate on the empty seat in the third row, glaring in Scoot's absence. Caleb and the other kids played soccer and attended church and flirted with the opposite sex like they knew what they were doing. They prayed for themselves and for others, and they ate what they could fish, what they could hunt in the woods, whitetail and rabbit and squirrel, and they laughed, but all of it was just a well-orchestrated charade. They were acting, going through the motions, pretending like the world continued to move on as it always had, with Scoot in it, healthy and laughing and pranking kids smaller than him, when the impending apocalypse wasn't just a few moments beyond the horizon.

On a Thursday morning, Caleb and Catherine were fetching water from the well at the edge of the property when they stopped by the lake's edge. It was sweltering out, and a stiff wind flew up from the south and rustled the oak branches behind them. Everything was bright, and the air was wet and thick. It filled Caleb's nostrils and clogged his throat. He feared he, too, might be getting sick, but he didn't say anything. He hoped if he ignored it, if he boiled his water enough and cleaned his food the best he could, it would go away on its own.

He and Catherine stared out over the water, taking refuge in the moment, when they didn't have to think about Scoot locked up in his room suffering. She leaned in and kissed him. It took Caleb by surprise, and he jerked back, but she kissed him again, softer this time, letting her lips linger. He'd long thought of what it would be like to kiss a girl, fantasizing about it like it was some sort of magical thing, soft and mysterious and the most pleasurable thing in the world, like falling into a never-ending pillow, but it wasn't exciting at all. It just was. It came quickly and unexpectedly and was over before he knew it. She then stood up and walked away.

Two days later, Scoot's mother began to vomit. She'd been Scoot's primary caregiver since he'd become ill, feeding him, bathing him, providing him comfort and prayer. Ruth was her name, and she was the tallest woman Caleb knew. She was also the most giving and caring. Before the storm, she'd drop off some banana muffins at the community's school for the children, or pick up a toy or two at the Dollar Store for the smaller kids, little plastic slingshots and Marvel action figures, Captain America and Thor. She smiled incessantly and laughed with her entire body, her skin turning pink and her mouth wide. She was one person Caleb could spend every single day with and not grow tired of her presence. She just had that way with people—she always made everyone feel welcome. That afternoon, though, it was difficult to look at her. She'd been crying, and her cheeks and eyes were puffy and purple. Caleb could tell she was in pain, both physically and emotionally, seeing her boy suffer, not knowing exactly what to do to help him, knowing that she, too, was growing sick.

More followed. It always started with stomach pain. Then came the loss of appetite. Weight dripped off the ill like melting ice cream, then came the diarrhea. Aches in their muscles, their bones throbbing, gnawing at them until it felt like their bodies were disintegrating. Their fevers ballooned until their skin turned pink, then red, and was hot to the touch. They'd be bedridden, moaning under sweat-stained sheets. Most faced it bravely, not allowing themselves to complain, to place a burden on their caretakers, but their agony was apparent. They wore it on their faces like Halloween masks. It was the only way Caleb could think of them without crippling under immense sadness and helplessness. His prayers he uttered with as much fervor as he could muster, but he knew there would be no recompense in this life, only in the next, after Revelation had come.

"Unyielding faith is important," his mother said. The healthy had congregated at the church. Their numbers had started to dwindle, from thirty-six to thirty to twenty-five, now more than a dozen sick and at home, struggling to sleep. "It's something noble. It's something rewarded both here and in the afterlife. And you have it. I know it. I know it as I know the sun is yellow and the grass is green and that God looks down upon us and smiles. And in the coming days, in the coming weeks, in the coming months, you will need to remember that. You'll need to remember your faith. You'll need to remember your God, because the end of times is upon us."

She looked tired, more tired than Caleb ever remembered seeing her. Her hair was streaked gray, and her skin sagged and pruned as if soaked with lake water.

"The Fourth Seal has broken," she said. "'And I looked, and behold a pale horse: and his name that sat on him was Death, and hell followed with him. And power was given unto them over the fourth part of the earth, to kill with sword, and with hunger, and with death, and with the beasts of the earth.'

"Our own are sick. Scoot Finch. A young boy. A strong boy. He's been afflicted. His mother. Several others. And they're going to die. There's nothing we can do to stop it. We may be sad. We may be angry. We may be confused. But we should not be afraid, for this is God's plan. He has chosen us.

"'Then I looked, and behold, on Mount Zion stood the Lamb, and with him 144,000 who had his name and his Father's name written on their foreheads. And I heard a voice from heaven like the roar of many waters and like the sound of loud thunder. The voice I heard was like the sound of harpists playing on their harps, and they were singing a new song before the throne and before the four living creatures and before the elders. No one could learn that song except the 144,000 who had been redeemed from the earth. It is these who have not defiled themselves with women, for they are virgins. It is these who follow the Lamb wherever he goes. These have been redeemed from mankind as first fruits for God and the Lamb, and in their mouth no lie was found, for they are blameless.'"

Caleb's mother walked from the pulpit. She walked down the aisle through the middle of the congregation, and she left the worship hall. The remaining congregants didn't move. They sat in the pews as if they were awaiting further instructions. For several minutes they sat like that, preparing themselves, each in their own individual way, for they all, deep down, knew Caleb's mother was correct. The end was coming. Death was upon them. They were powerless to stop it. Even if they wanted to, death and destruction and the end of times were near. It was a strange moment for Caleb, realizing this, that the world was going to end and he would be there to see it. He had to make peace with it. And he had to face it head-on.

Eventually, a few got up to leave, one or two or three at a time. No one said a word as they did so. They didn't have to. It was all imprinted on their faces: a sweet mixture of fear and glee, for they would see the world burn.

CHAPTER 8

LARGE TRUCKS RUMBLED DOWN THE HIGHWAY, helicopters soared overhead, and National Guard troops clad in heavy boots and assault rifles marched toward town. Caleb heard them before he saw them. They were louder than he would have expected, a pulse that he could feel just as much as he could hear. There were three helicopters that first morning. He and Brandon were digging an irrigation ditch along the west side of the property when they flew overhead. Caleb had never seen a helicopter so close. The blades thrummed in his eardrums a staccato beat, oscillating like a giant ceiling fan. They were so close he thought he could reach out and touch them. Neither Caleb nor Brandon said a word. Caleb was in too much shock to say anything. It was the oddest thing he'd ever seen. He would've been less surprised to see the sky tear open and for all the angels of heaven to come pouring out.

Then came the trucks. Rows and rows of them. Humvees painted Vallejo green and eighteen-wheelers carrying what Caleb could only assume was food, water, and medicine. It wasn't just soldiers filling the trucks. There were also aid workers, doctors, and volunteers. They wore plainclothes, white-collared shirts, dark denim jeans, and work boots instead of the long-sleeved camouflage and black combat boots of the National Guardsmen. Caleb felt an immediate sense of relief when he saw them. Perhaps, he thought, the end of the world might not be coming. Perhaps Scoot and his mother and the rest of the congregation wouldn't die. Perhaps they'd be saved, and all would return to normal in a few weeks. Fall would return, and with it the turning of the leaves, maybe the hum of motorboats, the laughter of families out on the water, sunburnt and happy. Perhaps his mother was wrong.

Caleb dropped his shovel and raced back toward home. He found his mother there, washing dishes. Her arms were soaked, bubbles up to her elbows from soap they'd made from lard. Sam had taught them how to do it, melting the fat into a large pot, pouring in lye, and stirring hard to a creamy mixture. The smell was something awful, and it made Caleb nauseated just thinking about it, the mixture of innards and chemical curdling his stomach.

He and Brandon told his mother what they'd seen.

"What was on them?" she asked.

"I'm sorry?"

"The helicopters, did they have paintings on them?"

"Paintings? They were dark green."

"A logo. A red cross in a white circle. The flag. Anything."

"I don't remember."

She stopped washing a coffee mug, letting it float in the basin before it filled with water and sank below the surface. She dried her hands with an old towel full of holes and loose threads.

"Were they filled with soldiers?"

"The trucks were," Brandon said.

"But there were others, too," Caleb said. "Doctors possibly. Volunteers. We could be saved."

"Saved from what?" she asked. "From God?"

"They could come to help. Maybe they have medicine for Scoot. For his mom. The others. Food. Water. Things could go back to normal."

"Normal?" she asked. "What's normal about this? A disaster. Plague. Soldiers marching into town. What seems normal about this to you, son?"

"I don't understand. I thought this was a good thing."

"Think about it, Caleb. You're smarter than this."

He knew his mother was testing him. He hated when she did this. He always felt like he disappointed her when he couldn't find the right answer, and this gnawed at him, turned his brain into sandpaper and jagged edges, but then it came to him. "The Fifth Seal?" he asked, like answering a question on a game show they'd used to watch together after school in Bartlesville. *Jeopardy!*, Caleb remembered. That seemed so long ago.

She nodded. " 'And when he had opened the fifth seal, I saw under the altar the souls of them that were slain for the word of God, and for the testimony which they held.'"

They found Sam at his house praying, and together they rounded up the healthy members of the congregation. They met in the worship hall, and most of them had heard and seen the helicopters and the trucks themselves. Rumors had already spread. Some thought they only came to help, that they would cure the sick, feed the hungry, and shelter the cold. Others still thought they were demons incarnate, sent from the devil himself, there to wage the final battle between heaven and hell. One by one they spoke, all of them uncertain, despondent, unsure of themselves and what to do next.

"We should send a few into town," Scoot's father said. "See why they've come. See for ourselves what they intend to do."

A few of the others agreed, younger members with small children in tow, locked on their mothers' hips. All of them were tired, hungry, and afraid. Caleb could tell by the way they collapsed in on themselves, their eyes desperate, their hands wringing and bleeding. It was like he could even read their thoughts. What if they were the next to get sick? Their children? What, exactly, would they do then?

"They could harm us," Caleb's mother said. "Imprison us. Kill us. It's too big of a risk."

"We have to do something," Scoot's father said. "People are sick, Evelyn. They could die. My wife might die. My son. I'll lose everything."

"You're not losing anything. You're gaining eternal bliss. Can't you see that? We're being tested. God is testing us. Now is not the time to lose our faith."

"I am not losing my faith. Do not question my faith. I just don't want to see my family die."

"It's the end of times. We're all going to die."

"But that doesn't mean we can't look out for each other. We are the chosen, right? The faithful are to help the least amongst us."

"Do you remember how they treated us?" she asked, pointing in the direction of town. "Do you remember being ridiculed and mocked? Do you remember when they set fire to my home? They've already tried to kill us. What makes you think they won't shoot you down on the spot?"

Caleb's mother spoke with a fervor and passion Caleb had grown to expect from her. She'd always had it, but it had hardened in the past few months, its edges sharpened, charged with static electricity. It was impossible to argue with her, though some tried and failed because of her hot moral outrage. It seethed from her, escaped from her pores, attacked everyone within earshot. It both frightened and excited Caleb to be her offspring, her golden child. It made him teem with pride but also shake with fear he'd never live up to her expectations.

"I have to go," Scoot's father said. "Whether you like it or not."

"Maybe he's right," Sam said. "Maybe it's worth checking out."

She sighed, threw up her hands. "Fine," she said. "But I'm coming with you."

Caleb's mother didn't allow him to go into town with the rest. She said he was too important to risk, that he had to stay there with the sick and the frightened and comfort them, and so he did. While he waited, he visited Scoot. Both he and his mother were in bed, their breaths raspy and weak. Scoot had lost perhaps twenty pounds since falling ill, his skin turning the color of an infected sore. He was conscious of his surroundings maybe only an hour or two a day. During that time, his father tried to make him eat, but he refused, citing nausea and pain. Scoot was giving up, and Caleb didn't blame him. Faced with the same symptoms, Caleb would more than likely do the same, waste away until he was nothing but a bag of bones.

Dr. Cox had told them he'd been lobbying for help from the state and the federal government. Maybe they'd finally heeded his warnings. Maybe they brought with them IVs to replenish fluids, clean water, and antibiotics. Maybe they'd cure the sick and rebuild the town. Maybe in a few days they'd eat fresh fruit again, an apple or a banana or even a pineapple. He could taste its tartness now, feel its juices spilling over his tongue, feel his belly full, his muscles regaining their strength. Natural disasters happened. They had since the beginning of time. There were earthquakes and fires and volcanos and hurricanes and tsunamis. Every day they occurred. Eventually, though, the devastation would subside, and the victims would band together to grieve the departed and relish the chance to start anew. God could be testing them, but maybe the Seals hadn't been broken.

Caleb passed the time by repeating a bedtime prayer over and over. "Now I lay me down to sleep, I pray the Lord my soul to keep. For if I die before I wake, I pray the Lord my soul to take. Now I lay me down to sleep, I pray the Lord my soul to keep. For if I die before I wake, I pray the Lord my soul to take. Now I lay me down to sleep, I pray the Lord my soul to keep. For if I die before I wake, I pray the Lord my soul to take." He didn't know what else he could do. He wished he could comfort Scoot, but Caleb didn't have any pain medication, any antibiotics. All he had was his words, and they did no good in this world. Only in the next.

When his mother returned, she gathered the congregation in the worship hall and told them what they'd seen.

"It's worse than we thought," she said. She reported the town had been overrun with National Guardsmen and was suffering under martial law. Soldiers patrolled the streets with assault rifles and riot gear, and the sick had been quarantined in the middle of the city, imprisoned in a makeshift jail. No one went in or out. No one cared for them. Even though they'd perched hidden more than a hundred yards away, they could hear the sick wailing. It had been the most terrible thing she'd ever heard in her life. It was worse than when she'd been a kid and her father took her to a slaughterhouse. She remembered the cows screaming as they were bludgeoned to death. Corralled in steel pens, they'd moved in a single-file line to the killing floor, where a man with a sledgehammer waited. Sometimes it took more than one swing. Three, maybe four, the man rearing back, bringing the hammer down between the eyes. It wasn't unlike that, she said. Men, women, children, all of them treated like animals.

Scoot's father remained quiet while she spoke. He stood off to the side, a lighter in his hand. He kept striking it, letting the flame burn for a few seconds, then letting it extinguish, his mouth puckered as if swallowing his own tongue.

Dr. Cox visited the compound a couple days later. He came after breakfast, dressed in street clothes. It was the first time Caleb had seen the doctor without his tools, a stethoscope hanging around his neck, smelling of hand sanitizer. The trailer park now had a barbed-wire fence around it, the driveways barricaded by cast-iron gates. When the doctor arrived, he came in a Humvee escorted by three National Guardsmen. They parked at the gate, exited their vehicle, and the doctor stood there with his hands folded in front of him like a paperboy awaiting his holiday tip. It was odd seeing a man of such stature in the community in such a way, sporting a simple blue oxford shirt and chinos, his loafers turning dusty under the harsh wind. It was also odd because his clothes appeared clean, recently pressed, like he'd just picked them up from the dry cleaners. Since the storm, Caleb hadn't seen a man dress so nicely. It was unnerving in a way—if everyone else had it so poorly, why did the doctor have it so good?

Caleb, his mother, and Sam greeted Dr. Cox at the gate and bid him enter. He accompanied them to Sam's house. While they walked down the long drive, the doctor took in his surroundings. Compared to the ravages of town, he must have been surprised by what he saw.

Instead of crumbled buildings, toppled power lines, and makeshift tent cities, the congregation enjoyed newly built shelters. They had dug wells and tilled fields and raised chickens. Those who were still healthy worked as a community, mending fences, washing clothes, preparing lunches of venison and squirrel. They were still leading a life here, not what they'd been accustomed to prior to the storm, a bit harder, more uncertain, the angst of the end bearing down upon them, but it was a life nonetheless.

Sam brewed the doctor some fresh coffee and served him toast, which the doctor didn't eat. He picked up a slice, turned it over as if he'd never seen something so insipid before in his life, and laid it back down. They didn't have much else to offer him, though. Their remaining stores they had to ration and were already running low, and they dared not travel to town for supplies, leery of what they would find, the hatred and judgment and fear in their fellow townspeople's eyes. If they had learned one thing, it was that a fearful man was most certainly a dangerous man.

"I think you probably have a good understanding of why I'm here," the doctor said. He had the countenance of a patient man. He leaned forward as if sitting bedside with a terminal patient, comforting her before she passed. Caleb knew his mother wouldn't take too kindly to such a demeanor, especially in her own community.

"We do not, actually," Caleb's mother said. She stirred her coffee with a spoon despite it being served black. They didn't have any cream or sugar. "Why don't you enlighten us?"

"I didn't come here to be confrontational. I don't mind what you're doing here. I'm all for a man and woman praying to their god however they see fit. I don't listen to the rumors, and I don't care to. My entire reason for being here is the sick. Whoever may be sick. That is all. No more, no less. You have my word."

"Your word?"

"Yes, ma'am. My word."

"And what are these rumors you've been hearing?"

"Like I said, I don't care to listen to them."

"But surely you've heard them, whether or not you care to listen. People talk, do they not?"

"Yes, ma'am. They do." The doctor fidgeted in his seat and cleared his throat. "I'm sure they're untrue and not worth listing here."

"No, please. By all means."

The doctor was obviously uncomfortable. Being a man of medicine, Caleb was sure he'd spent the majority of his days in a position of authority, his word taken as gospel, his advice and care irrefutable. He was the one with the degree, after all. He was the one who'd been elected to the state house for three consecutive terms. Why would any layman ever question him?

"Some say you're a cult out here," he said. "Not that I subscribe to that notion."

"A cult? Really? And what, exactly, makes us a cult?"

"Well," he said. "People say you're predicting the end of the world. And that you believe your son is the Second Coming of Jesus."

The doctor looked at Caleb for the first time since arriving, and in his gaze wasn't the fear and judgment Caleb had grown accustomed to receiving. Rather, there was a curiosity there, and pity. He felt sorry for Caleb, and Caleb couldn't help but feel a little comforted by this.

"Are you a God-fearing man, Doctor?" Caleb's mother asked.

The doctor shrugged. "God-fearing? Probably not."

"But you believe in God?"

"At different times in my life, I have. I suppose you could call me an agnostic."

"Then you don't. You either do or you don't. There's no in between with God."

"If you say so."

Caleb's mother dragged her teeth across her bottom lip, turning it a chalky white. "Why are you here really?"

"Like I said, for the wellbeing of the sick. You came to me for help. At the time I couldn't provide it. Now help has arrived. We have medicine. More doctors. Shelter. You should come with us. Let us help you."

"And what, exactly, do you mean by the sick's wellbeing?"

"There's no denying it. Several are sick. This is dangerous. They need medical attention."

"Antibiotics, IVs, rehydration therapy?"

"Yes. Exactly."

"You think you can save their lives, is that it?"

"I can't promise you anything, but I can tell you—"

"You want to play God? You think you know better than God's plan?"

The doctor sighed loudly through his nose. It was part exasperation, part impatience—he just couldn't believe he was being questioned over this. Caleb couldn't help but feel a little sorry for the doctor. In his mind it was worth a shot. If it was God's plan for them to die, then they'd die. If it wasn't, then they'd live, but he couldn't speak out against his mother.

"Let me tell you how this will go. If you refuse treatment, I'll be forced to contact the Department of Human Services. There will be an inquiry, an investigation. If you're found to be endangering people, children especially, that is a felony." The doctor turned to Scoot's father. "Scoot and Brandon and Catherine might very well be taken from you, and you could face prosecution. Mr. Finch, you could go to jail. For a long time. And, worse yet, through all of this, your son and wife will continue to get sicker. Eventually they'll die because you refused to give them help."

Scoot's father hadn't said anything since the doctor had arrived; instead, he stared at the floor, his hands clasped in front of him, his fingers trembling.

"Are you scared of death, Dr. Cox?" Caleb's mother asked.

"I'm speaking with Mr. Finch now. You have absolutely no say in this matter, and I'm only allowing this conversation to continue out of deference to Mr. Finch's wishes."

"Allowing?"

"Yes. Allowing. I should not be discussing the treatment options of a minor with an uninvolved party."

Evelyn stood. "We're a family here, Dr. Cox, whether you understand that notion or not. We do not recognize man's law over God's law here, and it's best you realize that sooner rather than later."

"I think you should leave, Dr. Cox," Sam said.

Dr. Cox leaned forward, trying to catch Mr. Finch's eye, but he refused to look up. He just stared at the carpet as if he were holding a conversation with it, the Berber fibers recalling a story of a love long lost or the passing of a favorite aunt.

"Is that what you want, Mr. Finch? You want me to leave?"

It took awhile for him to answer, the words caught in his throat. "Yes," he said. "It would be for the best."

CHAPTER 9

THE DRILLS STARTED THEREAFTER. AT LEAST once per day the sirens blared. The first time it happened, Caleb was in school with the other kids, seven chairs empty due to more getting sick. Caleb knew the sirens were coming, having been told the night before, but the rest of the students did not. They looked at each other, confused, trying to glean how they should react from their peers, but each one of them was as perplexed as the next. Being from Oklahoma, all of them were accustomed to the tornado sirens that sounded sporadically throughout the spring, both at all hours of the night during freak thunderstorms and also noon on Saturdays for the weekly test, but this was different. It wailed so closely they could feel the soundwaves tickling their skin.

Caleb's mother rose to her feet and stood at the front of the classroom, instructing everyone to form a single-file line, to do so calmly and in an orderly fashion. Each of the children obeyed. Caleb's mother was at the front of the line, and Caleb was at the back to ensure no one was lost in transit. The children were instructed to place their hands on the shoulders of the person in front of them as they marched. Outside they found similar lines heading toward the worship hall. Sam led one, a few church elders leading others. Every single congregant was rounded up, wherever they happened to be, cutting firewood or mending a fence, tending to a sick child or washing laundry. Many of them had come from inside, their hats left behind, squinting under the blinding sun.

The siren originated from four speakers bolted to the corners of the worship hall and got louder as they approached. Many of the children and some of the adults placed their hands over their ears. Conversation was futile. Even if they were screaming, they wouldn't be able to hear anything. This was by design, Caleb had been told. Mom and Sam wanted the congregants to be able to hear the siren sounding from the farthest reaches of the compound, even beyond their borders to the lake if need be. They couldn't afford to lose a single member when the time came. Too much was at stake. They also wanted to drown out anything and everything else that might be around. Keep the congregation focused on one thing, the noise, luring them to safety.

Once they reached the worship hall, they crammed into the pews. The first group moved into the front row where Caleb's mother stayed, and the next took a seat behind them, new groups coming in one by one until they filled out the remainder. The group leaders then began a head count, and when they gave the all-clear, Caleb's mother signaled to barricade the windows with storm shutters. It turned pitch black for a moment, and everyone sat in silence, the only noise the soft fidgeting of nervous parishioners in their seats. Then fluorescent lamps hummed on one by one and illuminated the hall in a soft white glow. Shadows fell in every direction, granting the room an eerie quality, reminding Caleb of a house of mirrors. The doors were locked, and

Sam and Mr. Finch fortified them with two-by-fours. In a matter of minutes, they were safely inside, barring any intruder who wanted to get in, and then the siren was cut.

When they were finished, Mr. Finch and Sam took down the two-by-fours and removed the storm shutters from the windows. The lamps were extinguished, and the parishioners all blinked and rubbed their eyes, adjusting to the natural light. They then began to exit, meandering through the door one by one, their feet shuffling against the wooden floors.

It wasn't long before it wasn't just a drill. A week after Dr. Cox's visit, the National Guard and the OSBI arrived in camouflaged Humvees and black Suburbans. Their vehicles blocked the only exit from the property. Standing alongside them were soldiers with assault rifles and OSBI agents. They wore wind jackets with the letters emblazoned in yellow, and spoke into cell phones and walkie-talkies. Many of them were smoking, taking turns filling the air with their plumage. When they'd first arrived, Evelyn had tripped the siren, and the congregation filed into the worship hall. Caleb's mom, Sam, Mr. Finch, and Caleb watched them from the worship hall. It scared Caleb, seeing them out there. He could feel the separation between them, a wide and vast ocean. The soldiers and agents were uneasy and cautious travelers; Caleb and his mother and the rest of the congregation an indigenous people watching them approach.

"What do you think they want?" Caleb asked.

"Nothing good," his mom said.

"We shouldn't rush to judgment," Sam said, though he looked genuinely concerned. He wiped his mouth with a handkerchief though his lips and chin were dry.

"It's not like they're here to read scripture," Caleb's mom said. "They're here to invade us. They're here because they're scared of us, and when people get scared, they get violent."

"You don't know that," Caleb said. "They might just be here to help us, like Dr. Cox said."

"This isn't going to end well," she said. "We need to prepare."

"We need to remain calm," Sam said. "Maybe they'll go away. Leave us in peace."

"Don't be naïve. They're not going to be happy until we're destroyed."

There were ten cars in all, about forty agents. They meandered about, huddling in smaller groups of five or six, and stared at the worship hall through binoculars. They took position behind the hoods of their cars like the congregants might at any second open fire. Their sunglasses reflected the morning sun, and Caleb wondered what they thought of the place, if they were, deep down, despite their distrust, their fear of the unknown, impressed. The congregation had risen up after the storm. They'd faced meager food supplies, complete destruction of their homes and livelihoods, but yet they'd built a life there, even if it was in wait of the end of everything. They'd lived despite imminent apocalypse. There had to be some admiration in that fact, even if it was marred by sin.

"Do you think this is it?" Caleb asked his mother. "Do you think this could be the Sixth Seal?"

"There's absolutely no doubt in my mind."

The agents didn't make contact right away. Caleb wasn't sure why they waited, but he figured they wanted to instill fear into the congregation. The uncertainty their presence caused they wanted to let fester. And it did. It boiled inside of them. Caleb stared at the agents out the window, too worried and afraid of what might happen next to even blink. His mother paced, stopping at different members of the congregation, reassuring them God had everything under control, to trust in him, that soon they'd be arm-in-arm in paradise. Sam sat in the corner with his head in his hands. He had the look of a man facing life in prison with only the slimmest of chances of being set free. The Finches stayed with Scoot and prayed, repeating the Lord's Prayer while their son slept, moaned, and sweated.

Scoot had been getting worse. He was in a lot of pain, which they couldn't manage. They didn't have any more meds to give him, having run out of what Tylenol and Ibuprofen and Aleve they could scrape together, but none of it helped anyway. He just moaned. He couldn't stand. He couldn't walk. He had to stay in bed. When the agents came, Brandon and Mr. Finch had to carry him. They placed him on the ground in front of the altar atop a couple blankets with a single pillow behind his head, and that was where he remained, along with the rest of the sick. Most of the time he just slept. It was the only relief he got, but he still didn't seem peaceful. He still was flush, his eyebrows arched into a scowl. Caleb wished he could do something to alleviate his pain, but the only thing he knew was to pray, and so he joined Scoot's father, hand in hand at the foot of his pallet, and did just that: "Our Father, who art in heaven, hallowed be Thy name, Thy kingdom come, Thy will be done on earth as it is in heaven. Give us this day our daily bread; and forgive us our trespasses as we forgive those who trespass against us; and lead us not into temptation, but deliver us from evil. For thine is the kingdom and the power and the glory forever."

A knock came at the door. They all jumped in unison when it

did, its thumps reverberating throughout the worship hall, but no one moved to answer it. They just blinked at each other. Eventually, Caleb's mother went to the door and opened it. No one was there. She returned a few seconds later with a cell phone. It then rang.

Caleb's mother looked to Sam.

"Should I answer it?" she asked.

Sam bit at a piece of dry skin on his lip. He nodded, and Caleb's mother pressed a button and put it on speakerphone.

"Hello?" she asked.

It was quiet for a moment. In the background Caleb thought he could hear whispering, or it could've just been the wind.

"Hello," a disembodied voice said. It was younger than Caleb expected, full of energy and angst. "This is Lieutenant Walter Lippman with the Oklahoma State Bureau of Investigation. May I ask who I'm speaking with?"

"There's no place for niceties here, Mr. Lippman. You know damn well who you're speaking with," Caleb's mother said. "Just tell us what you want. We'll tell you we can't provide it, and then you can go on your merry way."

"Is this Mrs. Gunter? Evelyn Gunter?"

"Names are unimportant. Tell us what you want and what it will take to get you out of here."

"First, if I could just understand who I'm speaking with—"

"Fine. Yes, this is Evelyn Gunter."

"Good. Great. That's a good start. Let's just try to keep everything calm. Okay, Mrs. Gunter?"

"It's hard to keep calm when we have dozens of law enforcement bearing down on our home, Mr. Lippman."

"I understand. Is it okay if I call you Evelyn?"

"So, we're getting friendly now, huh?"

"I can continue to call you Mrs. Gunter if that's what you prefer."

"Evelyn's fine if it'll get this to move any faster."

"Thank you, Evelyn. First and foremost, we want to remain calm. That's our overriding concern at this juncture, just for everyone to remain calm. Second, we'd like to know if everyone is safe. Is everyone okay, Evelyn?"

"I suppose that depends on your definition of 'okay.'"

"Is anyone injured?"

"Physically? No. Not yet. Their souls, on the other hand . . ."

"We'd like to see everyone if that's okay. Just to make sure."

"We're a little indisposed at the moment."

"It would put a lot of people's minds at ease if we could just hear their voices. See the children. I'm sure you can understand that."

"They're fine. All of you, however . . ."

"All of us?"

"You have no idea what is coming for you."

"I'd like to think you're not threatening us, Evelyn. That would be a grave—"

"I think you may have this situation confused, Mr. Lippman."

"How is that?"

"We didn't come to your home. We're not parked outside of your house with guns and strangers and threats of taking your children, now, are we?"

"Now, Mrs. Gunter. Let's just talk about this. Valid concerns have been—"

"Let me just stop you right there. None of our children will be going with you. Do you understand me? None. I don't expect you to understand it. I don't expect you to like it. But I do expect you to accept it. This is a fact. It will not be changed."

There was a long silence on the other end of the line. Caleb couldn't even hear the wind blowing through the speaker. Lippman had muted the phone, and Caleb imagined they were discussing their best course of action going forward. He wondered what their conversation consisted of. Nothing good, Caleb assumed.

The line clicked back on. Caleb heard static, followed by Mr. Lippman clearing his throat.

"I think that's probably enough for now, Evelyn," Mr. Lippman said. "We'll be back in touch soon."

THE CONGREGATION HOLED UP IN the service hall, crowded, cramped, and uncomfortable. They were scared. All of them. They bit their lips and spit brown, tobacco-soaked spit. Their faces long and desperate, they avoided eye contact with their brethren. They forewent their usual handshakes and hugs, their blessings and words of love. Instead, they sat down in the pews as a disparate group of individuals. They were thinking of themselves, their wives, their husbands, their children, not the community as a whole. A doubt permeated them, Caleb too, and it vibrated over their heads as something palpable and real. Caleb could feel it like the heat coming off a hot stove.

After they had all settled, Sam opened the floor to questions. And they had several, pointed questions, questions that jumped off the tongue in desperation.

"What are they planning to do?" they asked.

"Are they here to hurt us?"

"Are they going to make us leave?"

"Is this it? Is this the end of times?"

"Just what, exactly, are we going to do?"

The best answer Caleb's mother could provide them was the same answer she'd been giving for months: "Yes," she said. "This is the end of times." She tried to calm them. She spoke slowly and assuredly, but the congregation argued, some even becoming defiant, a man standing, Ralph was his name, saying she was lying, that she and Sam and the rest of them were hiding something from the congregation, that this wasn't the end; they were just trying to scare them. Several heads nodded in assent, but Sam and Caleb's mother assured them, told them they knew this was scary, but "We must trust in the Lord. We will hide nothing from you. God has a purpose for us. He has chosen us. He has graced us with his Son. No matter what the devil places at our doorstep, no matter the trials, the tribulations, the very devil himself cannot walk into our home and compel us to give up our faith."

"But how can you be sure?" the congregation asked. "How do you know for sure?"

Sam dabbed at his forehead with a handkerchief, wiping up the sweat that beaded his brow. He'd lost a lot of weight since the tornado, fifteen pounds, Caleb guessed, and now his skin hung off his bones like laundry on a clothesline. More and more, he frightened Caleb. Not for his safety, but what might happen to Sam. Caleb wouldn't have been surprised if he dropped dead at any moment, collapsing where he stood. He needed a doctor. All of them did.

"I have prayed about this," Sam said. "Last night I prayed, and without the slightest bit of doubt, I'm certain. The Sixth Seal has been broken. Some of us will die. I may even die, but it has been opened, and the end of the world is upon us."

The congregation was silent. They sat, and they listened. They fidgeted in their seats, but they didn't seem surprised. In their faces were resignation and acceptance, perhaps sullied with doubt, but resignation nonetheless—they'd followed Sam and Caleb's mother this far, and they couldn't turn back now. Everything they'd fought so hard for would turn out to be a lie.

The congregation took each other's hands, bowed their heads, and prayed. They prayed to God to give them strength, for safety. They prayed for their souls and the federal agents' souls and all the souls of humankind on earth. They prayed for all to end well. They prayed to be welcomed into his bosom and the kingdom of heaven. They prayed for all these things with all the earnestness they could muster, and along with them, so did Caleb. He prayed with his heart and his mind and his soul. He prayed with everything he had, imploring God Almighty to grant them the reason to know what they were doing.

That night, the congregation slept in the service hall, or tried to. Mostly they squirmed and groaned, trying to find some comfort on the oak floor. They hadn't dared go out for blankets and pillows while the agents waited for them outside their gates, too afraid of what they might do. This worried Caleb. Despite the OSBI agents and soldiers outside their gate, they still had work to do: water to tote, clothes to mend, hunting and fishing so they could eat, so they could maintain the semblance of humanity, but no one was allowed to leave. When they'd boarded themselves into the service hall they only grabbed the bare essentials, an extra pair of socks and undergarments, a toothbrush, a cherished memento passed down through the generations. And so, without the comforts of home, they sprawled out as best they could, feet to head, along the aisles and in the pews. It smelled of sweat and smoke. The humidity sat on top of Caleb, making it hard to breathe. His tongue swelled, and he was soaked with sweat.

Caleb heard the agents stirring outside, a car engine rumbling, and the screeching of a radio connecting with the correct frequency. He heard commands shouted across a crowd of otherwise distracted agents. Probably most disconcerting were the voices. They collected and reverberated throughout the service hall, a cacophony of hushed tones and whispers that had no discernible shape, words transmuted into the rattling of an invisible ghost, waiting for the congregants outside their own halls. At least once per hour, the phone in the service hall rang. Caleb knew it to be Agent Lippman, but no one answered, too afraid, Caleb supposed, of what might happen next.

Caleb took refuge near the pulpit. Sitting next to him was Catherine.

"What do you think is going to happen?" she asked. She wore nylon gym shorts and a Grove Ridgerunner sweatshirt two sizes too large for her. She smelled of wood smoke and peanut butter, and little red scratches spiderwebbed her calves, the victim of underbrush while hauling wood.

"I don't know," Caleb said.

"I thought you were supposed to know everything," she said. "I thought you could see the future or whatever."

"It doesn't work like that."

"You don't know God's plan? He doesn't tell you those things?"

She sounded worried. She sounded confused.

"It's difficult to explain."

"Try," she said.

Caleb sat up straighter, blinked to see her better in the dark, and searched for the right words.

"God comes to me in fragments," he said. "It's like coming in on a conversation that has already started, and I'm only able to hear about every third or fourth word. God comes to me in images, but they're jumbled. They're upside-down and pixelated, and they don't make much sense. I have to dwell upon them. I have to study them. I have to decipher them through context and signs and the interactions I have here on earth before I can make sense of them. It's like learning a foreign language but without a teacher or guide to help you along. So, for now, I don't know what will happen. But I do know I trust in the Lord."

"So, you don't know this is right," she said. "You don't know for sure that this is the end."

"What do you mean?"

"Scoot's sick. My mother. I thought we were supposed to be the good ones. They're saying the doctors could help him."

"Who's saying that?"

She scraped dirt out from underneath her fingernail. "It's not important who. The point is, if we don't do anything, he's going to die."

She was right, but he couldn't bring himself to say it. He would die if they didn't do anything.

A bright light illuminated the service hall. It was something piercing, alien even. It accosted the pupils and caused sharp pains in the back of Caleb's eyeballs. It blinded him, and he feared when he opened his eyes next, he wouldn't be able to see.

Accompanying the light was a loud shriek of static. It sounded like a radio tuned to a long-dead frequency. There was abrupt scratching, followed by intermittent sections of white noise. Catherine and Caleb covered their ears. It was so loud he could feel the enamel of his teeth rattle. Babies cried and frightened yelps escaped the lips of a congregation already on edge. After a few moments, a song played over a loudspeaker. It was Chumbawamba's "Tubthumping." It played loud, and the sound was terrible, the bass cackling in the background. The noise made Caleb grind his teeth. It made his temples throb. It made his blood scrape the insides of his capillaries.

CHAPTER 10

IT WASN'T LONG BEFORE THE CONGREGATION ran out of food. It had been a week since the OSBI agents had shown up at the property. The congregation only dared to go outside one or two at a time, sneaking back to homes for basic supplies, blankets and pillows and clothes, too afraid of what might happen if they lingered outside the service hall for too long. Before the occupation, they'd survived on hunting whitetail, rabbit, squirrel, and quail, but with the OSBI outside their gate, they had to ration their food. They only used water to drink anymore, all of them having gone days without bathing. It caused the service hall to smell ripe, the air thick with sweat. After a while, they just had corn to eat. They ate corn for breakfast, for lunch, and for dinner. They ran out of butter and flour and so all they could do was boil it, choke it down with tepid water, and pray for a turn of events, but it never came.

Evelyn, Sam, the Finches, and Caleb slept near the pulpit, furthest away from the door, elevated so they could see the entire congregation. The sick had deteriorated the past month or so since Scoot first started showing symptoms. They slept mostly, their breaths weak and raspy, but Scoot was the worst. He'd turned yellow, then pale, then bluish, to the point his skin seemed almost transparent. When he was awake, he simply moaned. It wasn't loud. It wasn't urgent. It was barely audible. He no longer had the energy to even let the rest know he was in pain.

"Mom," Caleb said. "We need food. We need to go hunting."

Caleb's mother looked haggard and worn, like she hadn't slept in days—skin jaundiced, face bruised, eyes the color of eggshells. Caleb had only seen her like this once before, right after his papa had died. She'd stopped eating and sleeping, instead surviving off coffee and cigarettes. Her state scared Caleb. She had trouble pronouncing words, the consonants sliding off her tongue without purpose. Clothes hung off her like on a hanger, and she often got dizzy, having to bend and grab her knees so she wouldn't faint.

"It's too dangerous, Caleb. We don't know what will happen."

"But we do know what'll happen if we don't. We'll starve. There's no other choice."

"There's always a choice, sweetheart. Always."

"And we need to make the right one."

"He's right," Sam said. "The boy's right."

Sam sat in the corner. His eyes darted and his movements were shifty like he'd drunk too much caffeine.

"We're going to die if we don't do something. Just look at us. We're weak. We're hurting."

Scoot coughed, choked, and turned his head to the side, a bit of blood and phlegm painting the corner of his mouth. His mother sat next to him, using a damp rag to dab his face, trying to keep him cool despite suffering herself. Mr. Finch sat by the window. It had been boarded with plywood, and Mr. Finch had his back to it. Occasionally, he looked toward it like he could see the OSBI lining the street in front of the property. Of course, he couldn't, but the congregation didn't need to see them to know they were there. They still blared pop music at all hours of the day, and they still surrounded the property on all three sides, cornering the congregation into the lake at the back of the property. Caleb's mother paced. Or tried to. The place was so crowded she had to step over legs and congregants napping on the floor.

"This is a bad idea," she said. "A very, very bad idea."

"We need to eat," Caleb said. "We need food."

"It's a mistake. I just know it. It's a mistake."

Three of them volunteered to go hunting: Sam, Mr. Finch, and Caleb. His mother urged him not to go, but Caleb insisted, and his mother, too weak to fight him, relented. The rifles were kept in Sam's house, locked in a safe. Caleb hadn't been outside since the OSBI had descended onto their compound, and though he was afraid to do so, he felt compelled to help the congregation. They were hungry and weak and scared. They deserved to feel normal for a little while. They deserved a good meal.

There was only one exit to the service hall, and it faced the main gate of the compound. About a hundred yards separated them from the nearest OSBI agent. When they opened the door, Caleb could feel their collective eyes on them as they exited and made their way to Sam's house. He tried to ignore them, but they were in plain view. They hid behind the hoods of their Suburbans, watching through binoculars. A few of them made excessive gestures, waving their arms above their heads and signaling with their hands. Caleb thought he could see their mouths moving, but he couldn't make anything out over the music. An electronic dance song reverberated over the countryside, drowning out all noise and making communication impossible. Despite this, though, Caleb knew they were prepared for the worst. He could feel their scopes trained on him, their crosshairs aimed at a kill shot if he even so much as looked like he was being threatening.

Once inside Sam's house, they took a moment to collect themselves, plan their next move. It was hot in there, humid like a sweat lodge. The guns were kept upstairs in an extra room. Caleb stayed downstairs to keep a lookout, peering out at the army of agents lest they decided to ambush, and counted. One Mississippi, two Mississippi, three Mississippi, four Mississippi. Five Mississippi, six Mississippi, seven Mississippi, eight Mississippi. He wondered what was taking Sam and Mr. Finch so long, why he couldn't hear them upstairs, and for a moment he thought maybe they'd abandoned him, that this was a trap, that they had signaled to the soldiers and the OSBI that the cause of all the problems was alone, downstairs, and the OSBI was about to pounce. They didn't, though. They didn't even move.

Sam and Mr. Finch returned with three rifles and a box of ammunition. Knowing they couldn't simply walk outside carrying arms, they placed them in a large duffel bag, and Mr. Finch hoisted it onto his shoulders. He labored underneath the weight, his back arched at an awkward angle, but he declined any help. "If things go south," he said, "you two will need to run."

Caleb, Sam, and Mr. Finch exited through the back door and headed east toward the lake, their backs to the agents. Caleb kept telling himself not to look back, but he couldn't help himself. He peered over his shoulder. The agents were still there, growing smaller in the distance. They didn't appear to be reacting to Caleb, Sam, and Mr. Finch. Caleb didn't see a group of them convening or tracking, and he didn't know whether to be encouraged or scared by this. They were cautious. Patient. They simply watched from the safe confines of the road.

In the cover of the woods, Caleb, Sam, and Mr. Finch each took a rifle and loaded it. The gun felt heavy in Caleb's hand, burdensome. He'd never particularly liked guns, but viewed them as a necessity, one of survival. And he'd gotten pretty good with them. Since moving to Grove, he and Sam had gone hunting many times, and now he could hit a deer in the heart from a hundred yards away. He was proud of this fact, taking it as evidence that he was maturing, growing into a self-sufficient man. And he liked the attention, the way Sam would ruffle his hair, smile with pride, and tell him "Good shot, son. That was one hell of a shot."

They ventured into the underbrush parallel with the lake. It was dark in there, the early morning sun covered by white clouds, and quiet. Caleb didn't have much hope they would find anything. The music still blared in the distance, electronic bass beats reverberating over the canopy, probably scaring any type of game for miles, spooking them to take off out of earshot from the strange, deafening sound. Despite this, Sam, Caleb, and Mr. Finch trekked in a single line, their eyes darting back and forth for any sign of movement. Caleb couldn't see much of anything, just an endless barrage of oak and Bradford pears, his line of vision no more than fifteen yards in each direction.

Caleb searched for any sign of life, whether animal or human. It was the latter that worried him the most, National Guardsmen with assault rifles and scared OSBI agents with itchy trigger fingers. Though, if he thought about it, not finding a deer was equally as frightening. His flock, his friends, his family, they were starving. They'd been a couple days without food, and they were growing weak, their spirits waning, questioning if they were doing the right thing. He couldn't let them down. With each step they took through the woods, Caleb felt the urgency pulse through him as if the earth itself was trembling.

For hours they walked. Mile after mile until they grew tired and sore. Caleb's muscles suffered from spasms and soon they had to stop. They took refuge by the lake, just inside the tree line, and shared a canteen of water. It tasted cool and crisp against Caleb's tongue, and they didn't say anything. They didn't have to. With each passing minute, their failure crept up on them. They'd have to go back empty-handed, tell the congregation not to worry, that they'd try again later, the next day and the next and the next if they had to, that God would provide for them if they just trusted in him, but Caleb didn't quite know if he believed that anymore.

A twig snapped behind them. Branches rattled. Fear gripped Caleb. He reached for his rifle and turned behind him, searching for the cause of the noise. All he saw were trees. Rows and rows of them. But then there was movement, just a flash in his periphery. He scanned the trees back and forth, his tongue swelling in his mouth, and then he saw it. It was a single buck about thirty yards ahead. Caleb exhaled, finally. He could only make out his antlers and hindquarters, sticking out from behind a tree trunk. Thank God, he thought. Thank you, God.

Caleb, Sam, and Mr. Finch ducked behind a ridge. No clear shot. The deer was alone and seemingly lost. It would trot east toward the lake five or six steps, coming closer to them, but then it would turn its nose up into the air as if it was trying to locate something by smell, and turn around. Caleb, Sam, and Mr. Finch stooped about twenty yards from it, downwind so it couldn't smell them.

"He's chasing a doe," Sam said. "Lost her."

The buck stopped behind some trees, and so they didn't have a clear shot. Only its stomach showed, and if they hit it there, it would take off and die a slow and agonizing death. It would be much more difficult to find it, and with the OSBI outside their property, they wouldn't be able to chase it far.

"Who wants the shot?" Sam whispered.

"I got it," Caleb said.

Sam peered at Caleb. "You sure?" he asked.

Caleb nodded and got into position, his rifle poised on the ridge for balance, and clicked off the safety. The buck was behind some trees but still moving—all Caleb had to do was wait until it stopped in a clearing. Caleb's mouth watered in anticipation, anxious to take the shot, scared he might miss. The entire congregation was depending on him to come through so they could eat, so they could, for a little while anyway, curb the hunger pains in their stomachs and go to bed full and happy and with one less worry on their minds.

The deer moved again, closer to a clearing. Three more steps and Caleb would have a clear shot. Two. One. Caleb licked his lips, placed his finger on the trigger, and centered the deer at the end of the sight. He aimed a little high and to the left, just above the kill zone, so as to take into consideration wind and distance, and squeezed the trigger. The kick rocketed Caleb back, and his shoulder throbbed. Smoke billowed from the barrel, and the deer shot up in a panic and sprinted into the woods, leaping in a zigzag motion. Caleb had hit it, but well enough to kill it? He wasn't sure.

The deer headed northwest, and Sam, Mr. Finch, and Caleb stood all at once and took off after it. Where it had been hit, they found a splattering of blood. It was dark and crimson and trailed through the woods. Along the way they found prints. They were erratic and easy to locate at first. The deer weaved as it moved, its prints heavy against the soil, but after a while the blood and the prints were harder to locate. The blood was scarcer, the drops smaller, spread thin, and the prints were lighter as the deer slowed. Eventually they lost the trail; either it wasn't there or it was too weak to be noticed in the underbrush.

"Looks like you might've hit it in the shoulder," Sam said. "We could be following this thing for hours."

"I'm sorry," Caleb said.

"Don't be sorry," he said. "Look around for scrapes. Broken limbs, twigs, droppings, anything."

"I'm sorry," Caleb said again. "I'm not used to this rifle."

"It happens," Sam said. "I should've taken the shot."

Sam laid a heavy hand on Caleb's shoulder, trying to comfort him, but it only weighed Caleb down.

"I think I have something," Mr. Finch said. He pointed to a trunk that had been scraped of its bark. It wasn't a clean scrape but something done haphazardly, leading east toward the edge of the property line.

They followed the trail as quietly as they could, and though they didn't say anything, Caleb knew they were all thinking it—the OSBI agents and the National Guard would've heard Caleb's rifle shot. They'd search for it, scared and anxious at what they might find, and so Caleb knew they were running against a short clock. They would have to find the deer, field dress it, and carry what meat they could back to the worship hall as quickly as possible. He didn't want to think what might happen if they didn't make it back in time.

After about a hundred yards, they came upon the deer. It was still alive, though barely—its breath weak and eyes closed.

"We need to put it out of its misery," Sam said.

Caleb raised his rifle to his shoulder.

"No," Sam said and pulled out a knife. "Save the bullet."

Sam pulled out a knife and placed his hand on the deer's neck. The deer trembled from shock, and Sam placed the knife's edge against its jawline, pulled the blade across its neck, and spilled its blood. Warmth emanated from the wound, like opening the hood to an idling car engine. The smell was awful—a mixture of infection and rotting meat and spoiled food. It caused Caleb to gag, dry heave, and finally vomit, but he didn't have anything in his stomach to really puke. It was just phlegm, thick and gelatinous, choking him.

Sam field dressed the deer. He stabbed the deer in its lower abdomen and sawed upward to its neck. The ribcage gave him trouble, but the blade sliced through. He pulled out the intestines and the bladder, careful not to puncture it and spill out the contents all over the meat. When he pulled out the heart, Caleb couldn't help but think how large it was, how just a few moments before it had been beating with life. He felt bad about this. He grieved for the deer. He had, after all, just taken its life. But he brushed the sentiment aside. Its utility outweighed its death, and so he said a prayer for its soul and then was done with it.

Sam quartered it so they could carry it back home, and for the first time in weeks, Caleb felt good. They would have a warm meal, a good meal, and he was thankful for that. They placed the meat and the hide into the duffel bag, and Mr. Finch hoisted it again onto his shoulders.

The guns didn't fit, and so they had to carry them back.

They were a couple of miles away from the worship hall, and moving through the woods was slow going. There were no trails to follow, only thick underbrush, spindly and grating. Though it was about noon, it was darker than before, the clouds fully covering the sun. Caleb couldn't make out the sky through the thick canopy, but it smelled like rain. A storm might be coming, and this worried Caleb. They wouldn't be able to survive another storm. Of that, he was certain.

After about a half hour, Caleb thought he heard something ahead and to their left. A snap, followed by whispers. Mr. Finch stopped, held up his hand. Caleb scanned the woods, but he couldn't make anything out. He could still hear it. Whatever it was moved alongside them, and Caleb prayed. He prayed it was another deer, the doe the buck had been chasing, searching for its mate. Please God, he begged, let it be a fox, or a coyote, anything, but then he spotted them. There were five of them, two National Guardsmen and three OSBI agents, wandering the woods, guns drawn, searching for the source of the gunshot, Caleb's gunshot. Mr. Finch, Sam, and Caleb took cover behind three separate trees, crouching low. The footsteps grew louder until they were right upon them. Caleb shut his eyes and prayed. He prayed the soldiers and agents wouldn't see them, prayed that God would shield them, but it was to no avail. When he opened his eyes, he saw the agents and soldiers, and they saw him. They froze and pointed their weapons. Sam and Mr. Finch did the same.

"Listen," Sam said. "We're just hunting. We're hungry."

The agents and soldiers didn't say a word. They just pointed their weapons.

"We just want to go back home. That's all."

"Put down your weapons," they said. "Put down your weapons and get on the ground."

"We've done nothing wrong," Sam said. "We were just hunting. We've done nothing wrong."

"Put down your weapons!"

They were screaming now, barking orders, and fear rose up into Caleb's chest. He felt it in his throat and behind his tongue. He choked on it.

"Put down your weapons, or we'll have to open fire."

A shot rang out. Caleb wasn't sure who fired first, if it was the soldiers or agents or Sam or Mr. Finch, but two people went down: one of them, and Sam. There was screaming, and Caleb hid behind a tree. Sam fired and they fired and Caleb froze, but after a few seconds the agents retreated west through the woods toward the property line. When everything was done, Mr. Finch and Caleb stood there breathing, unsure what to do. It was Sam, finally, who told them to move.

"Pick me up," he said. "Let's go home."

SAM HAD BEEN SHOT IN the side, just below the ribcage. It was a clean entry and exit, and Caleb's mother worked to bandage him up. They were back in the worship hall, and Sam was laid in the first pew. Evelyn dabbed at the wound with gauze, doused it with water, but they didn't have any antibiotics, no iodine solution, no hydrogen peroxide. The blood just gushed out of it. They applied pressure, wrapping his midsection in white cloth, but the blood soaked it deep. It scared Caleb. Sam turned pale, sweat-drenched. It took a long time to get the bleeding under control, too long, Caleb thought. Sam squirmed from the pain, and they didn't have much to give him. They didn't have Tylenol or prescription medication or morphine, and they had no way to get them. All they could do was change his bandages every few hours and pray the wound didn't get infected.

The OSBI and National Guard doubled in numbers. News vans parked behind the perimeter, filming the worship hall with high-definition, long-range lenses. The FBI were called in. Outside the compound were military vehicles: tanks and Humvees armed with large-caliber machine guns. Helicopters flew overhead. Soldiers in full body armor manned the roadside, pointing assault rifles at the service hall filled with frightened, panicked congregants. They cried more often. The sick moaned, and the others murmured. "We should surrender," they said. "We should give in to their demands. The Lord would understand."

"Did he understand the citizens of Sodom and Gomorrah?" Evelyn asked. "Did the Lord show mercy when he flooded the world? Tell me, does God show mercy in Revelation, when the final judgment is cast down upon mankind? God is a vengeful God, and we must respect his wrath. We shouldn't surrender. We should arm ourselves. Give all the men and women rifles. If a child is over thirteen and can shoot, they should be armed, too."

Caleb's mother strained as she spoke, like her muscles were trying to pry free from her body. She looked deranged, pupils dilated, fingers curled into hooks. She scared Caleb. He wouldn't have been surprised if she bit the air while she spoke, or even him if he dared step too close.

"They have tanks, Evelyn. How're we supposed to fight tanks?"

"We have to defend ourselves. We have to. The Lord requires us. We are to be raised to heaven in a shining ray of light, not gunned down in a hail of gunfire. I've seen this before. I've seen what mob mentality can do. I've been cast away in exile, and I will not bear the shame of it again. I will not let my child live through that again."

She pointed at Caleb, and he couldn't help but feel small and powerless and weak. He couldn't help but think of Jesus when Judas had betrayed him. He couldn't help but think how Jesus faced the onslaught of the Roman army and accepted his martyrdom with calm and grace. It was a courage he feared he did not possess. Doubt filled him up. It filled him so that he breathed it and tasted it and felt it swimming in the pit of his stomach, and for the first time in his life, he wasn't sure it was a good thing.

"They're just scared," Sam said. "People fear what they don't understand. If we explained what happened. If they hear our side of the story—"

"Maybe Sam's right," Caleb said. "Maybe we're wrong."

"Don't be a fool, Caleb," she said. "They've already reached their conclusions. No amount of evidence will change their minds. Look how they openly defy God. Look at their continued sloth. Their greed. Their avarice. You can't deny their abominations. You can't overlook their lack of reason."

Sam scratched his forehead and reached for his cigarettes, but they weren't there, hadn't been since the storm, but it was a practiced motion, too ingrained into his identity for his hands to let him forget. He was scared, and Caleb was scared, and his mom was angry, and everyone was looking to them for answers. Caleb could feel them waiting. He could feel them huddling next to each other, praying and wondering why they weren't doing anything, why they weren't helping them prepare for what they thought might be the final judgment.

Even if they were wrong, they needed to be comforted. They needed help to survive the agents tearing down their walls.

"You're right," Caleb said. "I'm sorry."

They armed themselves and barricaded the service hall. They took up hammers and nailed two-by-fours over the windows. They risked their lives when they stood guard on the roof, exposed to the government's much larger, much deadlier weapons. And Caleb's mom thanked them for it. She blessed them and prayed for them and told them paradise awaited them in the afterlife, that it wouldn't be long now; the end was near, and they were doing their part to secure the congregation's place next to God in the kingdom of heaven.

Some, though, still protested. Rumors spread of defection. Whispers could be heard from some of the members. They harbored doubt, were instilled by it. They questioned the church leadership's decisions, their fundamental belief system, and Caleb didn't blame them. He, too, was asking the same questions.

"How certain are you the world is going to end?"

"Absolutely," Caleb's mother told them.

"How do you know we're the chosen ones?"

"He speaks to me."

"How come we can't hear him?"

"You have to trust me."

Agent Lippman called again, and this time Caleb's mom answered and put the conversation on speakerphone. "The governor wants us to storm the place," he said. "The public. The media. They're all telling me to send in troops, but I don't want it to end that way."

"It will end how God sees fit."

"You killed an OSBI agent. You understand that, don't you? You have to work with me here. Give me something. Give me the children."

"We obey no other law but God's."

"How is that working out for you?"

"You'll soon see. When the dead rise up and the rivers run with blood. You'll see how it works out for us."

There was silence. For a second, Caleb thought the line had been cut off or perhaps Agent Lippman had hung up, resigned to the fact he'd have to give in to the governor's wishes, but then he spoke.

"You have one day," he said. "No more."

That night Caleb volunteered for guard duty and took his post on the roof. He had his rifle in hand, pointed toward the agents, watching them through his scope, safety already off, finger near the trigger, when he heard something. It sounded like a log landing against hard, cracked earth. He looked down where the sound originated and saw a window opening, followed by a bag dropping, and then three people. He couldn't really recognize them in the dark. There was a man, a woman, and a child. Other than that, their faces were shrouded in darkness. When they hit the ground and gathered their things, they ran. They ran toward the agents as fast as they could, the man carrying the child across the field. It was a disheartening sight. Not because they were leaving but rather the method by which they fled, through a window under the darkness of night, as if it was the congregation who they should be scared of, not what waited for them outside the walls.

CHAPTER 11

SCOOT LOOKED LIKE HE WAS GOING TO DIE.
Without antibiotics, without IV drips, and without pain medication,
he slipped into what seemed like a coma. He hardly woke, and when
he did, he only moaned. His breaths were belabored, short, and sporadic. He lost more weight. In his face and his arms, his legs and his
stomach. He was just bones. He suffered from bedsores, these quarter-
sized infected wounds that smelled like copper and spoiled meat. Despite Caleb's best attempts not to be, he was scared. He was scared to
sit next to him. He was scared to be by his side. He was scared to hold
his hand or to comfort him. And others followed. The sick had grown
in number from six to eight to ten to twelve, more people coughing,
more people suffering from fever, disorientation, diarrhea, vomiting
into a bucket. A third of the congregation had fallen ill, and more were
catching it each day, becoming infected, becoming weak, susceptible
to doubt and fear and hunger, their faith wavering with each hour that
passed by.

Scoot's father hardly left his son's and wife's sides. He slept near
them. He ate breakfast, lunch, and dinner with them, spooning their
meager portions into their mouths, trying to prevent them from chok-

ing as they tried to swallow. It was disheartening seeing their trans-formation. Mr. Finch appeared sickly himself, like he, too, could die at any moment. It made it all that much harder to provide them with hope when they clasped at Caleb's hands and they cried and they asked him if it was in God's plan to have them die like this. Caleb had to tell them he didn't know. He was sorry, but he just didn't know.

"But you told me they wouldn't suffer," Mr. Finch said. There was anger in his voice, sharp and jagged, laced with dismay, desperation, and a deep, abiding sadness. "You told me God would take them. You told me God would comfort us. You told me we'd all be taken in this halo of light. Where is the light, Caleb? Where is God now?"

Scoot's mother was weeping. Her hands covered her face.

"I'm sorry," Caleb said. "I thought—I still believe . . ."

"Stop," he said. "No more lies. No more empty promises. I want you to look at me straight. I want you to tell my wife the truth. My son. Your friend. I want to hear you say you lied to us."

"I didn't lie. I really thought—"

"We disobeyed the doctor's orders. They could've been saved. We could've beaten this. We believed you."

"I know," Caleb said. "I'm sorry. I thought what we were doing was right. I was wrong. I'm sorry."

Scoot's father sat back down, scratching his neck and face until he bled. He no longer had any faith. He stared at nothing. There was this glaze over his eyes, like an opaque film marred his vision. He'd lost hope. He'd lost his belief in God, and in its place remained an emptiness, a barren cavity his soul had once filled, and Caleb knew he'd caused this. Nothing like this ever would've happened if he and his mother hadn't come here. They were the reason this man and his wife no longer carried any hope. They were the reason they'd lost faith in God, and there was nothing, Caleb knew, that could remedy this.

THAT NIGHT, CATHERINE WOKE CALEB. It was dark out, even darker in the service hall, all the candles having been extinguished hours before. The room resounded with faint snores, a collective breathing from the congregation, spurting in odd and uneven intervals.

"We're leaving," she said.

Caleb's head was fuzzy, still lethargic from sleep, and so he didn't answer her, instead rubbing his eyes, waiting for them to adjust.

"Brandon and me. Mom and Dad. We're taking Scoot with us."

Caleb had been dreaming about playing baseball back in Bartlesville. He was playing second base, and it was an important game, the championship game. The stadium lights were bright, and the stands were filled with faceless fans, dozens of them, maybe a hundred, all of them riled and raucous. They screamed obscenities and shook the chain-link fences. Caleb was scared, but none of his teammates or the opposing players were bothered by them, and so he took his position, slapped his glove, and readied for the pitch.

"Come with us," Catherine said. "Please."

The pitcher was a mountain of a kid, tall, skinny as a pencil, his torso curved, arms long, elbows bent too low. He had no features. He vibrated in pixels, dark and churning like a thundercloud. When he threw the ball, it came out like fire, and the hitter swung and connected, launching a rocket of a groundball in Caleb's direction. He moved his feet to get in front of it, timing his steps to field it on a good hop, but before it reached him, it struck a pebble and ricocheted high and to his left. He couldn't adjust in time, and the ball struck his shoulder, showering sparks and marking his jersey in black soot. The ball dribbled away from him, and the batter reached first safely. The crowd became enraged, cussing and pointing their fingers.

"I can't," Caleb said.

"Sure you can," Catherine said. "Just get up and walk out the door."

The next batter came to the plate, and the runner took his lead off first base. Caleb cheated toward second base a little to get into double-play position. The dark, giant pitcher came set and then delivered a fastball. The hitter made contact and chopped it off the plate. The flaming ball bounced high into the air and over the pitcher's head. Caleb charged the ball and tried to field it as it descended, but he couldn't make it in time, and the ball short hopped off his knee. Runners on first and second, both errors committed by Caleb. The crowd grew angrier. They seethed. They called him out by name.

"I can't leave my mom."

"Please, Caleb. This is getting out of hand. It's getting dangerous. Please come with us."

The next batter dug in and on the first pitch roped a line drive toward Caleb. It came at him so fast he didn't have time to react. He didn't have time to blink, and he raised his glove to grab it, but it just burned a hole straight through his glove and through his chest until all that remained was a simmering hole. But there wasn't any pain. None at all. The heat and the wind flowed through him, and the runner on second rounded third and was on his way home. The crowd yelled for him to get the ball, get the ball, throw it home, but he couldn't find it. He looked behind him and there was nothing, just a vast, endless right field. The runner scored, and Caleb's team lost and the crowd became furious. They threw rocks. They foamed at the mouth. They climbed the fence and were coming for Caleb.

"You have to, Caleb. You have to. We're all going to die if we stay here. Please." She grabbed Caleb's hand and tugged. "Please. I'm begging you. Just come with us."

The funny thing was, Caleb didn't even try to run from them. He stood his ground and waited. He dropped his glove into the dirt and raised his arms and turned his face toward the deep, black sky, and when the first one reached him and grabbed his collar, Caleb didn't fight back.

"I'm sorry," Caleb said. "I can't leave my mother."

Half the congregation left with the Finches. The rest remained in the service hall, the room dimly lit by candles. They were tired, unable to sleep or bathe. The room filled with the stench of sweat and body odor. No longer did they carry with them a resolute confidence. They'd lost. And they knew it. Caleb could see it in the way they avoided eye contact, instead staring at their feet, the ceiling, the landscape outside the windows they once called home.

Caleb's mom and Sam were as disheveled as the rest of the congregation. Sam hadn't shaved in weeks, and scraggly facial hair covered his chin and near his sideburns, his cheeks still noticeably bare. His hair curled away, clumped together by grease, making him appear childlike despite his wrinkled and dark features, his overgrown nose hair and bushy eyebrows. He doubled over in pain from the gunshot wound. Mired in his expression was a mixture of fear, anger, confusion, and angst. But not Caleb's mom. Despite her haggard appearance, bones pushing out her flesh like tent poles, she maintained an air of resolution. Despite all that had happened, she remained steadfast in her convictions.

"Remember Job," she said to the congregation. The ones who had the strength sat in the pews. The sick mostly slept in the aisles, moaning under their fever and delirium. "He was a pious man, a man of God. He had bountiful fields and oxen, seven sons and three daughters. He was a blessed man. He prayed and he tithed and he devoted himself to the Lord, but the devil, undeterred, made a bet with God. He said, 'See that man right there; he has lived a pious life, a fulfilled life, a life blessed with riches and family. That is why he is a pious man. That is why he praises You, because You have made him rich. Take that away, and he will curse Your name. You watch, God. Watch and learn. Man is a selfish lot. He is a greedy lot. Take away from them all they hold dear, and they will turn away from You.'

"God accepted the devil's bet, and the devil, pleased and confident, went to the earth, and he burned Job's fields. He killed Job's oxen, his sheep. He killed Job's sons, his daughters, and when Job learned of all his losses, he praised the Lord. He said the Lord giveth and the Lord taketh away. He did not sin. He prayed, and he revered the Lord. 'See,' the Lord told the devil, 'See my son Job. He is an upright man, a good man, a godly man,' and the devil replied, 'Yes, take away a man's riches, his family, he will still love the Lord, but touch a man's own flesh, and he will curse Your name.' And so the devil returned to the earth, and he plagued poor Job with leprosy. His skin boiled and ruptured, turned malignant and sour. Even Job's wife turned on him, mocked him for still revering God, laughing at his piety, his conviction and determination. But Job did not relent. He still loved the Lord. Despite all that happened, he remained loyal to God, and with this, the Lord was pleased.

"Hearing about his plight, Job's neighbors visited him. Three came, but they didn't even recognize Job. For seven days and seven nights they sat with Job as he suffered until finally Job spoke, and they debated Job's plight. They argued as to whether Job's punishment was justified, on what he could do to win favor once again with God, but Job disregarded their advice. He remained silent until finally claiming his friends false. Man cannot understand God's intentions through worldly righteousness or wickedness. Man's gains or losses have no bearing on the divine. Only God gives and only God takes away, and Man is unfit to know why. God acts for his own purpose, his alone, and does not consider Man's wishes or wants. Whether he be rich, poor, old, wise, powerful, or wicked, it is God's will, and Man shall not question the Lord.

"Then God showed himself to Job, and Job revered his God, and the merciful God provided twice as much as before. The Lord gave unto Job thousands of oxen, of sheep, his fields and his family. Job went on to live 140 years, and it was written that Job will rise again with those whom the Lord raises up, all because he remained faithful and obedient."

LATER THAT NIGHT, THE FBI raided the service hall. They sent in a dozen armed agents and twice as many National Guard soldiers. The FBI agents wore bulletproof vests and carried semi-automatic hand-guns, some of them approaching the door with a battering ram, and the National Guard carried M-16 rifles and were in full combat gear.

It was when they started to beat down the door that Caleb became aware of them. Sam, Caleb, and his mother hurried the remaining members of the congregation who were well enough upstairs to the storage room. The sick they left downstairs. They begged to be carried, to be helped, but there wasn't enough time. They barricaded the door with boxes and unused bricks and lumber, and they waited. They waited for God to come. They waited for him to tell them they'd done the right thing. They waited until they heard a loud crash from downstairs.

Caleb's mother moved to the window and looked down.

"Get a gun," she said.

"What?"

"Do what I say!"

She grabbed a handgun. She checked the clip to make sure it was loaded, and then she pointed the barrel out the window. Caleb waited for her to fire, but she didn't right away. She was mumbling something, and she kept jarring the barrel from one target to the next like she couldn't decide whom to shoot first.

Then she looked back at Caleb. "Get your gun. There's no time to waste."

"We've gone too far," Caleb said. "We've gone too far. We've gone too far. We've gone too far."

"Pull yourself together, Caleb. I'm counting on you."

She turned back to the window and fired. Caleb couldn't see it, but he knew people were getting hurt. He knew people were getting shot. He knew people were dying—he could hear their screams when they were hit, and each one made it feel as though he were being stabbed in the chest, and he couldn't help but think this was his fault. All of it. Every last bit.

"They're dead, Mom. All those people downstairs. All of us up here. They're dead. Sam's going to die. Me and you. It's all our fault. Don't you see that?"

"These people need us. We're saving them. Not hurting them. Please tell me you understand that." She put down her gun and placed her hands on Caleb's cheeks. "Please tell me you know we're saving their souls."

"We're going to die, Mom."

"And we will be welcomed into the kingdom of heaven."

"It wasn't supposed to turn out this way. You said—"

"I know what I said."

She grabbed ahold of Caleb's wrists and she shook him. She put her face right up against his, her eyes a vein-ribbed red, and said, "Sometimes terrible things happen. And you just have to get right back up and walk it. Do you understand me?"

She looked deranged. She looked like she'd snapped. Eyes bugged. Hair disheveled. Her face and neck and forearms scratched up. She looked scared, too, like she didn't know what might happen next, and for the first time in his life, Caleb was scared of her.

"We've got to turn ourselves in." Caleb tried to get up, but she pushed him back down. "We have to make this stop."

"Don't you dare," she said. "Don't you dare do that to me."

Something exploded, followed by a bright flash. Caleb looked outside and saw a ball of light streaking up into the sky like a flare. It looked like a shooting star, and for a moment everything was peaceful, serene even. There was just the flare illuminating the sky, making it so bright as to drown out the stars behind it, and there appeared to be a halo over the worship hall, a celestial glow burning bright and cascading down in emblazoned embers, and he thought everything might be okay. Maybe it was all over, and he and his friends might live. But then came pounding on the door. The congregation cried and screamed and begged for help, and Caleb's mother turned from the window. She reloaded her gun and pointed it at the noise. More pounding. The door buckled and splintered, bending away from its hinges. Caleb's mother tightened her grip and fired. She fired at Mr. Goldsby. Then Mrs. Goldsby. Then their twin sons, Devon and Luke. She shot Barbara Eggleston and Peyton Wouk, Martin Sanders and Mary Atler. All of them were pleading with her, begging her, "No, please, don't, spare me!" But she didn't. She shot one after another after another until the trigger clicked. Finally, the door gave way, and gas canisters were launched inside.

Caleb was surprised at first, frozen in a state of shock. He couldn't breathe. He couldn't see. His eyes stung, and tears streamed down his face. There was nothing but gray, stinging haze. He could taste the smoke. It tasted like sulfur and smelled even worse. He could hear screaming. A high-pitched panicked scream. A deep scream full of fear. A loud moan from Sam, like he needed to make noise to convince himself he was still alive.

Another explosion sounded. Caleb couldn't pinpoint the source, but he heard more yelling, commands this time, screaming to get down, get down, "Get on your hands and knees, motherfuckers," followed by the stampede of heavy boots and, finally, the volley of machine-gun fire. And then he felt heat, then smoke. Someone had set a fire. Caleb dropped to the ground, and it burned hot and it burned bright, and he knew there was no way to get out safely. He panicked, and he thought this was it—this truly was the end of times.

He'd have thought there'd be some sort of acceptance or seren-
ity in this realization. He'd find calm, and St. Peter would greet him
at the gates of heaven, and standing next to him would be Scoot and
Brandon and Catherine and Sam and his father and his brother and
his mother, and they'd all be happy and free from sin, free from pain
and suffering and the bitter angst that buried him under the blackest
of soil, but that wasn't what happened. There was just sheer and utter
panic. He was scared, and he was distraught—he was going to die, and
he still hadn't yet made peace with God.

As the National Guard made it deeper into the room, his mother
tried to shield him. She somehow managed to find him in the smoke
and the confusion, and she pushed him to the ground and lay on top
of him. Her body was heavy, and her weight bore down on Caleb,
making it hard for him to breathe. He coughed, and he choked, the
smoke and the ash and the heat crawling deep inside of him, filling
his lungs until there wasn't any more room for oxygen, and she kept
saying something over and over and over, repeating the same syllables
in a hushed and hurried whisper above his ear. "I'm sorry. I'm sorry.
I'm sorry."

THE BOOK OF REVELATION

CHAPTER 1

I WAS RELEASED FROM THE JUVENILE DETEN-
tion center when I was eighteen years old. The FBI gave me a new
name, Billie Booker, a new social security number, five hundred dollars, and told me I could move anywhere I wanted. I didn't have any-
place to go to—I didn't know where my father and brother were at,
and the authorities told me not to look for them anyway, for their
safety and mine. I didn't have any friends to speak of. The congregation had, of course, long ago disbanded, the survivors having lost faith
in us and in themselves and in the God we'd preached to them. I had
nothing and nowhere, and so I chose Oklahoma City. The FBI tried to
get me to move out of state, but I refused. Having never left the state
of Oklahoma, I was too scared to, incapable of taking on even more of
the unknown when I was so uncertain in myself.

Oklahoma City was a nice place with nice people and nice homes
and nice dogs and hand-painted wooden advertisements and mega
churches. People drove Ford F-150s and wore plaid shirts and Wran-
gler jeans and polo shirts to work. On Saturday mornings it smelled
of donuts and gasoline. The wind blew so hard it stung the eyes, and it
was bigger than any place I'd ever lived. Though a small city compared

to Chicago or New York or L.A., there were people everywhere. They went for walks and shopped for new tires and commuted to work, and although I didn't know a soul there, I never felt alone. I always felt in the presence of people, and I found comfort in that—when I was eighteen and scared and unsure what I would do with my life, how I would live, how I would support myself, how I would find my next meal or a roof over my head or someone I could confide in, it was enough. It was familiar enough to give me confidence in being on my own, but different enough I could start over. I think the hardest thing to get used to was the new name. Billie Booker. Billie Booker. It just sounded foreign in my mouth, tripping over my tongue. The first thing I did when I was released was go to a Conoco station just down the road and stand in the bathroom for an hour, just standing there in front of the mirror, repeating, "I am Billie Booker. I am Billie Booker. I am Billie Booker." But no matter how many times I said it, I couldn't quite get myself to believe it.

I used a part of the five hundred bucks to put a deposit down on an apartment and looked for a job. Inside juvie, counselors had taught me some life skills, how to cook and clean and balance my checkbook. I learned how to stamp license plates and pick up trash on the side of the road. An electrician came in to teach us how to wire a house and repair small appliances, but most of the time he just read magazines and didn't teach us a thing. I did get my GED, and I was proud of that, but I really didn't have any valuable skills. I couldn't weld or carpenter. I couldn't read a balance sheet or design detailed blueprints. I was an unskilled laborer, and I was okay with that. I found solace in what this entailed, mainly anonymity. I would be a product or service, a barista or mailman or carpet cleaner, not Caleb, the false prophet, the leader of a cult, a murderer.

I found a job with a pyramid scheme called SlashCo, selling cutlery sharp enough to slice through polycarbonate and copper. Not that it was a competitive hiring process; they simply hired whoever replied to the company's help wanted advertisement. It wasn't a bad job, per se. Their business model was centered upon recruitment. They made money by the number of recruits they could convince to hock their wares, not necessarily by the skillset of their sales team. There were some good salespeople, but mostly it was just kids who had $139 to put down as a deposit in order to sell some knives to their parents and aunts and uncles. The problem was, I'd just been released from five years in juvenile detention, knew nobody in the area, and was in witness protection.

But, to his credit, my manager helped me out. Named Pinkett, he was a heavyset, jolly guy with a short beard who fueled his relentless energy with Mountain Dew and Wendy's chicken nuggets. He smelled of pot smoke and listened to Phish songs and rooted for the Texas Longhorns. Every chance he could, he brought up Dallas, how he missed it and how much better it was than Oklahoma City, or anywhere for that matter. To him it wasn't the United States—it was Texas and its forty-nine little sisters. He wasn't a bad guy, though. I looked up to him. And he looked out for me. When I told him I didn't have any leads, he was undeterred.

"No problem," he said. "What we can do is, we'll train you to be the service guy, a knife sharpener. When an old customer calls in and needs their knives sharpened or new ones, we'll send you out there, and you can upsell them and build leads for new sales that way. No problem."

I liked the guy. His energy was infectious, and so when the service calls came in, I tried to relate the same type of energy into my demos. I'd listen to songs Pinkett recommended, Phish jam-band tunes with winding and intricate melodies, sometimes a little metal like GWAR to get me pumped up. I drank Mountain Dew and ate pounds of Wendy's chicken nuggets. I bought ties from Target and gray, pin-striped suits, stuffing white handkerchiefs in the breast pocket so I'd even look like him. He was young and successful and everything I thought I wanted to be. Pinkett encouraged it, too, giving me tips on how to style my hair, hardening it with a quarter-sized dollop of gel.

In the demos I met the most interesting people: WWII veterans and math prodigies, cello players and conspiracy theorists. There were dog groomers and civil war reenactors. I met bucktoothed equestrian riders and Beanie Babies collectors and even a professional bowler. And I loved it. While a ward of the juvenile correctional facility, I'd met very few people. There were the guards and then there were the inmates. There were the counselors, and there were more guards. My world was confined to cinderblock walls and fluorescent lights and doors that locked from the outside. I didn't have access to a computer. I had nobody to write. I kept to myself. I played a lot of solitaire and read anything I could get my hands on: gossip magazines, cookbooks, OSHA pamphlets, whatever was at hand. But outside, it was different. I could move freely and talk to whomever I wished. It was exhilarating, like learning to walk all over again.

My first service call was with a housewife. She lived in a nice-sized home with a nice-sized fence and had two nice-sized toddlers. Family portraits lined her walls, the children posing in awkward angles, resting their chins in their hands and kicking their feet up behind them as they lay on their bellies. They were prescribed poses, pretense masquerading as everyday life, photoshopped and directed, but that was okay. I tended to prefer these types of photos to candid shots, shots where people's faces were long and their eyes were full of sadness. I'd had enough of that.

While I sharpened her knives, she sat at the island and sipped from a coffee mug filled with white wine, half-heartedly reprimanding her two toddlers as they sprinted around the house, touching everything they could in their wake, the walls and books and art and couch and chairs and even my ultra-sharp knives.

"Don't worry about it," she said when her three-year-old picked up shears that could slice through copper. "If she loses a finger, she'll learn a lesson."

"I'm not sure my manager would agree," I said as I recovered the shears, and the wife shrugged.

It was a simple, domestic scene, one I imagined occurred countless times each day across America: unruly children, an unkempt home, a bored housewife tipsily chatting up a complete stranger, thankful just to have someone to speak to who wasn't in diapers, but it intrigued me in a way that was hard to articulate. I felt like a sociologist might, or maybe an astronaut first making contact with alien life, there to study and to listen and to record and then report back home with my findings. I realize this was silly, but I couldn't help it. Anything that might even hint at normalcy was still novel to me.

"The thing is," my customer, Mrs. Applebury, said, "I really don't mind they bought the motorcycle. I really don't." She was speaking of her next-door neighbor. "He's just one of those guys who thinks he's hot shit. Whatever you want to do with your money is fine by me.

As long as you pay taxes like the rest of us, it's your God-given right to buy whatever the hell you want, but to ride that thing at eleven at night? Revving up the engine like he's in some cock-measuring contest? I've got kids, for Christ's sake. Young kids. And once they wake up, they don't get back to bed." She shook her head like she was being offered food she didn't like. "Up all hours of the goddamn night. Crying and screaming and just throwing a fit. Only way I can get them to shut up is to rub a little whiskey on their gums. Not that I'd ever admit to that."

"Sounds terrible," I said. "I noticed you only have a couple of our knives, Mrs. Applebury. Do you cook often?" I asked.

She poured herself another glass of wine, her third since I'd been there, and scolded her children for jumping on the sofa. "The thing that gets me the most is that I've talked to him about it. I asked him politely to please ride before nine p.m. I said please and thank you. I said that. 'Please.' To him. To that narcissistic, walking hard-on. You know I caught him looking at my ass the other day? Broad daylight and everything. Right in the middle of his driveway like this was some goddamn peep show. Tongue out, eyes wide. Goddamn disgusting. Made me want to puke. Why do men think they can just do that? Eye a woman like she can be owned?"

"You know, if you do, you might benefit by taking a look at our Homemaker Special. It's got everything you would ever need: a chef's knife, utility knife, paring knife, a serrated spreader, bread knife, butcher knife. You name it. Not to mention it comes with a lifetime warranty. Doesn't matter if it's in one year, five years, ten years, if you need a piece fixed or replaced, we'll do it at no charge to you."

"And you know what he did when he noticed I'd caught him? He winked! Can you believe that? Like I would ever in a million years let that cretin lay a hand on me."

"If you're interested, I might even be able to throw in a vegetable peeler for free."

Her head snapped toward me. "Vegetable peeler?"

That was my first sale. A nine-hundred-dollar block of knives that netted me ninety bucks. And I'd only been in there for an hour. When I left the Appleburys' home, I vibrated. It was like I levitated. I hadn't felt that good in years, since my mother and I had arrived in Grove, before we'd promised Scoot something we couldn't deliver, when everything had been sincere and altruistic, when we'd been doing some good in the world. I felt so good, in fact, I couldn't wait to call Pinkett and tell him the news.

"Boom!" he yelled through the phone. "Booker for the homemaker! Go big or go home, son!"

And it didn't diminish after that. After every sale, my skin tingled and my heart rate quickened. My tongue constricted, and I salivated. I could feel the rush of adrenaline and serotonin flood my system because for the first time in a long time, I felt needed and wanted and like I was accomplishing something bigger than myself, and it felt good to feel that way again, even if it was just for a little while, even if it was for selling knives. It felt good to be appreciated.

After work, I explored town. I'd leave my apartment without reason or destination and just walk. Oklahoma City was so much different than Bartlesville or Grove, definitely different than juvenile detention. It sprawled in every direction. There were homes and antique shops and bookstores and mechanic's garages and cafés and museums and bars and restaurants. I visited the Oklahoma City Bombing Memorial on one of the first nights I was out. It was dusk when I visited, the place mostly empty with the exception of one family, a mother and father and young son, perhaps five or six, old enough, it seemed, to understand the words his parents were saying but young enough to not yet grasp the gravity of the situation.

The memorial itself was a beautiful place. A large black archway guarded the entrance, the numbers 9:02 sketched into the façade, marking the time the bomb exploded. A reflecting pool illuminated chairs, representing each of the 168 victims. Their names were carved into the chairs, a placard of sorts, not allowing us to forget what had happened that morning in April 1995. The Survivor Tree, an American elm on the north side of the memorial, had provided shade for visitors in the parking lot across the street from the Murrah Building. About a hundred years old, it had been heavily damaged in the bombing, and after investigators had retrieved evidence embedded in the bark, it was slated to be cut down. But it never was, and one year after the blast, survivors and friends and family of the victims had met there for a memorial ceremony when they noticed it had started to bloom. It came to symbolize the Oklahoma spirit, our inimitable will to keep going despite the misery.

I'd been just a child when the bombing happened. I was in elementary school at the time, maybe third or fourth grade. We were living in Bartlesville, and my classmates were competing in a math game, a race to complete multiplication problems on the chalkboard. Two students stood up at the front of the class, and the teacher, behind us, stated aloud a problem, five times eight, say, and the students would have to write the problem on the board along with the solution. When done, the first student to turn around and face the classroom won. I was up at the board, and I had won several in a row. The other students revolved through one by one, and I defeated all of them in turn. I'd made it around the class two or three times, each of them defeated, and finally the teacher, Mrs. Brown, a young, pregnant teacher, said, "Sounds like you need some competition." She stood and cradled her belly with her hands. "How about this: you beat me, and you can teach math for the rest of the semester."

Mrs. Brown joined me at the front of the class. I was nervous before we started, my palms a wet paper cup. I was taking on the teacher, the modicum of authority in our day-to-day lives. If I was to beat her, it was like anything was possible. We could rise up and start a revolution. We, for once, the children and not the adults, could be in charge. I'd read *Lord of the Flies* the previous summer, and I thought everything would be different if I were in charge. Everything would be so much better. Just so much better.

"Let's make it difficult, though," she said. "Nothing off our times tables. Let's get big numbers involved here. Everything has to be greater than twelve. Got it, class?"

"Yes, Mrs. Brown," they chanted back in unison.

Mrs. Brown selected a student to randomly choose a problem, and she and I stood side by side, me on the right of the chalkboard, and she on the left, chalk and eraser in hand.

"One hundred seventy-four times two hundred eighty-eight."

We began, writing as fast as we could. I wrote a two, a nine, a three, a one, next line, a zero, a two, a nine, a three, a one, and my hand started to cramp. I'd been writing and writing and writing, and my fingers were slippery with perspiration. Next line, a zero, a zero, an eight, a four, a three, and my pulse quickened, my tongue flexed in anticipation, the electrical synapses firing in my brain because I was ahead; I was doing it; I was going to win. A two, a one, a one, a zero, a five, and I turned around. I'd done it. I'd done it. I'd beat the teacher.

That's when Mr. Owen, the principal, burst into the classroom. He looked scared and worried, like a man afraid of heights on the edge of a skyscraper, knowing if he just made one wrong move he'd fall straight down to his death.

"Everyone," he said. "To the library."

We lined up in a single-file line, and each of us was confused and a little frightened. Nothing like this had ever happened before. We didn't know what to expect when we got there, and nothing could have prepared us for the images on the large television screen. The front of the building was gone. Like a giant had just sliced it off. There was smoke, and the façade had been burnt black. From the pile of rubble, soot-covered victims ran. They didn't even know where they were running. They just zigzagged. It didn't even matter where, just as long as it was away from there. And I couldn't help but break down. The victims didn't deserve to suffer. They didn't deserve to die. It had seemed so random, so unpreventable. It was the first time in my life I'd been struck paralyzed by how important it was to be good to people, how tenuous that goodness was, and how easy it was for someone to take it all away.

CHAPTER 2

I MET A GIRL. SHE WORKED AT SLASHCO AS
Pinkett's assistant. She answered phones, scheduled interviews, and
maintained sales records. She was dark-haired and fair-skinned and
named Atchley. She didn't pay much attention to me when we met.
Later she told me it was because she'd thought I was a nerd and boring, probably not worth getting to know, but at the time I chalked
it up to her being new to the city. She'd come from a small town in
southwest Oklahoma called Empire, and right away I was attracted
to her. She had this quiet confidence, always so sure of herself. When
asked a question, she blinked with disbelief at your inherent stupidity,
then answered without inflection but somehow full of aplomb, just the
sincerest reply, uttered in the most monotone voice she could muster.
She wore dark lipstick and took large bites of bananas and double-
decker SONIC Cheeseburgers. She smelled like men's deodorant and
typed by pounding the keys, and every chance I could I tried to talk
to her.

Of course, I really didn't know how to act. During those awkward
teenage years when you first started becoming aware of your attrac-
tion to other human beings in a way that didn't involve action figures

and BMX bikes, I didn't have any contact with girls. Inside juvie, there were just teenage boys, horny, hormone-ridden, pubescent boys. And we had no alone time, which meant we had no opportunity for release. Showers were communal, no curtain, nothing. Three boys to a room. Even the toilets didn't have stalls in them. We never had privacy. We never had the opportunity like other boys to find our parents' porn mags or peruse naughty websites because our parents weren't savvy enough to turn on parental controls. Instead, we were always watched. Guards, counselors, cameras, other inmates, didn't matter if we were naked or clothed, horny or not, someone was always aware of where our hands were at, if our shorts protruded a little farther than they should. Sometimes it became too much, and the bunks shook late at night when one of my roommates thought I'd fallen asleep. I never said a word to them, though, and they never said anything to me, either, when I did the same thing.

The first time I met Atchley was at a work meeting late one night. We always had our meetings about nine p.m. so our days could be filled with sales calls. We were in the big conference room, and in the rows of metal folding chairs sat a very unusual-looking group. There were people of every race and socioeconomic status, Polo-wearing natives and Carhart hillbillies, Maserati-driving rich kids and tattooed black guys. In the back sat a blond-haired girl who eyed the place like she had made a grave mistake. An elderly man with a walker and a hearing aid looked around with the same look, but for probably different reasons. There were moms with oversized purses and twenty-somethings with long beards. Most sat by themselves and didn't speak to anyone else, obviously not knowing another attendee, myself included. Other than Pinkett, I knew no one. Since starting a week prior, I hadn't met a single other person who worked for the company. At the time, I didn't find any of this strange or worrisome because I had no other relative work experience to compare my situation to.

Pinkett stood at the front of the room alongside a table draped by a white sheet, clapping his hands as The String Cheese Incident blared through a decade-old boom box. As with the other times I'd met with him, he bounced with relentless energy, dancing and moving his shoulders and legs and head, out of sync with the music. Pinkett's complete lack of shame and inhibition reminded me of Sam in a way—here was a true leader, someone who could inspire others to do better, to do more than they'd originally thought possible. I knew I'd attach myself to him even before I did so. It was almost like an electric magnetism. I felt drawn to him, and there was little I could do to stop it.

Underneath the sheet were bulbous shapes, and behind Pinkett was the sales leaderboard, the five top salespeople's names illuminated by glitter and neon Sharpie. There was a leader for the week, for the month, and for the year, the three big boards, Pinkett called them. This was the first of such meetings for me, and I couldn't help but feel a little excited.

"Welcome!" Pinkett said as we all found our seats. He gyrated with energy, his jowls jiggling like a fruitcake. "Take a seat, meet your neighbor, have a Dew, come in, sit down, get comfortable! We got some exciting fucking things going on tonight."

Pinkett circled the room like he was sizing each of us up. He power-walked, pumping his elbows, and he sweated profusely. His white oxford shirt was drenched, and he smelled overwhelmingly of French fries. I wouldn't have been surprised if he hadn't slept in days. He was in a delirious frenzy, and it was contagious. I could see others affected by his energy, beginning to bounce their heads and tap their shoes. I was, I have to admit, one of them.

"I am extremely proud of this group. I am proud of Hubert and Henry and Adam and Suzanne. I'm proud of you and you and you and you. I am monumentally, exasperatingly, meteorically, flamboyantly, almost erotically proud of this fucking group. Do you know how good you guys are?"

No one said a word, looking at each other confused, intrigued, bewildered, but no one responded.

"I say again, do you know how fucking great you guys are?"

"Great!" I shouted. A few of the others looked back at me, including Pinkett. He beamed. He turned red in the face, and he smiled with his whole body, bouncing up and down.

"How good are you?" Pinkett held his hand to his ear.

"Great!" more of us yelled.

"How fucking great are you?"

"Fucking great!"

Pinkett performed jumping jacks and skipped his way back up to the front of the room, his knees high, his hands pumping up and down. The music reached a crescendo, and we all joined him in clapping along to the rising melody.

"Stand up!" Pinkett ordered. "I want to hear you!"

We rose to our feet and cheered and clapped and bellowed our approval. It reminded me of church, a communal and singular belief in ourselves, in what we were doing. It was intoxicating, and all of it, down to me jumping up and down and hollering and clapping, felt monumentally right.

"This week has been a very good week. An epic week. One of

those weeks when you just know everything we've worked so hard for has come together. This week, we're unveiling a new leaderboard to add to our Big Three up here, and this one is very, very, very exciting. This week we're going to unveil the regional leaderboard, and it will show all the offices in the southwest division. And we want to be the best, right?"

"Right!" we yelled.

"We want to destroy them, right?"

"Right!"

"What do we want to do?"

"Destroy them!"

"What?"

"Destroy them!"

"I can't hear you!"

"Destroy them!"

"You know what?" Pinkett continued. He paced at the front of the room, arms swinging like he was securing a rebound. "I actually can't wait any longer. Let's go ahead and bring that out. Atchley."

That was when I first saw her. And, looking back, it wasn't all that spectacular. My heart didn't palpitate, and I didn't sweat. Time didn't stand still. There wasn't love at first sight, or second, or even third for that matter. None of that crap crammed down our throats in romantic comedy after generic romantic comedy. There was just a girl, and the reason she stood out was not because she was beautiful or sexy or smelled like lemon-drop rainbows—what grabbed my attention was she was so aloof. Here we were, yelling and clapping and stomping along in some euphoric, communal jubilation, and yet she wasn't affected like the rest of us. She was calm and disinterested, mouth set firm in a line, eyes sleepy and devoid of makeup. She had her hair pulled up into a ponytail and wore jeans so wrinkled they appeared they hadn't been washed in weeks. And it wasn't that I found this charming or attractive. I was intrigued. What made this girl so immune to her surroundings when the rest of us couldn't help but follow along?

"Drumroll please!" Pinkett said, as we all started drumming on our laps. "And Bam!"

Atchley pulled out the leaderboard. It was made from construction paper and glued to white Styrofoam board. In big block letters at the top, it read, "Southwest Assassins," our regional name, and below it were five empty slots.

"Let's start us off with number five, shall we?" Pinkett continued. "Coming in at $45,872 is Shreveport, Louisiana."

Pinkett pointed up at the board like a game-show host as Atchley reached underneath the white sheet, pulled out the Shreveport panel, and attached it to the leaderboard with Velcro, all the while her expression unchanged, one of complete and utter boredom.

"At number four, totaling $63,294 in sales for this period, is, dun da duh, Round Rock, Texas!"

Again, Pinkett pointed up at the board as Atchley posted it, the rest of us booing Round Rock and all that they stood for.

"And now, ladies and gentlemen, for our current bronze finishers is, wait for it, wait for it . . . Oklahoma City!"

A collective groan erupted from the crowd.

"Now, now," Pinkett said, "it's okay." Atchley put OKC up on the board in third place, and some of the veterans at the front balled up pieces of paper and chucked them toward the leaderboard. Atchley stepped to the side and stuffed her hands into her pockets.

"We've come a long way now. Two weeks ago, we were ranked seventh. Last week fifth. This week third. If we keep this up, guys, we'll take over first place. I just know it. Nobody is going to be able to stop you."

Atchley placed the second- and first-place cities up on the leaderboard, Phoenix and Dallas, respectively. Pinkett put the music back on and acted like he was riding an invisible horse, lapping the table, the rest of us clapping and urging him on.

"And now the fun stuff!" Pinkett said as he stopped behind the table, pulled the sheet, and revealed a set of cleavers and butcher knives. They were large and shiny and I wanted them. I didn't really know why, but I wanted them. "First, we're going to unveil the top salespeople of the week. Atchley, if you please." Atchley picked up the first name to be placed on the leaderboard, but she didn't reveal who it was, instead holding it backward so that we couldn't read the name. "Coming in fifth place, we have Zach Hughes!"

Everyone clapped and Zach stood to take a bow.

"As a reward for Zach's gallant efforts this week, he has earned a new toy. A bread knife." Pinkett held up the knife and handed it to Zach as if bestowing a sword to a samurai, head bowed, grip offered in reverence. Pinkett continued in this way, giving out bigger prizes to fourth place, a sharpener; third place, a chef's knife; second place, a butcher's knife, until he made it to the top prize of the week, the coveted first place. "This is a very exciting week," Pinkett said. For the first time since starting the meeting, he didn't shout. Instead he took a serious tone and demeanor. "For the first time in the history of the Oklahoma City office, our top salesman for the week is a newbie. Yes, that's right, a brand-new salesperson outdid our top candidates. And by a long shot. By a wide margin. In fact, it wasn't even close. Coming in at $4,593 in sales, nearly doubling our second-place finisher, is the one and only, fresh and ornery, Billie B-B-B-Booker!"

My stomach dropped. I felt queasy. I felt nauseated. Besides that, though, I felt happy. Ever since I'd been locked up in juvenile detention, I'd been marginalized and drummed down, beaten up and scolded, my conscience unbearable, my living conditions worse. The other inmates derided me, called me the false prophet. They called me crazy and held me down and stuffed dirty socks into my mouth. When I complained, the counselors were disinterested, their attention and resources already spread too thin by an ever-increasing population of traumatized and unruly boys, and so I'd felt alone and useless, beaten down into an automaton, a biological shell that ate and shit and pissed and drank and slept and stared, but nothing else. But this was different. For the first time since the church, someone believed in me, recognized me, made me feel as though I amounted to something, mattered to somebody. I was special, and—I couldn't lie—it felt good.

"Come up here, Billie," Pinkett said as he waved me up onstage like Bob Barker. When I joined him, he handed me a cleaver and unveiled a watermelon. "Here," he said. "Take this."

I blinked at him.

"Go ahead. Smash it. Destroy it. Make that fruit your bitch."

I blinked again, unsure.

"It's okay," he said. "I promise."

And so I swung. I swung the cleaver like an axe. I brought it over my head and used my entire weight to bring it down. I did it again. And again. And again. Until pieces of watermelon splashed the entire first row, Pinkett, and me. I swung until the table splintered in two. I swung until my hands were bruised, and the cleaver slipped from my hands. And then we all just stopped. Everyone looked stunned. The salesmen, Pinkett, everybody. Their jaws dropped and their eyes were like saucers, until Pinkett raised his arms in triumph and let out a shriek and the rest of the crowd followed suit, all of them standing and jumping and whistling, with the exception of Atchley. She just brushed the fruit from her clothes and walked out of the room, a piece of watermelon still dangling from her hair.

I SPENT ALL MY TIME at the office after that. The first couple of hours, I sat with Pinkett while he conducted interviews. The entire interview process was a sales pitch. From the ad to the phone call to the scheduling to the moment the applicant walked through the door. The entire act was scripted. Pinkett sold the job like we were supposed to sell knives, and he was good at it. He made you feel special, like you were bestowed this wonderful gift for being selected when in reality anyone who showed up was hired.

"Don't tell anyone, though," he said. "This stays between us."

I also spent time with Atchley, asking her questions, mentally cataloguing her answers, jotting them down in a notebook when I got home at night. I tried to come off as genuinely interested in her, which I was, but looking back I must have seemed crazy, this odd interrogator asking endless, bizarre questions: "How do you like to cook your eggs?" "Have you ever broken a bone?" "What song most often gets stuck in your head?" To her credit, she answered every single one, no matter how off-putting or random it seemed, and she never made me feel stupid for asking either. She gave each of her answers genuine thought and consideration, sometimes even saying she would get back to me on something, then three or four days later giving me an answer, always with a straight face, always with poise.

"Why do you want to know these things?" she once asked me, a couple weeks after I'd started with SlashCo. We were at her desk, where she shared a space with her counterpart, Kari, the other girl charged with scheduling interviews. As always, Atchley was genuine when she asked, not distancing herself from my interest with sarcasm or derision. I found this irresistible and charming. I felt remarkably sane with her, not consumed with crippling self-doubt and loneliness.

"I don't know," I told her, though that was a lie. I asked her personal questions because I wanted to know everything there was to know about her. I wanted to know her so well I could predict what she was going to do even before she did it. I wanted to anticipate where she would be and what she'd be doing twenty years from now so I'd never be surprised by her, so I could be there for every important moment in her life, revel in her successes, comfort her in her failures. It was a strange impulse, I knew, but it was there nevertheless, and I knew I wouldn't be able to diminish it.

"Okay," she said, staring straight at me. Not in a way that made me uncomfortable, but in a way that emboldened me. "Ask away."

"What is the most embarrassing moment of your life?"

"Easy," she said. "I once peed myself while on a first date. The waiter made me laugh so hard I pissed all down the front of my dress. It pooled on the floor, and a busboy slipped in it."

"Where were you when the Oklahoma City bombing happened?"

"I was in elementary school, Mrs. Sullivan's class. We were working on spelling words, and she was getting aggravated because we kept misspelling the words on purpose. She wanted to scream at us. She wanted to yell and throw things and beat the ever-living crap out of us because we were just laughing at her, and there was nothing she could do about it."

"Who do you hate most in the world?"

"Oprah."

"Really?"

"She buys her audience with appliances. Seems disingenuous."

"Okay, then. Oprah it is. Have you ever been arrested?"

"Once for public drunkenness and once for stealing."

"What'd you steal?"

"Temporary tattoos and a Snapple."

"You like Snapple?"

She shrugged. "I like the Snapple lady."

"If you could change one thing about yourself, what would it be?"

She squinted at me like she was sizing up the veracity of my question, and if I was somehow going to use the information to hurt her in some way. For a while she just sat there and stared at me. "I wish I wasn't so much of a coward," she said, and left it at that.

I smiled, and she smiled, and that was all there was to say.

"For fuck's sake, you guys," Kari said. "You guys are weird."

At ten a.m. I made my sales calls, scheduling appointments for that afternoon. Most of the time, I met with women, because they generally were the ones who did the cooking for the family, but every once in a while, I met with a man. One afternoon I met with a guy who owned a military-surplus store, and in his spare time he liked to cook. He watched Food Network and followed Rachel Ray on Facebook, and he owned every single item SlashCo had to offer.

"You a Republican or a Democrat?" he asked as soon as he answered the door. The way he said "Democrat," with his tongue splayed against his teeth, I already knew the right answer.

"Republican," I said. "We got a good one in W. Kerry would've been a disaster."

"Good man," he said and opened the door wider, letting me inside.

His house was filled with dead animals. On his walls were buck mounts and his chandeliers were made from antlers. A bearskin rug lay on the floor, and in the corner prowled a full-sized stuffed mountain lion. It reminded me of home in a way. My father had always been a hunter, and though Mom didn't allow him to hang his trophies like this man did, the fall always smelled of venison cooking, a ten-point buck hanging from the ceiling in the garage, waiting to be sent to the butcher. I suppose this man's house made me nostalgic in a way I hadn't been before, missing my father, missing home before everything had crumbled around us.

The man's SlashCo collection was impressive. He had the Ultimate, which was every single kitchen knife SlashCo manufactured, stored in a massive, 84-unit butcher block. The thing completely covered his kitchen island.

"Try to get them sharpened every few months," the man said. "Nothing worse than a dull knife."

I eyed the collection, knowing it would take me well over six hours to finish the job. Six hours of work while this man cleaned his guns at the kitchen table. He had an arsenal, 30.06 rifles and 9 mm semi-automatic handguns. He had a Colt .45 and a snub-nosed .48 and a shotgun. Having them all sitting there made me nervous. I hadn't seen any guns since the night the feds raided the worship hall, and my throat constricted and my lungs threatened to collapse. To make matters worse, the room smelled of gun oil, and I had a hard time catching my breath. It made me dizzy, like I'd lost an inordinate amount of blood.

"So, tell me," he said. "What is it about W that excites you? Not too often you find a young Republican such as yourself. Always seems like it takes a few dozen years before the stupid falls out. Know what I mean?"

"His support of the military, sir," I said. "He did the right thing taking out Saddam."

He nodded. "I know what you mean. You can trust a man like that. At least, you can trust him way before that traitor son of a bitch who turned his back on his buddies in Vietnam." He picked up the snub-nosed revolver, unlatched the cylinder, and popped it open. The gun, to my surprise, was loaded. "You ever think about joining the service? I was in the Army myself. Two tours in the first Gulf War."

"I haven't. No, sir." The room spun, and the man split into two.

"To me, I think military service should be mandatory. Maybe the country wouldn't be going to hell in a handbasket. Teach people respect. Responsibility. A sense of duty and reverence. Important things."

He smiled and elbowed me like we were in cahoots. His teeth were yellowed and a large gap separated his two front teeth. I could clearly make out his tongue behind them, and I thought I might be sick. My breaths were short and sporadic, sweat poured from my brow, and I wanted nothing more than to run. In a moment, I was transported back to that night at the worship hall. I heard bullets firing. I heard people screaming. I smelled the worship hall burning.

"You okay, boy?" he asked.

My shirt was drenched. Everything went wavy. I was steeped in vertigo, and I reached out to catch my balance, but instead I knocked the customer's butcher block to the floor. Knives spilled everywhere, and I fell. I fell and tried to catch myself but couldn't. I landed on a butcher knife, my hand splitting at the heel. The cut was deep, and blood spewed from the wound.

"Jesus," the man said. "Jesus fucking Christ."

I could make out bone. It glinted underneath the fluorescent lighting. The pain was intense. It shot up my forearm and through my shoulder and panged my chest like it was hammering my heart. Blood squirted everywhere. It shot up and out like water from a hose.

"Oh wow," the man said. "Crazy, man."

Blood splattered the island and the floor and his knives, and the man kneeled next to me, but I was so woozy and disoriented he no longer looked like the man. He seemed much shorter. His hair straighter and brown, parted in the middle. His complexion turned darker, and his voice an octave higher, though still gravelly. His voice was my mother's voice, and in the distance I could hear the firing of gunshots, Sam screaming, and myself crying.

The man called an ambulance, and it took me to the hospital to stitch me up. It wasn't far from the customer's home, a short ten-minute jaunt by the turnpike. When I got there, two EMTs escorted me into the emergency room, instructing me to keep my hand elevated. It still bled, the loosely wrapped gauze stained a deep crimson. The pain was severe. I didn't cringe or buckle over, but it was there, more pronounced than a dull ache, rather a monotonous stabbing agony. Strangely, I could feel my individual muscles contracting and relaxing underneath the wound, more acutely aware of how my body worked than before. It was a strange feeling in a way, unbearable and persistent, but one I was surprised to find I somewhat enjoyed.

The doctor who treated me was young. She wore a ponytail and stylish glasses and smelled of soap. She was gentle, touching my hand with the care of a curator examining a rare artifact.

"Nasty little bugger you have here," she said, dabbing at the wound with gauze. The wound still bled, blocking her view of the incision. "Does it hurt?"

"Yes," I said.

"Scale of one to ten, one being 'meh' and ten being cataclysmic, mind-numbing torture."

"I don't know. Eight maybe?"

"You don't seem sure."

"It hurts. It hurts like a son of a bitch."

"We'll call that 7.5 then."

"Sure."

The doctor had a suture kit displayed on a rolling chrome table. There were scissors with their blades curved at the end, black thread, a needle sharp enough to puncture flesh. All of it sterilized, lying on a nondescript blue towel.

"You have anyone with you?" she asked.

"What do you mean?"

"Waiting in the lobby. Someone to make sure you get home after this?"

I shook my head no.

"The pain's just going to get worse," she said. "It might seem bad now, but once you leave here, the pain will intensify. You nicked the bone. Good, too. And later you'll bump it. You'll roll over it in your sleep. You'll overwork it. Happens every time."

"No. I don't have anyone to take me home."

"Someone you can call then? Your mom or dad or a friend."

"Nobody."

"Maybe a neighbor or somebody? You'll need pain meds, but they'll make you disoriented. Groggy. You won't be able to drive."

"I don't drive."

She nodded her head, her eyes still locked on her work. She had me lay my hand on the table, the wound facing up. She used a local anesthetic to numb it, then cleaned it with iodine and alcohol.

"I can't give you anything for the pain if you don't have anyone to get you. Are you sure you don't have anyone to call? A brother, an aunt, some guy that tried to sell you pest control door to door?"

I racked my brain. There was Pinkett, of course, and Atchley. They were really the only friends I had since being set free, but I didn't feel right calling them. I'd only known them for a couple weeks, our inter-actions consisting solely of motivational team meetings, backslapping and exuberant congratulations, a quick lunch chowing down some chicken nuggets, some mild workplace flirtation. We didn't ask each other to help us move. We didn't hang out on the weekends, hitting up clubs or catching a movie together or the nightcap doubleheader for the Oklahoma City Redhawks. I didn't know what their reaction would be if I were to call them, if they'd be flattered or surprised or both. Mostly, I didn't want them to feel sorry for me. Eighteen years old and the only person I could call was a relative stranger. What would they think of me then?

"You know," the doctor said. "My husband and I were getting

ready to go on a date the other night. Dinner, movie, nothing really special, but with our work schedules it was the first time we'd been free in a long time, so I wanted to look nice, you know?"

"Sure," I said.

She readied the thread and needle and punctured my skin. I flinched a little, expecting at least a slight pinch, but there was nothing. My hand was completely numb.

"And so, I went to my closet. I tried on dress after dress after dress. I must've tried on like fourteen outfits or something, but I couldn't find anything I liked. I felt like I looked fat in all of them, and so I started complaining to my husband. I tell him I want to go shopping, that nothing I have fits me right, and that I look fat and so on and so on, and he doesn't even say a word. Finally, I'm like, you know, you could give me a compliment, make me feel a little better. And you know what he said?"

I shook my head.

"He said that at least my eyesight is good."

She laughed and laughed and laughed. She snorted, she laughed so hard. It was infectious, really, like her laughter was a shared, intimate memory, and I couldn't help but laugh myself. I laughed so hard I began to feel a little bit better.

When she was done, she gave me two painkillers. "Percocet," she said. "Take one when you get home, the other one four hours later. That'll get you through the night." I took the packet from her and thanked her for her kindness.

"Of course," she said. "You be careful now with those knives," she said. "Though I like you, I don't ever want to see you in here again, you hear?"

She stood to leave, and I did as well, my hand now bandaged but still numb. I stood there a moment, not knowing exactly what to do. I had no idea where I was at, really, or where I could find the closest bus station. My demo knives were still at the client's house, and that was about a mile or two away, though I wasn't really sure. I wasn't even sure how to get there from the hospital. The ambulance ride over, I hadn't been able to see the street, and I didn't pay attention to the turns being made. I had no money for a taxi. No cell phone to call for directions. I really had no idea what to do.

I must've had a concerned expression on my face, because the doctor said, "Listen. I usually don't do this, but"—she took out a pen and wrote out a phone number on a prescription pad—"you call me when you get home, okay? Just so I know you made it all right."

I thanked her again and walked out into the lobby. It was chaotic in there, people with head wounds, the sick, the frightened. A family huddled in the corner, crying, leaning against each other for support. The place teemed with people. They coughed, and they slept, some watching television from a set that hung from the ceiling. It was on a news station, but it was muted without captioning, just a man's face, a picture beside him of a town devastated. I didn't know where the picture was taken, but it looked as though a bomb had dropped, destroying buildings, a city in rubble. Finally, I went to the front desk, and they were able to tell me the address where I'd been picked up, gave me directions on how to get back. And so I walked. I walked for an hour, getting lost a couple times, wandering streets in an unfamiliar neighborhood, but finally I found it. The man was home, surprised I'd returned, and handed me back my knives. He then told me where I could catch the bus.

When I got home, I took the painkiller with an entire glass of wa-ter, gulping it down, refilling the glass, and then gulping it down again, surprised at how thirsty I was, but I didn't call the doctor. I thought about it, staring at her number, phone in hand. A couple of times I even dialed the first three numbers before hanging up, thinking of her still at the emergency room, caring for the sick, the injured, suturing wounds and diagnosing a persistent cough or vomiting, wondering if she was thinking about me at that moment, worried I hadn't reached out to her yet, or if she was too busy with her patients to have given me a second thought once I'd walked out the doors. I hoped the for-mer. I really did, but I couldn't bring myself to call her. Instead, I just taped her number to my fridge. At the very least, I liked the idea I had somebody to call if I absolutely needed to.

CHAPTER 3

WHEN I ARRIVED AT WORK THE FOLLOWING DAY, arm in sling, hand bandaged and splinted, everyone showed concern: Pinkett, Atchley, even Kari. They offered their sympathies, asking if they could do anything for me, get me a Mountain Dew, a sausage biscuit from Johnnies, carry my demo bag full of knives. They fussed over me like a concerned parent might, their tone full of angst and sincerity. It was like waking up to smell your mother cooking pancakes.

"There is one thing," I said.

"Of course," they said. "Anything. Just name it."

"You guys want to hang out sometime?"

They blinked at me, surprised by the question.

"Sure," they said. "Yeah. Sure. Any time."

That evening we all hung out after work. We went to Pinkett's apartment, this small place a minute or two from the office, carpet stained and doors chipped. In the living room there was a pleather couch, a lamp devoid of its shade, and an old glass coffee table marked by condensation rings. It was a one-bedroom with an open-style concept, the small kitchen overlooking the living room. The sink was full of mismatched dishes, plastic cups from various burger and pizza joints around town, bowls that still contained bits of popcorn. The only things worth any money in the place were his set of SlashCo knives and his video game consoles: Playstation, Xbox, N64, the Wii. Two bookshelves full of video games framed the big-screen TV. *Mario Kart* and *Call of Duty* and *Halo* and *Resident Evil* and *Legend of Zelda* and sports games, NBA basketball and NFL football and Major League Baseball, even hockey and soccer. There must've been five hundred of them, dating back from the mid-nineties to new releases out that very week.

Pinkett stashed his keys on the coffee table and slung his suit jacket on the couch's armrest.

"Home sweet home," he said, and the awkwardness was palpable. No one really knew what to say or do, avoiding eye contact, holding their hands in front of them, not moving more than a few feet into the apartment, eyes searching the ceiling, the kitchen, the blinds covered in dust. It seemed it was the first time any of them had hung out together outside of the office.

"I don't have much in the way of refreshments," Pinkett said. "Got water." He opened his fridge. A smell emanated from it: soured milk and bologna. "Beer. Got a few beers, too."

No one said anything right away. Kari, Atchley, and I stood at the entrance, and Pinkett kept looking at us. Well, at Atchley, really. Every chance he could, he stared at her.

"I'll take a beer," Atchley said, and Pinkett smiled. He grabbed a Natural Light and tossed her the can. Atchley grabbed it, popped the tab, and took a long, deep gulp, burping when she was finished, and everyone laughed.

Beers in hand, we relaxed. We drank, and we gossiped, laughing at our customers, at other sales reps on the team, poking fun at their insecurities and their eccentricities, finding common ground in pointing out their flaws and gaffes.

"You remember Daryl?" Pinkett asked. He was referring to a young kid, a senior in high school, who had been hired a few weeks back. He'd showed up to his interview with a short-sleeved oxford buttoned all the way up to his neck and tucked into chinos a size too small. "I shit you not, the first sales call he goes on is his friend's mother, and he gets there, and he starts on the demo, cutting the penny and the rope and going over all the options, and the entire time he's nervous as hell. He's stuttering and shaking, and it takes him like five or six tries just to cut the penny, and his friend's mom is laughing at him. He tells me all this. She starts to laugh at him, and he gets all embarrassed, and he goes into this panic attack and guess what happens?"

"What?" we asked, our eyes slits and bloodshot red.

"He pisses himself."

We burst out laughing, Kari actually spitting out a mouthful of beer.

Pinkett nods. "Honest to God. Just straight up pisses his pants right there in the lady's kitchen, and then you know what he does? He comes to the office. Doesn't go home. Doesn't change his pants. Just drives straight to the office, smelling like piss and his pants soaked. I can see the stain on his crotch, and he just hands me his demo bag back and says he can't do it anymore."

"I wondered what the hell happened to him," I said, all of us laughing until we cried, doubled over in pain.

"Best thing was, it worked. Kid sold the lady a Homemaker. A $900 knife set because she felt sorry for the little fuck. Damnedest thing I've ever heard."

The night continued on like that. Pinkett left to go get more beer, and we kept drinking. The entire time, Pinkett kept scooting closer to Atchley. He touched her. He touched her hand, and he touched her shoulder. He rested his knee against hers and brushed her hair from her face, and Atchley didn't rebuke his advances. She welcomed them, actually, returning his flirtations with her own, parting her lips into a small, enticing circle. And with each lingering glance and grazing fingernail tease, the bile in my stomach churned. They were going to spend the night together, and I couldn't stop it. I wasn't the object of her affection, he was, and the cut I felt was even deeper than the one to my hand.

Around two-thirty that morning, we decided to call it a night. All of us were too drunk to drive, so Pinkett gave Kari and I a couple pillows, some sheets, and a blanket. Kari took the couch while I made a pallet on the floor. Atchley retired to Pinkett's bedroom with him, their hushed voices and giggles audible through the cheap, thin door, all the while Kari asking me, "Are you still awake, Billie?" nudging my shoulder, tracing her fingers along my hairline. "Billie, you still awake?"

BACK AT WORK THE NEXT day, Pinkett and Atchley acted like nothing had happened. Pinkett conducted his interviews and counseled newly minted sales reps. Atchley answered Pinkett's phone and got his dry cleaning and prepped materials for our weekly team meetings. They didn't eat lunch together or have private conversations in Pinkett's office. They didn't hold hands or kiss each other goodbye, making plans to see each other that evening, to go see a movie or catch a concert at the Blue Door. Their conversations were professional, polite, and to the point, often clipped with one-word answers: "Print this out for me?"

"Sure."

"Clean the butcher block?"

"Yeah."

"Got the orders ready?"

"Yup."

I looked for clues they were a couple now, reading into their inflections, how they pronounced the last syllable in a question, if it flipped off the tongue an octave higher or remained flat. I read their emails over their shoulders, looking for emojis, a sentence in all caps followed by a dozen exclamation points. Did they take bathroom breaks around the same time or carry on a private conversation by text? Every little move or action they took, I deconstructed, turned it over in my head, analyzed it from every angle, reading into everything that they were indeed an item, fucking in the facilities-management closet on the first floor, planning a vacation to Hawaii, their marriage, kids, moving far, far away, until I couldn't take it anymore, until I was convinced they were maddeningly, deeply, irrevocably in love.

"You don't have anything to worry about," Kari said. We were sitting in the lobby to the office, prepping materials for the next interview that was about to start. "It was a one-night stand. That's all."

"I don't know what you're talking about."

"Don't play dumb. I know you like her."

"Atchley?"

Kari shot me a look like a mother catching her child eating raw cookie dough.

"They're not a thing. Seriously. You should talk to her."

I glanced through the door. Atchley and Pinkett were in the large conference room. They weren't working. They weren't setting up for the interview like I'd thought they were. They just sat in two metal folding chairs, talking. I tried to make out their conversation, but their tones were hushed, their lip movements unintelligible. They could've been talking about innocuous things, the state bird for example, or their favorite cartoon growing up, but I couldn't help but think they were planning on running away from here, starting a life someplace new, a future shared just between the two of them. They'd end up someplace tropical probably, drinking rum punches and digging their toes in the sand, making love in their studio apartment, the surf audible through an open window. They'd probably even laugh about me. "Remember that kid?" they'd ask each other. "Remember Billie? How he used to swoon over you?" Sad guy, they'd say. Hope everything turned out okay.

"No," I said. "I don't know what you're talking about."

Afterward, everything took on shape. I had a routine. I had a purpose. I was doing well, and people looked up to me. I was the number one in the office, week after week. I became Pinkett's assistant manager. I started conducting my own interviews. I made friends and won awards and became known throughout the region as an up-and-comer, a candidate to be a district manager one day. Hell, maybe even a regional one. For a while I thought it would continue on like this forever. All I had to do was avoid any triggers. Stay away from guns, loud noises, law enforcement officers, the pulpit. All I had to do was sell knives and stay drunk and everything would be okay.

The four of us hung out more. Most nights, we just went to Pinkett's apartment, drank beer, chain-smoked cigarettes, took bong rips, and snorted Adderall. Every day was the same routine: wake up at seven a.m., shower, shave, put on our suits, head to the office, conduct interviews, go on sales calls, coach new reps, book more appointments, then head back to Pinkett's for a thirty rack of whatever beer was cheapest and a night of substance abuse until our eyes drooped and our bodies couldn't take any more. It became a ritual in a way, one I looked forward to regardless of the toll it was taking. After several weeks, I started to feel exhausted, my limbs heavy, my organs labored. It became harder to breathe, to walk upstairs, to carry my demo bag full of knives. But it wasn't just physical; it was mental, too. My mood changed. When drunk, I was happy, carousing alongside Pinkett as we played *Guitar Hero*, but during the day, my anxiety levels peaked. I constantly thought the newer sales reps were talking about me behind my back, laughing at me, at how I mimicked Pinkett and how I secretly pined for just a few more seconds of conversation with Atchley, for her to look in my direction, for her to choose me instead of Pinkett.

To their credit, they kept their relationship hidden. They never had public displays of affection, making out at the office or even holding hands, but that didn't mean there weren't some clues they were seeing each other. Atchley wore more makeup for one, a dark purple lipstick, a smoky charcoal eye shadow. She never wore sweatpants to the office anymore, opting for tight jeans, a low-cut top. Our conversations became less frequent, she always having some important task to complete for Pinkett. Some nights Pinkett would make an excuse as to why we couldn't hang out at his apartment, saying he had to travel to Dallas that evening for business or that his mother was in town. Strangely, his business trips only lasted that evening; he'd be back in the office the very next morning, and his mother never visited the office. Those nights, Atchley, Kari, and I would never hang out, our friendship hinging on the glue of Pinkett bringing us together, sustainable as a foursome but disintegrating if he was missing. I never saw them together, but I always had a sinking feeling they were sneaking around so as not to arouse the rumor mill around the office.

After a while, Atchley started to question my aloofness.

"You mad at me or something?" she asked.

I jumped at her question. We were at lunch at the Wendy's down the street, my thoughts elsewhere as I worked on my fries and read a three-month-old *Sports Illustrated*. It was the college football preview issue, and the Oklahoma Sooners had been a top-three team in the country in the preseason polls, but they lost their first game of the year to a Division I-AA school on a last-second field goal, and their entire season had been ruined right from the get-go.

"I'm sorry?"

"You mad at me or something? Seems like you've been avoiding me."

"No," I said.

She had a tray with her, and on it rested her lunch: a grilled chicken salad and a chocolate shake.

"Okay," she said, sitting across from me. "What is it then? You don't like me? You think I'm boring?"

"I hang out with you almost every night."

"You hang out with Pinkett. You hardly even talk to me. Never look at me. Did I do something to piss you off?"

Yes, I thought. Yes. You chose him.

"No. Just been busy, that's all. Trying to get number-one rep in the region."

"Uh-huh."

"Seriously."

"Okay," she said, stuffing her face with a bite of salad. A bit of ranch dressing stuck to her bottom lip. I licked my own, thinking she might get the hint, but she didn't. "If that's how you want to play it, that's fine with me."

That night, Pinkett, Kari, Atchley, and I did as we always did: we drank beers and chain-smoked cigarettes. The girls watched Pinkett and I play old video games and talk shit the way young men do, emasculating one another as we shot turtles out of our go-karts captained by a digital Donkey Kong. The girls took their turns playing, but mostly they just watched, passing the bong back and forth and discussing a freak fall thunderstorm that had produced lightning so bad it had struck an elementary school down the street, setting it on fire.

"Sounded like a bomb went off," Kari said.

"Just think how fucked all those kids would've been if it had been during the day."

"Crazy."

Besides the four of us, a few other sales reps joined us. Pinkett only had a couple controllers for *Mario Kart*, so after a while the others got tired of watching and wanted to turn it to TV. We had, in one drunken hazy night, lost the remote, and so we changed the channel like it was the nineties again, pressing the button with a Dow rod we'd picked up at Lowe's for eighty-five cents, and as Pinkett surfed the channels, there it was, a picture of my mother.

"Whoa, whoa, whoa, hold up," Barry, a new sales rep, said. "Go back." And so Pinkett did; he pushed the channel up. "No, no, too far. Go back. Channel five."

"The news?"

My stomach dropped like we'd hit a pocket of turbulence.

"Yeah."

A collective groan washed over the group, and I begged silently, *please, oh please. Please don't turn it back.*

"Come on, man. The fucking news?" Pinkett said.

"Seriously. Turn it back!"

Barry grabbed the Dow rod from Pinkett and changed the channel. My mother's picture illuminated the screen as a woman's voice narrated a news story, calling our community a cult, describing the violence that had erupted, the hoarding of arms, Scoot's passing, the fire, the raid, the dozens dead.

"Yeah, man," Barry said. "This is it. I remember when this shit went down. It was crazy."

My mother looked terrible. The picture shown was a recent one, a still from an interview recently conducted regarding her incarceration, her unwavering faith, and her decision to cease the appeals process on her death sentence. In it she looked haggard, her hair having turned the color of a dirty ashtray, her flesh drooping like she was more sensitive to the effects of gravity than the rest of us. She was missing a tooth, one right incisor, and it made her look a little mad, like she might just try to bite you if you got too close. It was harrowing seeing her like this, so unlike the woman I had known, the woman who had raised me.

"This sick bitch right here," Barry continued, "turned a gun on all these brainwashed sons a bitches. Just boom, boom, boom." He made a gun with his hands and pointed it at Atchley, Pinkett, and Kari. "Fucking SWAT team busted down their doors, and the only ones left alive were this bitch and her son and the preacher. The preacher rolled, ended up testifying against the woman. Crazy, man. Just crazy."

"Jesus Christ," Pinkett said.

"That's who she said told her to do it," Barry said. "I ain't guilty—God made me do it."

"Let's just play video games," I said, trying to keep my voice from wavering.

"Hold on," Barry said. "I want to see when this bitch is set to die."

Turned out it was December 14th at ten p.m., just three months away. It was hard to hear the words being said, delivered in a somber, Midwestern timbre like a sports announcer delivering news a star player had been ejected from the game. With it came a certainty hard to deal with. There was no manual for how to react in such a situation. Anything could've been justified: denial, anger, depression. I could've upended the coffee table or broken the bong over Barry's head. I could've taken a razor to my arm and like that stupid owl and his Tootsie Pop counted how many cuts it would take to reach bone. I could've just gotten up and walked away and gone back to my own place, acted like nothing had even happened. Instead, though, I just clasped Atchley's hand and squeezed. I did it without thinking. I squeezed tightly. I squeezed until my hand hurt and, to my surprise, she squeezed back.

CHAPTER 4

HALLOWEEN THAT YEAR, I DRESSED UP AS DOC Brown from *Back to the Future*, the scene in particular when the 1950s Doc met Marty for the first time. In the movie Doc is wearing a helmet made of light bulbs attached to a geo-dimensional steel frame, and he uses this contraption to try to read Marty's mind. I recreated this using twinkle lights, a battery-powered pocket generator, a bicycle helmet, cardboard, and duct tape. I looked good, I thought, and was anxious to show Atchley my outfit, having heard she was a fan of 1980s-era comedies like *The Goonies, Say Anything, Bill & Ted's Excellent Adventure, Caddyshack, Ferris Bueller's Day Off,* and, of course, the *Back to the Future* trilogy. The first two, at least. The third, she claimed, nearly ruined the franchise.

It wasn't a date. A neighbor of mine, Clay, was having a Halloween party, and I'd been invited—the entire apartment building had, actually—and I used it as an excuse to hang out with Atchley alone. Pinkett was out of town, visiting his parents down in Dallas, but to keep it from looking like a date, I invited Barry along as well, masquerading my invitation as a group outing, hoping it would conceal my ulterior motives. Which were, I admit, a bit of a mystery even to me. I knew I was attracted to Atchley, but being locked up for the majority of my hormonal teenage years, I was unsure how to act around girls, how to ask them out on a date or attempt something even more forward like kissing them. The thought petrified me, and so I did the only thing I could think of: I asked Atchley out to a party thrown by a guy I hardly even knew.

Atchley dressed as a zombie. When I showed up to her place, an apartment downtown overlooking the bombing memorial, she was applying her makeup, pancake powder and copious amounts of dried, deep-red blood caked around her mouth, jawline, and neck. She wore colored contact lenses to make her eyes look milky white, without iris or pupil. It was off-putting, and when she opened the door I actually flinched, but she didn't make fun. She just invited me in and asked if I wanted something to drink.

"I have Fresca, I think. Or tap water. No beer or anything."

"I'm fine."

"It's no problem," she said. "The Fresca might be warm, but I think I have a clean glass somewhere."

"No, really. I'm okay."

"Okay," she said like she was unconvinced. "I'll just be a minute. I want to look as dead as possible."

Her place wasn't as I'd pictured at all. Although I had no idea what a twenty-year-old woman's apartment should look like, never having been in one, I had the idea of pink and zebra prints and picture collages and single-word knickknacks demanding we live and laugh and love. Instead, though, there wasn't much in the way of decorations. There was a wrought-iron TV stand and an old bulbous Magnavox. A glass coffee table. A worn checkered loveseat. Mismatched dining

260

chairs and a circular table that wobbled. Everything looked second-hand, and all of it was dirty, covered in dust and mustard-covered plates.

"I don't stay here much," Atchley said when she returned, and there was something in her voice that unnerved me. She wasn't just stating a fact; there was a deep sincerity in her voice as well, verging on the apologetic. "Actually," she said, "I don't like staying here at all."

And so, we didn't. We picked Barry up and headed back to my apartment complex, where we could hear the party had already started. House music blared, the bass vibrating my bone marrow. Fake smoke filled the apartment, and it was dark, the only light from crisscrossing lasers and a strobe. A scream soundtrack underlay the music, and fake blood caked the bathroom sink and walls and kitchen tile. Werewolves and goblins and sexy cats danced in the living room as Clay served punch from a large plastic trashcan. We got drinks and made our way to a couch where we sat by ourselves. I knew nobody there, and neither did my guests, and so we sat in silence and sipped the sugary punch and stared straight ahead to keep from having to talk to one another. I kept coming up with different conversation starters, an anecdote about a customer nearly cutting his thumb off during a service call, or this homeless guy across the street that kept throwing soup on passersby, but everything sounded so stupid in my head.

"I once ruptured my spleen," Atchley said.

"I'm sorry?"

"My spleen. I ruptured it."

I wasn't sure if I heard her right.

"I was young and playing on a swing set, and these kids next to me kept swinging up as high as they could and then jumping off. They were a lot bigger than me, but still, I wanted to be like them, and so I swung as hard and as fast as I could, and when I started to get scared because I was higher than I'd ever been before, I let go. At first, I remember being exhilarated. All the fear evaporated, and for a moment all I felt was the most extreme joy, but that didn't last long. I came down on the wooden rail surrounding the swings. The kids next to me got scared and ran off. I ended up passing out, and I wasn't found until about twenty minutes later, bleeding from the mouth."

I didn't know what to say to this, so I decided not to say anything. And she didn't say anything else, either, instead turning to face the dancers in front of us. I couldn't tell why she stopped talking, if she might've been embarrassed for revealing such a story to someone who didn't say a word in response, but she wore so much fake blood I couldn't tell if she blushed or not. I would've been surprised, though, if she had—she didn't seem to have the same filter the rest of us did, where we cared too deeply about what others thought of us.

"I got a scar," I said as I pulled up my shirt. On my ribcage was a jagged, peach-colored scar running from my waistline up to my armpit. "Got jumped in the shower once."

She ran her finger alongside it and smiled. It was hardly noticeable, just a sly upturn at the corner of her lip. "What'd you do?" she asked.

"What?"

"What'd you do to get jumped?"

"I was new."

She nodded as though this made perfect sense.

"When I was sixteen," she said, "I was driving out on Route 66, and it was late at night and I'd been drinking, and for some reason I kept going faster and faster and faster. To this day, I'm not sure why I did it, but I kept accelerating until I reached around ninety. It was just this impulse, an urge to do something dangerous. I felt compelled to do it. I lost control around a slight curve to the left, and the car spun out before slamming down on its side. I almost killed myself and my best friend."

"I haven't spoken to my brother or my father in years," I said. "I don't even know where they're at. Or if they're even alive still. The last time we spoke I was just so angry at them. I told them to leave and not to come back, and though they reached out a couple more times, eventually they stopped."

"Looks like we've both made mistakes," she said.

Later, as she was exiting the bathroom and I was entering, she pinned me against the wall and kissed me. It took me by surprise, and we butted teeth, but she didn't stop. She exerted even more pressure, and I returned the kiss.

When she pulled away, she asked, "Want to get out of here?" and all I could say in return was, "Sure."

"Good," she said. "Good."

"What about Barry?" I asked.

"Fuck Barry."

We left him there and went to my apartment. We hadn't even made it off the elevator before we were at each other, biting each other's lips, throwing off our clothes, and clawing at each other as we made our way to my bedroom. Atchley pushed some dirty laundry off my bed, and we climbed aboard. She was on top, and it was such a strange sight, her mouth and neck drenched in red, her eyes lifeless and blank, but the rest of her body alive and well, rocking rhythmically on top of me. She grabbed ahold of my chest, and I tried to last as long as I could, counting one, two, three, four, five, six until I couldn't hold back anymore. I came inside of her even though I didn't mean to.

When done, she lay pressed up next to me, her head on my chest as she ran her fingertips around my nipple. I felt at ease, more so than I had in years, since I'd been a child, in fact, when I'd been convinced everything I was doing was right and good and divined by God himself. I was so at peace I could feel myself dozing off to sleep—good, hard, rejuvenating sleep—drifting seamlessly between dream and reality, but then Atchley spoke, jerking me awake.

"You're Caleb Gunter," she said. "Aren't you?"

ATCHLEY DIDN'T TELL ANYONE MY secret. In exchange, I didn't tell anyone about us. What "us" entailed, I wasn't exactly sure. After work, I'd call her and wait outside her apartment building until she answered, sometimes forty or fifty minutes having passed, but finally she'd ring me up and I'd go inside and we'd have sex. When we were done, we'd watch old *Full House* episodes on TV Land, and then she'd kick me out before midnight. The next morning at work she'd act like nothing had happened, and she told me she wanted to keep it that way. "Don't shit where you eat," she called it, and I obliged—I certainly didn't want the sex to stop.

The thing I liked most about Atchley was that she didn't ask a lot of questions. Or any at all, really. She didn't ask about the congregation or my belief in being the Second Coming of Christ or what it was like to have your house raided, to have your mother kill a dozen innocent people, to have been complicit, if at least in some way, in the death of a child because his father refused medical treatment. After she'd asked me if I was Caleb Gunter, the same false child prophet seen on the news, I prepared for her to bombard with me such questions. I formulated long, thoughtful responses wherein I would tell her I wasn't brainwashed—it wasn't like that, because in order to be brainwashed, the person convincing you must realize they're telling you lies. In my case, it couldn't be any different—my mother truly believed I was Jesus Christ reborn, and so why wouldn't I believe her? She was, after all, my mother. She birthed me and raised me and fed me and taught me, and so why wouldn't I trust her? My very life depended on her. But I think Atchley understood I wasn't ready to talk about it yet, not bringing it up again after asking me if I was who she thought I was. The night she'd asked, I couldn't lie to her, and so I simply nodded yes, and she dropped it after that.

The rest of the world, however, did not. For the first time in years, my family dominated the news. Local news, alternative weeklies, radio pundits, and national TV personalities all had one thing running almost 24/7, the Gunter family and the Church of the Seven Seals. CNN replayed the footage of the night the FBI had raided the worship hall, the night sky illuminated by fluorescent tear gas and flares and the flash of an assault rifle's muzzle. I always jumped when I watched the service hall erupt into flames, like I was reliving the moment again. To this day, I'm not sure who started the fire, whether it was the FBI or if it was my mother. I don't think I'd be surprised either way—my mother would rather have died than give in to an authority she didn't recognize, and the FBI had already proven they'd use any force necessary to bring us to justice. Alive, dead—didn't make much difference to them. We'd killed one of their own.

Of course, along with the video of the raid and pictures of my mother and Sam, there were also pictures and videos of me, Caleb Gunter, with prognosticators speculating as to where I was living, by what name, and why. People called in from all over the country, claiming they'd spotted me at a Starbucks in Seattle or an REI Outfitters in Montreal, that I was living off the grid in North Dakota, plotting my revenge a là Unabomber. One even claimed I was a particularly well-known hedge-fund manager whiz kid out of Boston, beating the market by double-digit points, but, to my relief, nobody said I was still in Oklahoma, just three hours from where tragedy had befallen me and my family and my church, selling knives to middle-aged housewives and spending my nights drinking until I passed out, hoping I stayed awake long enough to sloppily grope a coworker. All of the pictures the media outlets showed, of course, were when I was several years younger, before puberty scarred my face with acne, before my cheeks thinned and my hair grew darker, my forehead more pronounced. The resemblance was there, of course, but it wasn't so stark as to be immediate.

"Maybe you should grow a beard," Atchley recommended.

"Yeah. Maybe," I said.

"Keep it trim. Nothing hipster-y, but something neat and short and groomed. I think you'd look cute."

"I don't know."

"Seriously. You'd kind of look like Charlie Day."

"From *Always Sunny*? That's not cute."

"Sure he is. In a gross sort of funny way."

"Gross, funny, cute?"

"Yeah, but in a good way."

But I didn't. I didn't change anything. I still got donuts at Krispy Kreme first thing in the morning, going in and ordering until I became a regular. I still showed up to work in my suit and tie, clean-shaven, hair a mess, still smelling of stale beer from the night before. I still went out to middle-class families' homes, people who watched the news and had the best chance of putting two and two together, but they never did. I suppose people never really look for that one-in-a-million right in front of them. People always think stuff like that will never happen to them. They'll go through life unscathed, never running across Dave Chappelle in a shopping mall parking lot or seeing a tornado take out a downtown skyscraper. Stuff just doesn't happen like that to normal people, so even if they perhaps noticed a bit of a resemblance between me and that kid on the news, they never said a word, convincing themselves I couldn't be him—that stuff just doesn't happen to them.

Eventually, though, someone else did recognize me.

We were at one of our weekly meetings at the office, and I was helping Pinkett prepare the night's events to unveil the new leaderboard as the other salespeople filtered into the room. It had been weeks since we'd been at Pinkett's and the news had broken of my mother's impending execution, and that night was the first we'd all been back together. I should've known something was different when Pinkett was a little standoffish as we prepared for the meeting, going outside to smoke cigarettes by himself on the fire escape rather than chugging Mountain Dew and perusing his notes like he normally did, but I didn't. I busied myself by helping Atchley organize the leaderboard materials and the prizes that would be given away that night. Once everyone had taken their seats, Pinkett returned and blared the music and began his routine, jumping up and down and pacing the room, trying to infect the rest with his energy and optimistic personality. He chanted and cheered and screamed utter nonsense until everyone was riled up, and then Pinkett stopped at the front of the room.

"First of all," he said, "I want to thank each and every single one of you for being here. Thank you and thank you and thank you." He skipped around the room like a schoolboy and pointed at all the new members of the sales team, which, of course, comprised the majority in attendance. "You have no idea how much it means to me you've decided to join something bigger than yourselves. To do what you're doing is truly special. You're not here for just a job, but you're a part of a family. You're with people who care about your success, and I will do everything in my power to make you realize all of your goals, all of them, be the very best you can be, and, of course," he said as he pulled out a wad of cash from his back pocket, "make you all a shit-ton of money."

The team hooted and hollered and clapped their hands.

"To do that, to see you guys happy, to achieve your goals, it makes me so monumentally, overjoyously, exasperatingly, un-fucking-believably fulfilled by your dedication and your devotion and your goddamnit-can't-quit fucking attitude that I can't help but just find me aroused."

The crowd started to really get into it now, clapping and whistling and chanting SlashCo, SlashCo, SlashCo, as Pinkett finally stopped at the front of the room.

"I got great news tonight, and I got even greater news tonight. The greatest goddamn news I could possibly ever give. We've got surprises and plot twists, lies and deceit. But it's all going to be revealed tonight.

All of it, and it makes me so fucking happy I can hardly even stand it. In fact, I don't even want to wait. In fact, I know I can't."

Pinkett paused a moment, peered at me, and it looked like he mouthed the words "fuck you" before he whistled and in popped a camera crew. At first, I was confused, and so was everyone else. Their clapping and whistling ebbed and became less resolute, their cheers ending with a higher-pitched inflection at the end, almost as if they were asking a question: SlashCo, SlashCo, SlashCoooOOOO? It started to make more sense, though, as soon as the camera crew's spotlights and microphones were directed at me. They circled me, the camera's light blinding so that I had to shield the glare with my hand. Slowly, my vision came into focus, and it was a young woman standing in front of me, blonde with mounds of makeup caked on her cheeks and eyes and lips.

"Tell us, Caleb Gunter, where have you been all these years? What have you been doing? Have you spoken with your mother? Do you have any regrets? Do you feel guilty, responsible, remorse for what you've done?"

Everything spun. Saliva flooded my mouth. I was nauseated. I couldn't catch my breath. I was having a panic attack, and despite the realization of what was happening, I couldn't stop it, which made it even more frightening. I was going to die, and no one would be able to help.

"Our assistant manager here, one Billie Booker—in our midst for months—has been keeping a secret from us," Pinkett continued. "Turns out, our beloved Billie's not who he says he is."

The camera crew was from a local news station, Channel 4, the NBC affiliate. The woman kept rattling off questions, not even waiting for me to respond. It felt aggressive. It felt like she was attacking me, and my fight-or-flight instinct kicked in. I had to hit her, hit Pinkett, beat the cameraman with his own equipment, or I had to flee. I had to do something. Standing there was not an option.

"Would you like to tell us who you are?" Pinkett asked.

I didn't say a word.

"No?" he asked. "Well, all right then. It turns out, our Billie here is the one and only, the dog and pony, Caleb Gunter!"

Time, after that, sped up. Something built up inside of me, something visceral, some central and intrinsic force. My heart rate quickened. My tongue swelled. Saliva dried up. There was a throb in the back of my neck, pulsating up my spinal cord and into my brain. Everything brightened. I could make out the smallest of imperfections on the cameraman's hands, a jagged hangnail, nicotine-stained fingers, and I started swinging. I swung at Pinkett. I swung at the camera, knocking it out of the man's hand. There was a producer behind him, telling him to pick the camera back up, to get it, get it, get it, and I ran. I burst through the door and ran down the hall and barreled down the stairs until I was out of the office building and heading nowhere at all.

CHAPTER 5

"YOU'RE GOING TO HAVE TO FACE IT SOONER OR later," Atchley said. We were in my apartment, had been for three days. Outside were dozens of news vans, camped out, trying to get me to give a statement of some kind, to apologize for my misdeeds, to condemn my mother, to show remorse or defiance or something, and I was sorry, I truly was. I'd agonized over what had happened for years, and every time I thought about what my mother and I'd done, a pain lurched in my chest and I dry-heaved until all I could do was choke, but I wasn't ready or able, much less both, to give the media what they wanted. Instead, I just stayed on the couch with Atchley and ate crackers and peanut butter and drank Fresca until all we had left was tap water. We binge-watched television and fucked like teenagers, all elbows and grunts and toothy kisses, and she told me the reason Pinkett had outed me.

"I've been fucking him, too," she said.

"I know."

"You did?"

"Sort of. I thought you might be."

"Why didn't you say anything?"

I hadn't because I'd hoped I was wrong. I knew they'd hooked up, had feared they were seeing each other for a while, but since Atchley and I had gotten together I'd hoped they hadn't been. I hoped it was all in my head, and that Kari had been right—it had been just a one-night stand. Turned out, Pinkett and Atchley had been an item, fuck-buddies or booty calls or whatever. It made sense. They'd known each other before I came along, spending eight, nine, ten, even eleven hours a day with each other, working and eating and getting drunk and stoned together. Eventually, something was bound to happen. They were both young and carefree and untethered by adult responsibility. But that didn't make it hurt any less. It made it hurt more, in fact.

"I'm done with him, though," she said. "I pick you. Only you." But it only made it a little bit better. I didn't feel betrayed, but the fact she continued to see us both for a time made me feel as though I was easily discarded, that if things had turned out just a little bit differently she'd have been on Pinkett's couch instead of mine, saying the exact same things, "I pick you, you, only you," but to him instead of me. It made what we had seem ephemeral and transient, like at any moment, if I even let her out of my sight for a second, she'd be gone and I would be all alone once again.

"I won't leave you. I promise. I'll be right here with you, but you have to face this."

I didn't have much of a choice either way. About a week after the news had leaked, Jonah showed up at my door. At first, I didn't recognize him—it had been close to five years since I'd seen him last. He and Dad had found me after the raid. They showed up to my trial and hired me an attorney, and they visited right after I'd been sentenced to juvenile detention, but I was just so angry with them at the time. I blamed them for what had happened. I blamed them for not stopping my mother, for not finding me after we'd taken off, and for not bringing me back home. None of it would've happened if my father had just fought for me a little bit harder, but he didn't, and a lot of people died because of that. For months I agonized over this while locked up in detention, staring up at the ceiling with nothing to do, and the last time they came and visited I told them to stop.

The visiting room was this large cinderblock place with fluorescent lights and long plastic tables, not unlike a school cafeteria.

"Why didn't you come looking for us?" I asked my father.

We'd skirted the issue during the trial. Too much to deal with in planning my defense, or at least that's what we'd told ourselves.

"I wish I had," he said. He chewed the inside of his cheek and rubbed his fingertips together. It was an old tic of his—he wanted a cigarette, but he couldn't smoke in there.

"That's not an answer. Why didn't you?"

"What can I say? I mean, whatever I say will come out wrong."

"Just tell me why. You have to tell me."

"You were just too much. Your mother had warped you. You weren't yourself anymore. And I couldn't deal with it. I thought everybody would be happier if you were with her and Jonah was with me."

"You thought it was too hard?"

"Yes."

"You thought I'd be too hard?"

"I'm sorry. But yes."

That was the last time I saw either one of them. I'd thought about them a lot since I'd been outed. I'd wondered if Jonah had changed, if he was still a skeptic, still tough and ornery and rebellious, and I'd wondered if Dad still chain-smoked and worked fourteen hours a day, and I'd wondered why, after they must have learned where I was at, after the news broke I was living in Oklahoma City, they didn't try to do anything to help. I was still their blood, after all. I was still their kin, despite what Mom and I had done. Were we not still family? Perhaps we'd just severed ties. Perhaps out of shame. Perhaps out of self-preservation. I wasn't sure. But I didn't blame them. I probably would've done the same if our roles had somehow been reversed.

But then Jonah showed up at my door. He wasn't the same as he'd been back then. For one, he was a full-grown man now, a wispy goatee covering his chin and upper lip, his cheeks covered in graphite-colored stubble. He wore a ballcap, and unkempt hair poked out from underneath. A gut protruded over his belt, but his arms had turned skinny, pale, and hairless. He looked sickly, like he desperately needed—but couldn't afford—dialysis.

"Caleb?" he said.

I didn't say anything.

"Caleb Gunter?"

"Jonah."

He smiled and came in. He sat next to Atchley, and he couldn't stop fidgeting. He bounced his knee and scratched his neck and pulled at his facial hair like he'd drunk a lot of coffee. He talked nonstop, his words slurring like his tongue couldn't keep up with his thoughts.

"It's just so great to see you, man. Just so, so, so great. You just have no idea. Like no idea what it's been like out here."

With every word he spoke, his hands and arms and head gesticulated. His energy surprised and scared me. He'd always been somewhat of a stoic kid. Rebellious, sure, but he was also quiet, reserved, and seemed to hold over his friends this mysterious power. He didn't have to say a word, and it was like they all thought he, and no one else, was their best friend. Now, though, it was like he vibrated, and the result was repulsive.

"You wouldn't believe what people are like. They ask you questions about Mom, questions that, like, you have no answers for. Why did she do what she did? Why did people believe her? What was it like living with her? Did she make me do stuff? Like weird cult stuff? Sexual stuff? Evil stuff? Like, it just never stops, man. You just can't ever hide from it. You know what I mean?"

I was beginning to learn. Yes, I knew what he meant.

"They won't let you forget, man. They just won't. Not ever, or ever, forever. They just won't let you ever forget. And you tell them, man, I don't know. I don't know. She was crazy. What do you want me to say? She said and did some crazy, weird shit, and for most of it I was along for the ride, but in the end, Pops and I got out, and I just don't know. I don't. I just don't know."

"You ever see Mom?" I asked.

"Like now?"

"Yeah. Do you ever go visit her?"

"God, man, no. Hells no. In the beginning, sure, a few times, yeah. I'd go there. I would say hi, but she wouldn't talk, man. She wouldn't. Just sat there and stared like beyond you. Know what I'm saying? Like she was looking right at you, but not seeing you. You get me?"

"And so you never went back?"

"Been five years. Five years. Wow. It's been five years."

"And Dad?"

"Dad. Wow. Yeah. You didn't hear?"

"Hear what?"

"Gone. Poof. Kablooey." Jonah held his fists by his ears and then opened them like they were exploding. "Everything just gone. Lights out. Doesn't remember a thing. Just sits there and drools and a nurse wipes his ass."

"What do you mean?"

"Had a stroke. It's like his brain imploded. Turned to mashed potatoes or whatever. Lights are on, but nobody's home. Feel me?"

"But he's still alive?"

He snorted. "If you call that living, man."

"And where is he?"

"Man, back home. Bartlesville. Where you think? I can't afford to move him out anywhere. At the old-folks' home there. Just wasting away."

"And you," I said. "What about you?"

He purged his story like a man in confessional. After the raid, he had to go into hiding. He dropped out of school, and he didn't leave the house. Vandals came. They threw bricks through his windows and shot roman candles at the house. Toilet paper adorned the trees and egg yolk the gutters. Every day it was something new. He took to drinking more. Ten beers a night. Twelve. Fifteen. A case by himself. Until he could shut his mind down long enough to sleep. He started gaming online, made up pseudonyms and pretended to be a teenage girl in chat rooms. He'd catfish people. He'd lead on lonely, middle-aged men, and then forward his conversations with these pedophiles to the FBI. After a few weeks, the vandalism subsided, and after a few more months, he summoned enough courage to leave the house. He tried to go back to school. He enrolled in classes at Oklahoma State and moved to Stillwater and had thoughts about majoring in journalism or perhaps history, something where he could chronicle life, make sense out of an otherwise senseless world, but soon he dropped out. He continued to drink, and he smoked pot, and then he was offered harder and harder stuff. Cocaine at first. Pills: Xanax and Zoloft and Oxy.

"Just enough to make my skin go numb," he said.

But that's when things got out of control. As soon as he woke up, he needed something to dull the edge, a drink, a snort, a smoke, and he went out looking for enough money for his next score. He stole copper wire from construction sites and collected cans from dumpsters to recycle and sold his bodily fluids, semen and plasma and whatever else he could just to make it by. He lost bigger and bigger blocks of time. He'd wake up naked and outside, mere yards from his house, but it seemed as though he didn't have the strength to make it up to his doorstep. He tried PCP and heroin and, finally, the love of his life, meth.

"It's like being God, man. Like being reborn, if you know what I'm saying."

I did. I knew exactly what he was saying.

Started off once a week, then every couple, then every day, until all his time and money and effort were spent procuring, smoking, and eventually cooking methamphetamine. It was lucrative, he said. More money than he could ever spend in a million lifetimes. Just fists full of cash. He hid it in his mattress, and when he couldn't fit any more in there, he hid it in the crawl space underneath his house, and when that was filled up, he filled an entire room full of pallets of cash. Hundreds of thousands of dollars. All his. But he couldn't spend it. He knew if he did, he'd be caught. What college student could afford a new Corvette or a 3,000-square foot home or a sailboat? Not anyone he knew, so he started asking around. He met local businessmen, Pizza Hut franchise owners and car wash proprietors and operators of tanning salons. He finally found what he was looking for in an owner of convenience stores and head shops. Carl Huntington. Jonah dropped out of school, became Carl's little protégé, cash went into Carl's businesses, and out came laundered money.

"Lemony fucking fresh."

The problem was that Jonah kept using his own product, and Carl had an eighteen-year-old daughter that looked twenty-five. She wore miniskirts and dark eye makeup and "could suck the chrome off a trailer hitch," Jonah said. She wound up pregnant, got it aborted, and Carl wound up with a gun in his hand, waving it in Jonah's face. He took a gunshot to the shoulder, but he was able to get out of there before he got hit anywhere else.

"Praise the fucking Lord."

But he lost it all. The money was gone and the connections gone and he was told if he ever sold another crystal in his life he'd be dead, and so he got out of the game. Ever since then he'd been working odd jobs: house painting and paper routes and hardware stores. Anything he could find, really, but he wasn't ever able to keep a job for too long. Never could break his habit. Never could stop using. Went to meetings and rehab and got himself a sponsor, but nothing worked. He wound up blowing all his money and living anywhere he could, crashing on old friends' couches or at the Y when beds were open or at the shelter. And that was about it for him. Nothing much else to tell.

"But I want you to know I forgive you," he said. "I do. It took me a long time, but you should know. You're forgiven."

I had to admit I was thankful for that. It was the first time anyone had ever said that to me. I was forgiven. Someone had forgiven me.

JONAH ENDED UP STAYING ON my couch. He wouldn't leave, actually. I'd expected him to. Eventually, anyway, I thought he would say farewell, walk out the door, make his way through the sea of reporters, and return to Bartlesville and our father, but he didn't. That first night, he slept on the couch, and the next day we all watched television together, hunched in shoulder to shoulder on my small sofa, sipping on ramen broth and binging on Hostess cakes. Another night passed and then another, and I found myself starting to worry about him, the fact he hadn't any clothes to change into, the fact he didn't have a toothbrush or clean underwear or money of his own, and so I went shopping. For the first time since I'd been outed, I left the house, with Atchley by my side, and I bought him shaving cream and Hanes T-shirts and a couple button-downs just in case we could line him up a job interview. It felt good to be doing this, to be thinking of someone else, to be needed. To have a purpose once again. It saved me, I think, in a way.

Jonah, of course, was thankful for all Atchley and I did for him. He showed his appreciation by cleaning the house. He vacuumed and washed dishes and even sprayed the windows. He even tried to shoo away the paparazzi. He'd take Atchley's dry cleaning and walk the three blocks to and from American Cleaners. He made sure our mail was laid out and organized our spice rack and changed lightbulbs, and the entire time we never discussed the fact he'd moved in with me. I didn't think we needed to. Everything seemed to be working out well, but Atchley, on the other hand, didn't think so.

"He's becoming dependent," she said. "He's running away from his problems. And so are you. It's like you two are building this parasitic bubble of denial."

"He just needs a little help. Everyone needs help every once in a while."

"He needs more help than you can give him. He's still using. He needs rehab. Something."

"He just needs some time, okay? Give him a break."

"And you?" she said. "What do you get out of this?"

We were out of the house on a rare date night, hitting up fall's last street festival at H & 8th before winter came with its winds and biting cold. We perused vendor tents hocking impromptu short poems and leather-bound, homemade journals, and ate tacos from a food truck. The cameras had started to lighten up a bit as Mom's story died down—only a few tabloids called the apartment anymore, wanting quotes about the rumors of a new cult I'd started, how I'd brainwashed the townspeople to turn into cannibal child killers—and so we were alone for the first time in weeks. I knew it was temporary, though. Mom's execution was set to happen in about a month, and I was sure the cameras would return along with the bright lights and nosy reporters, and so I tried to take advantage. I was worried Atchley would soon grow weary of the circus, deem me not worth the trouble, and leave the first chance she got.

"He's my brother. And he's suffered. Because of me, he's suffered. I owe him."

"So, you're alleviating some guilt? Is that it? You were a victim, too, Caleb."

I didn't say anything.

"You understand that, right? You're a victim, too."

Everyone was quick to point this out. While in juvenile detention, the counselors had repeatedly broached the subject of my victimhood, how I'd been manipulated and coerced by my mother's eccentric faith. That's what they called it—eccentric, as if it were some nervous tic or outlandish notion, and I tried to explain to them millions of people believe in God, in the word of the Bible, in Revelation: that one day the dead will rise and the streets will flow with blood and that Jesus will return to the earth and lead the chosen into the kingdom of heaven. This wasn't the eccentricity of one madwoman—the majority of the nation believes in these things. It just so happened my mother, and I, too, believed it was coming soon, and that we were to play a central role in the end of times. Perhaps we'd been wrong about that, but we weren't victims, and we weren't eccentric; it was just a matter of faith. My mother did some terrible things, and I should've done more to stop her once things were getting out of control, but I wasn't a victim. I was complicit. I was complicit in something I'd never be able to forgive myself for.

"And you still believe in God?" the counselors would ask me.

"Yes," I'd said every time. "Don't you?"

I tried to tell Atchley this, but she grabbed me by the wrists and tried to get me to face her. I obliged, and the other attendees streamed by us, a little annoyed we were blocking traffic, casting sideways glances as they took bites from their oversized corndogs.

"You were a child, Caleb. A child. Don't you see you can't be responsible for what your mother did? You didn't murder all those people. You couldn't be culpable. It's impossible. You have to stop blaming yourself."

"Let's just get a funnel cake and order a poem about a unicorn wearing a diaper," I said.

"I'm being serious here," she said.

"I am, too. My blood sugar dropped, and I think I could frame the poem and put it in front of the shitter. Give me some perspective while bored on the toilet."

Atchley screamed. It wasn't a high-pitched, shrilly scream either, but something full of anger and frustration and gut-wrenching exasperation. That was when she punched me. Hard. Balled up fist, arm flexed, thrown as hard as she could. It landed on my pec just above my heart, and I could feel it skip a beat. From the pain, from the surprise, but she didn't stop. She just kept throwing them. She swung and closed her eyes and then opened them again and kept on swinging, and I didn't have anywhere to flee. I just covered my face. I hunched over and tried to deflect the blows, but they kept on coming, and nobody was coming to help.

"Hey!" I said. "Hey! Stop! You're hurting me."

"You fucking, fuck, fuckety, fucking fucker."

"Jesus Christ, Atchley. You're hurting me here."

"I am so sick and fucking tired of you feeling sorry for yourself."

"I'm not feeling sorry for myself."

The blows were even harder now. They landed on my shoulders, my neck, the back of my head. I could hear people laughing now. I could feel their pointing, their leering, their wondering, "Is that—Is that Caleb Gunter?"

"Stop, Atchley. Please. You're making a scene."

"Good!" she said. "That's what I'm trying to do! Hey! Hey, everyone! Here's Caleb Gunter! The child prophet! The messiah! Get your cameras. Get your laughs. He's right here!"

The crowd continued on past. They gawked, but only fleetingly, their sneers temporary as they made their way to watch a blind man strum his guitar or to see a flash mob dance with hula hoops, but soon, as Atchley continued to swing, as she continued to berate me, a small crowd formed, egged Atchley on, screamed for her to swing harder, faster, to go for the kill shot.

"Here he is!" Atchley screamed. "The one and only, self-proclaimed Second Coming of Christ! In the flesh, folks, for your viewing fucking pleasure."

The crowd laughed and pointed and jeered. "Oh my God," they said. "It is him. Holy shit. Get your camera. Take a picture."

"Atchley, please. What are you doing?"

"Come and take a look! The messiah! Hide your children! Hide your wives! He's damning us all to hell!"

"Atchley, this isn't funny! What are you doing?"

"I'm trying to help!" she screamed.

She punched again and again, this time landing right on my chin. I bit my lip, and I could taste blood. It filled my mouth quickly, and some dribbled down my chin and onto my shirt. It tasted of copper. It tasted good.

"Fine!" I yelled. I threw my hands up and grabbed her wrists as she continued to swing, but I was stronger than her and could keep her from throwing any more punches. "I am Caleb Gunter. I am. I thought I was the Second Coming of Jesus Christ. I tried to help people. I failed. A lot of people got hurt. People died. And I'm sorry. I'm sorry that happened. I am. But there isn't anything I can do about it now. Happy?"

"Yes," she said. "I am."

CHAPTER 6

THE PRISON WAS WEST OF THE CITY IN A SMALL
Oklahoma town. It only had a population of about 1,500 people, and
most of them worked for the Department of Corrections. The prison itself towered over the town, a six-story cement-gray monstrosity.
Guard towers lined the perimeter, the fence protected with barbed
wire, dogs, and armed personnel. It was a desolate place and lonely,
bland and menacing all at once. To get into the prison, Atchley, Jonah, and I had to drive through this chain-link tunnel, several fences
closing behind us as we made our way to the main compound. It was
a depressing place, and almost instantaneously it was like I was transported back to my thirteen-year-old self, first checking in to juvenile
detention. There was the same fear, the same apprehension, the same
obstinate yearning, begging to go back, to please, let me go back in
time—I promise, I would do things differently.

"You sure you're up to this?" Atchley asked as we found a parking
spot. "We can come back," she said. "There's still time. If you want to
come back later."

The entrance was a singular, black steel door. There were no windows to speak of; only a few spotted the entire prison block, barred

and tinted so we couldn't see through them. The parking lot was gravel, and the rocks jabbed me through the soles of my shoes.

"No," I said. "I'm here. I have to do this."

"I can't," Jonah said. "I'm sorry, Caleb. I thought I could, but I just can't."

"You sure?"

"I'm sorry."

"No," I said. "Don't be. I understand."

Atchley and I left him in the car. Inside was a little entrance, wide enough for only one person, so Atchley had to stand on the threshold, door open. There was a window right when we walked in, and behind it sat a tired-looking lady, chewing gum and pointing to a sign-in sheet. At the top of the paper, it said, "Two forms of ID required. Pockets emptied. No metal beyond this point."

Underneath the window, the woman pushed a bin toward us. "Put your stuff in here," she said. "No belts, no shoes, no liquids. Act like you're at an airport."

We stripped. We took off our shoes, our watches, our belts, our bracelets and rings. We emptied our pockets. Handed over our phones and loose change and notes to pick up milk and eggs and bread at the store on our way home. I knew it was just protocol, that these precautions were in place for everyone's protection—ours, the inmates', and the security guards'—but it was disheartening in a way. I almost felt accused of something. Like I was in fact checking in for my own prison sentence rather than visiting my mother, sitting on death row.

I'd never been to a state prison before, let alone death row, so I was intrigued. I wanted to see the actual block where the inmates were kept. I pictured this long, concrete hallway, fortified by reinforced stone walls. It would be gray and bleak and dark. It would smell damp and be cold and lonely. The cells would be lined with steel bars and house a single twin bed, a toilet without a seat, and a sink that dispelled water in one temperature: tepid. The prisoners would spend their days making up games, variations of I Spy and the Name Game, and they would taunt each other, knowing full well they would never, ever get within arm's reach of one another. I knew this to be some gothic fantasy, however, ill-conceived notions wrought from reading too much Edgar Allen Poe and Oral Roberts. More than likely, the block would be bright, illuminated by a humming fluorescence. The cells would be painted white cinderblock, the doors floor-to-ceiling, painted-white steel. The bed would be new, newish anyway, and covered with thin white sheets. The pillow small. The sink chrome. The walls would be soundproof to keep the inmates from carrying on conversations about their appeals or about the letter their sisters did or did not write. It would be a lonely place and cold, but different from how I pictured it.

I didn't get to see the block, though. A young guard, plump and tall like a former athlete, ushered Atchley and I down a hallway and buzzed us through several doors. After the second or third, he turned to us and pulled up his belt.

"Only one of you from here on out," he said. "The other will have to stay here." He pointed toward a waiting room of sorts. It had a TV and magazines and a decades-old coffee table purchased sometime in the last century.

Atchley clutched my hand before I could go further. "You're very brave for doing this. You know that, don't you?"

I nodded, unconvinced.

"You are," she said. "And don't forget it."

The guard buzzed me through one last door, into another wing. There were various rooms on either side of the hallway, all of them small, furnished with two chairs and a single table. On the table and on the floor directly below it were metal hooks, bolted down. There were no windows. There were no vents. Only a camera mounted to the wall, a red light illuminated on the very top.

"We have these rooms for when lawyers visit. Family. Interviews. What have you." He pointed to the last room on the left and bid me sit. "When the inmate comes in," he said, "you are not to stand. You are not to touch the inmate. You are not to hand to or accept anything from the inmate. Do not lean forward. Do not tap the table. Keep your hands visible at all times. English must be spoken at all times. Do you understand me?"

I nodded.

"I need verbal confirmation."

"Yes. I understand."

"Arms out. Feet shoulder width."

The guard patted me down. Once satisfied I was clean, he told me to sit in the chair farthest from the door, and he took position on the far wall to my left, hands behind his back, jaw perched up as if standing at attention. While waiting, I tried to calm down, to regulate my breathing. To control my body temperature. To stop from sweating. Mind over matter. But I couldn't. It was like I couldn't catch my breath. I couldn't breathe. I tried short, sporadic bursts. In. Out. In. Out. In. Out. But I couldn't. It was like my throat had closed, and I started to panic.

"Relax," the guard said. "Just relax. Everything will be okay."

And, for some reason I still can't articulate, it worked. I relaxed. I caught my breath and the world returned to its normal color. That was when Mom came in, chaperoned by two armed guards. Her wrists and ankles were shackled, and she shuffled in a way that reminded me of a clumsy adult in a three-legged race. She looked much thinner than I remembered, her cheeks sunken and hollowed out, cheekbones like cue balls. Her expression was one of constant, repressed fear—mouth straight, neck muscles strained, eyes wide and red from lack of blinking. Later I would read about the effects of solitary confinement on the human psyche, how it caused in the victims a sort of chronic paranoid schizophrenia, hallucinations, violent and unpredictable impulses. At the time, though, I just thought she'd lost her mind. I suppose, in a way, I was right.

When she sat down, one of the guards locked her shackles to the table hook and to the floor. Mom didn't fight it. She just looked about the room. Corner to wall to door to wall. Everywhere but me.

"Hi, Mom," I said, trying to get her to make eye contact. "It's me. It's Caleb."

She peered at me like an Alzheimer's victim trying desperately to recognize a person whom she knew she should, but couldn't, place. Then it was like something clicked. Her gaze narrowed, her expression tightened. She was angry at me, like she was ready to come across the table if she wasn't bolted to it.

"Listen," she said. "I've already told you. A thousand times I've told you."

"What'd you tell me, Mom?" I asked, confused and a little scared— it was like I was a child again, being reprimanded for not knowing verse and chapter of a bible quote.

She groaned, exasperated. "Why do you have to be so stupid? Seriously. I want to know. Why are you just so damn dumb? Does it take practice or were you born this way?"

"Mom?"

"First you align the pages. It's got to be perfect. Perfect! Straight and even like it's a block of wood. Then you lock it into place. Got it?"

"Mom? What are you talking about?" I looked to the guards for clues, but they offered none. They just stared at my mother, ready to intervene should she make some unwanted, sudden move.

"Like this," she said, and she tried to raise her hands. They were open, her fingers arched like she was holding a basketball, but they were empty. Before she could get them to shoulder level, however, the chain reached its end length, and her hands snapped back into place on the table. The guards didn't move.

"I'm sorry, Mom. I don't know what you're talking about."

"Once you get it locked, that's when you scrape the edges. That's when you make your cuts. Every quarter inch. Got me?"

I didn't say anything. I knew she wasn't speaking to me. She was speaking to someone else, someone only she could see.

"Then you glue. Just a thin layer. Don't goop it in, and you got maybe thirty seconds tops to bind the twine. Thirty seconds. That's all. You understand?"

It was then that it hit me—she was describing how to bind a book. We'd learned together when I was about ten or eleven years old. I'd written a book, or at least tried to, an eighty- or ninety-page monstrosity about werewolves and gold and a young boy who would save the world and all the things a prepubescent boy can think of. After reading it, my mother decided it needed to be published, sent off to family members along with our Christmas cards, and I, desperate for attention and praise and to be told what I did mattered, wholeheart-edly agreed, and so we taught ourselves how to bind books. It wasn't as easy as we thought it would be. The equipment we found was all way too expensive, and so we had to build our own press from scratch. We bought lumber from Ace Hardware and borrowed my father's electric drill and saw. We put on goggles and measured and measured and then cut, our hands shaking from the vibration of the table saw. We cut four boards big enough to make a breadbox, sanded them down, and then drilled them together. The top was open, and we mounted an adjustable clamp. But it wasn't easy. We cut the boards too short and had to start over. We drilled our holes too deep, splitting the wood. The slide on the clamp was uneven, and we couldn't get it to remain parallel. Finally, after several days of work, we had a usable press, but it came at a cost: cut fingers and a box of Band-Aids and two tubes of A&D Ointment, Tylenol and callouses and nails pulled back away from our skin. We were bruised and hurt and sore, but we did it. Even-tually, we were able to start on what we aimed to do, bind a book I had written. This was what Mom was reliving, the sight of me somehow rekindling this moment as if I were a kid again, and she was hot and tired and aggravated.

"That's too much! Too much! What did I say? Just a little bit of glue! Jesus Christ. Now we have to start over."

"Mom, listen to me. We're not binding books. Do you know where you're at?"

"Just let me do it. Here. Give it to me."

Mom tried to stand. She leaned forward and reached her hands up, but the guards behind her grabbed her by her shoulder and shoved her hard back down into her seat. It scared me a bit, and I jumped.

Mom blinked up at them and then returned to me.

"Fine. You do it. But do it right."

It was hard seeing her like this. She didn't even look like the same person anymore. She was a crazy, psychotic shell of her former self, her mind eaten away by solitude and lack of empathy. I wanted nothing more than to reach out and hold her, tell her everything would be all right; I was there. I would be back every day if I could, until the end; I would be there, and I would never, ever give up on her.

"You always mess everything up," she said. "You always have to ruin everything."

Instead, though, I didn't say a word.

I VISITED HER EVERY WEEK after that. There were some good days, though most were bad. She oftentimes didn't recognize me. Sometimes she mistook me for Jonah or sometimes my father. She'd reach for my hand during those times, or ask to kiss me, and she'd rise up and the guards would push her back down, tell her, "No touching, inmate. No touching." This, I think, was the hardest. She seemed so hurt when she was rebuked, unable to hold or be held by the man she loved and missed and whom she'd hurt. When I didn't go to her, she often cried. Her sobs violent, her chest heaving, her back arching, and she'd wail and plead, please, please, please God just let him stay, let him stay, let him stay, but I couldn't. The guards would usher me out of the room, and she'd be dragged down the hallway in chains to be locked away in solitary confinement and medicated until all she did was drool on herself.

Other times she'd relive watching my brother wrestle at regionals in middle school, and she'd cheer him on and ask me if I saw that single leg or half nelson and she'd beam like a proud mother and chant his name as if watching him take home the championship. When she was happy like this, I couldn't help but partake in her delusion, cheering alongside her, wishing Jonah the best as he squared off against some imaginary wrestler in Mom's memory. We'd clap and whistle and the guards would roll their eyes, but I didn't care. If she could be happy, if only for a moment, then so be it.

Notably absent were flashbacks to when we'd been part of the church, what had happened that caused her to be incarcerated and facing her imminent execution. She didn't relive sermons or preach about the Seven Seals or the coming apocalypse or speak in tongues. She didn't relive moments telling my younger self I'd one day usher in the end of the world and save mankind. When I tried to broach the subject, if she remembered the worship hall, Sam, Scoot, the raid, any of it, turning the gun on so many people, she'd shake her head like she was trying to jar loose a memory, and then she'd change the subject, ask me about work or Atchley or if that cute weatherman was still on the news, the one with the hair and the eyes and the broad, broad shoulders. I supposed even when suffering from mental illness, her mind subconsciously repressed these memories, them being too painful to face. When I tried to talk about her case, she changed the subject, even going so far as defending her sentence and impending death, justifying her decision to end the appeals process.

"My attorneys are incompetent," Mom said. "All they would have done was stall the inevitable. Cost the taxpayers more money. Stealing from the survivors any notion of closure. Making everyone rehash what happened, analyze it, cast blame and guilt and all that nonsense.

It's just better this way."

"But there's still a chance, isn't there? I mean, there is religious freedom in this country. There was no notion of mens rea. No premeditation. You believed you were doing good. They all thought they were going to die. They knew what was going to happen. That has to mean something, right? It can't be a capital offense for second-degree murder, can it?"

"It's a black eye on the community. People need someone to blame. And I'm to blame. Sixteen people died. And they want retribution. An eye for an eye. Can't blame them for that."

"But the rule of law. That's not how the law is written."

"Doesn't matter. The judge writes the law. The court of public opinion. And they've ruled."

"But there's still the Federal Court of Appeals. The State Supreme Court. Hell, even the US Supreme Court. You still have options."

"That's enough, Caleb."

"Do you want to die? Is that it? Do you think there's some sort of bravery in that? Some sort of atonement?"

"It just is what it is."

"It is what it is?"

"It is what it is."

"That's the dumbest thing I've ever heard, Mom."

"Maybe so, but it's my choice."

"And it's a selfish one."

"Selfish?"

"Yes. Selfish. Haven't you thought what your death will mean to people? Haven't you thought of the consequences?"

"You mean for you?"

"Yes, for me."

"Yes." she said. "Yes, of course. How could I not?"

Mom made a clicking noise like she was trying to alleviate an itch in the back of her throat. While in prison, she accumulated habits she hadn't had before. She sniffed constantly, like she suffered from terrible allergies or maybe had a coke problem. When she spoke, she upturned her lip as if snarling. She curled her wrists, perhaps the result of constantly being handcuffed, when chaperoned to breakfast, back to her cell, to the infirmary for her annual health checks. She was as hardened and resolute and stubborn as she'd always been, but now instead of the underlying assumption that she was right, now she just seemed a delusional old fool, too set in her ways to admit she may have done some things wrong along the way.

"It doesn't seem right," I said. "To just give up like this. What happened to fight-or-flight? Why don't you want to save your life?"

"What kind of life would I be saving?" she asked. "You think they would ever let me out of here?"

No, they wouldn't. She'd be a lifer. Sooner or later, she'd die in prison. They'd more than likely keep her away from the general population, forcing her to spend most of her days in solitary confinement. They'd justify it as a means of protection, claiming the other inmates would shank her if they got a chance—too many people were affected by her crimes. An aunt or maybe a sister of one of the victims would find her in the shower, stick a toothbrush laced with a razor up underneath her ribcage, pack her mouth with a sock to keep her quiet as she bled out. Maybe they'd be right, but I wouldn't be surprised if they didn't get some twisted satisfaction out of it, watching her mind slowly deteriorate from the lack of any human connection, from any comforting touch or a nice word from a friend.

"It's okay," she said. "It is. I've made my peace with it. I'm ready to die."

"But I'm not ready, Mom. I'm not. You understand? I still need you."

"Oh, honey," she said. "Oh baby, oh sweetie, oh child. You don't."

Her last meal consisted of a sirloin steak cooked well, roasted potatoes, a cup of coffee, and a slice of key lime pie. The warden allowed me to eat with her, and it was the only time I saw her without her shackles. She seemed in good spirits despite the circumstances, chewing her food with gusto, savoring the flavors before swallowing. She talked quickly, food stuffed into her cheeks as we discussed various things, small talk about the weather and an unseasonal tornado that had touched down and killed eight people a few weeks before.

"A tornado," she said. "In November. Have you ever heard of such a thing?"

"It's strange," I said. "The news said it was the first time it had happened in over a hundred years."

"It's a sign," Mom said. "God's angry. He's angry, and he's punishing the people of this state."

It was difficult for me to consider that this would be the last time I'd ever speak with my mother. The thought was more abstract to me, like rocket propulsion or Descartes' demons. I knew the end was imminent, but there wasn't something to really mark the somberness of the situation. It was as if I expected the weather to turn severe, a thunderstorm to approach or perhaps an ice storm, for me to hear the crack of thunder or hail pounding the roof, but there wasn't. It was just me and Mom in a quiet, fluorescent-lit room, a guard on either side of her like always, like it had been for the weeks I'd been coming to see her. It was almost an affront in a way, the only marker for the act of my mother's death a piece of overcooked steak and coffee so weak I could see the bottom of the cup.

"You really think it's a sign, Mom?"

"You don't?"

"It just seems like a freak occurrence. That's all. A once-in-a-generation-type storm."

She peered at me with incredulity. "You really believe in coincidence? I thought I raised you better than that."

"Doesn't it seem more likely?"

She took a bite of steak and chewed the tough meat. It was difficult to swallow, and she washed it down with her now-cold coffee. "Let me tell you something," she said. "I've had a lot of time in here. A lot of time. And I've read, and I've thought, and I've come to some conclusions. I've read some of them science books that a lot of people claim disprove God. You ever hear about this quantum theory they got? Well, basically, we're all made up of these tiny, miniscule little atoms. Electrons and quarks and bosons and whatnot. I'm sure you've heard of this. And these things, they act in very strange ways. They appear to be in two different places at once. They seem to travel through every conceivable path. They disappear and reappear without warning, and they measure this phenomenon by what's called a probability wave. They can only know with certainty a single attribute of a quantum element. They can know its direction, say, but not its velocity. They can know its location but not its spin. You understand? They act in very bizarre ways; however, if you pinpoint one. If you look at just one little electron or one little boson, the probability wave collapses, and the electron is located in the most probable location in space-time, which just happens to be where we're observing. So, logically speaking, since we're all made of these quantum elements, we're all just in the most probable location. I'm in jail because it is the most probable location for me. You're here visiting me because it is the most probable location for you. That tornado hit and killed all them people because it was the most probable location for it. And if everything is in its most probable state, doesn't that probability insinuate premeditation? Does it not imply some sort of plan? Could that not be God? Could that not be his divine plan in action?"

I had to admit, it could be. On some level, she made sense, and it very well could have been God's plan. But I couldn't bring myself to say that out loud. I couldn't bring myself to consider she could be right, that she would ever be right again.

"I'm telling you, son. You might look out in the world and just see all this craziness. It may appear to be coincidence or accident or dumb luck or chance, but none of that really exists. It's an illusion. It's a smokescreen, sweetie, put there in place to make you think you actually have control of your life. Free will? The greatest lie the devil ever told mankind. You only have one choice in this world. Do you love God or don't you? The rest is just details."

Mom stared at her plate. The potatoes were gone, and so was her coffee. Just a bite of steak remained, one piece of carved meat, resting in a pool of grease. She stared at it for a while like a person deciding if she was too full to continue, but really, I think she was just stalling. Despite her tough talk, her certainty, she was racked with fear and doubt. She was about to die and pass on to the other side. She'd know soon enough if she'd been right or not, and there wasn't any recourse either way. She was to the point of judgment, or nothingness, and both were frightening propositions.

"It's time, Evelyn," the guard said. "It's time to go."

Mom stood, and the guards shackled her and then escorted her out of the room. The whole time, Mom kept staring at me, unblinking, like she was trying to sear the image into her mind, and I was pleading with myself to say something, to reach out to her, to touch her one last time, tell her that I loved her and that I forgave her and that she was saved, but I couldn't. I just couldn't bring myself to say anything. We both remained silent as she was escorted through the door, and it clicked shut behind her, locking in place.

The execution chamber was a small room with an examination table complete with leather straps to secure the condemned's head, arms, and legs. A large window constituted one wall, and outside of it was the viewing gallery, filled with aluminum folding chairs. In the gallery were a few reporters, my mother's attorney, the DA, the sheriff, a couple agents from the FBI, along with a handful of survivors. I recognized them from our time back in Grove, and they all leered at me as if they couldn't believe I had the gall to show my face in public. But they restrained themselves. I suppose watching the leader die was retribution enough, and so they left me be. I took a seat near the back and off to the side, close to the exit. I was surprised Sam hadn't shown, or maybe I wasn't. He was given five years for his role in the incident, having been given a deal by the DA since he testified against Mom. After his release, I'd heard he'd moved north and was still preaching up in Kansas. He'd always been a self-proclaimed pilgrim of God, and so when the dust settled, he'd moved on and wasn't about to return for any reason whatsoever, even if it was to say goodbye to his protégé, to take any sort of responsibility for his role in what had occurred. I suppose his lack of courage shouldn't have surprised me, but still it did, nagging at me like an upturned toenail, shooting pain with every step taken.

Guards escorted Mom into the chamber, and she kept her head down as they led her toward the examination table. A judge in a suit entered the room and read aloud her sentence.

"Evelyn June Gunter, for sixteen counts of murder, you have been sentenced by a jury of your peers to death. Do you have any last words?"

Mom shook her head no.

The guards unshackled Mom, had her lie upon the table, and then strapped her secure. A doctor entered, the executioner, a small case in hand, a stethoscope dangling from his neck. He laid his case down on a table next to my mother, and from it he readied three syringes. The first, I knew, was to paralyze my mother. The second was to render her unconscious. The third was to stop her heart. The doctor injected each methodically, stopping after each one to wait the prescribed two minutes before moving onto the next. Mom kept her eyes wide for as long as she could, refusing to blink, I suppose trying to bear witness to the world for as long as she could, hoping that if there was an afterlife like she believed, she'd be able to take with her as much of this life as she possibly could. I couldn't blame her for this impulse. No matter how resolute our faith, no matter if we've made peace with our creator, the moment of death is a terrifying prospect, because regardless of belief, there will exist a twinge of doubt, eating at you until the very last moment, nagging at you that you might be wrong.

After the second injection, my mother's eyes closed, and I could feel my heart rate quicken, my breathing slow, my vision narrow, turn dark, and I kept repeating to myself, silently, "Relax. Relax. Everything will be okay," and after a while I was able to breathe again and the world stopped its trembling. Everyone held their breath. The couple next to me held hands, the woman clutching a tissue. But she didn't cry. She just stared resolutely at my mother as she lay there motionless, like she was simply taking a nap, like she was just waiting for someone to wake her, ask her how she was doing.

After the third injection, the doctor watched the clock. One minute went by, then two. He put his stethoscope in place and placed the monitor on her chest. He moved it up, then down, then up again, searching for any trace of heartbeat, and I couldn't help but pray. Dear God, please, oh please, oh please, oh please, I begged, yearning for this to not be true, for her to rise up, to say something, anything, it didn't even matter what, just some sign she was still alive and would be alive and would be forever, but my prayers went unanswered. The doctor called her death, and yet no one moved. We all just sat there silently, uncertain what we were to do next.

CHAPTER 7

WE FOREWENT A FUNERAL, NOT THAT ANYONE would've shown anyway, but Jonah and I thought it best to keep it a private affair, to dispose of her ashes where she'd been happiest, back in Bartlesville before we'd moved to Grove, at our old house. It hadn't changed much since we'd moved years before. The tree that had once adorned our front yard had been cut down, and the basketball goal where Jonah and I had practiced our free throws had been removed, but the cement foundation in which the pole had stood was still there, the little circle filled in by a now-barren flowerpot. The roof had been replaced, and the walls shined with a new coat of paint, though it resembled the same color it had been when we lived there.

It was odd being back in Bartlesville. Everything seemed smaller somehow. The house and the street and the hill where Jonah and I had once sledded during winters. It even had a different smell, a mixture of gasoline and motor oil, wafting in from a new auto-repair garage that had been built a street over. I wondered if any of the same families still lived in the neighborhood. If Adam's mom, Jan, still lived across the street, if the Morrisons were still next to her, what they were doing now, if they were retired or moved on or still chugging away as they did years ago, working the same jobs and watching the same television shows and eating the same dinners. I wondered if they'd heard what had happened to us once we moved away, about the church and the raid and all those people who had died. I wondered if they told people at parties about us, an icebreaking anecdote: "Oh hey, did you hear about the Gunters? They used to be our neighbors. Crazy, right?" I'm sure others tried to distance themselves from us, act like they hadn't heard a thing, repress it as something disdainful, as if they could be guilty by association if anyone ever found out just how close we truly were.

At least one person realized what had happened. Clifton Mathews, a kid I'd gone to school with, had sent me a letter while I was inside at juvenile detention. It was a short letter, to the point, only saying, "I am so sorry this happened to you." I remembered just how odd it was to have received his letter out of the blue like that. It wasn't that Clifton and I had been close, and we didn't stay in touch after my mother and I'd moved to Grove. But he was the only one who reached out to me. I wish I could say his letter made me feel better, forgiven somehow, but it didn't. It made me angry. I didn't want his pity or his sympathy. It felt cheap and wrong, and I balled up the piece of paper and stuck it in my mouth and I chewed and tried to swallow it but couldn't. Instead, I choked, and I ended up vomiting it up into the corner of my cell. Standing there that night with Mom's ashes in my hand, I had half a mind to ring the doorbell, and if he answered, confess what I had done to his letter and tell him I was sorry for rebuking his gesture. But I didn't. I didn't and still don't have the courage to.

We spread Mom's ashes in the middle of the night. It was just me and Jonah and Atchley, and we didn't say anything. We just emptied her ashes onto the front yard, none of us knowing what to say or if there was anything to say, and so we didn't. There wasn't any wind, and so the ashes just lay there in a pile on the ground. It resembled an anthill in a way, larger, though, a mound of human dust, no more a person than the dirt it rested upon. We stood there for a minute, stared at the ashes on the ground, and then made our way back to our car to drive off.

Across town, the nursing home was a long white building. Out front were a few dead bushes, their branches brown and thin. The wood panels were warped from exposure to the elements. Paint chipped, revealing the worn, gray wood underneath. Though the windows were dark, I could make out a few ornaments hanging on the other side, little yarn knickknacks and dream catchers, a few Christmas decorations. A couple old men sat out front in wheelchairs, blankets draped over their legs, smoking cigarettes and looking cold and miserable. When we passed them, they didn't acknowledge our presence, still staring straight ahead, as if watching something far off in the distance. The place reminded me of juvenile detention in a way. It was cold and lonely, housing people who would rather be anywhere else. I immediately felt ashamed this was where my father would spend the rest of his days, blinking at daytime game shows and sitting in front of an unmarked bingo card as a disinterested and underpaid attendant read off the latest ping-pong ball. I felt as though I'd failed him. His situation was all my fault.

A young attendant greeted us with a sign-in sheet and a practiced smile, one I was sure she'd grown accustomed to giving unfamiliar faces, judgment reserved for the relatives of her charges who did not visit often enough. Despite her warm veneer, her twanged "hello," and her seasonal red-and-green manicured nails, I could feel the contempt she held for me, Caleb Gunter, the murderer and cult leader, visiting his father for the first time. Nothing in her reaction indicated she recognized me, but I'm sure she no doubt did, the rumors spreading across the home once it was learned Dad had once been married to the notorious Evelyn Gunter and that his son, now released from juvenile detention, might one day come to visit. I respected her restraint, her façade—I bet she was a practiced poker player, continually raking in the chips of an unsuspecting tourist—but despite her calmness, I could feel her eyes burning into the back of my head as I walked down the hall.

Dad we found near the back, in a small room by himself. He lay in a hospital bed, snoring, a blanket pulled up to his chin. The room itself was packed with Dad's belongings, old photographs dating back from his childhood to school pictures of Jonah and me when we'd been in elementary school. On a dresser was a picture of him and Mom at their wedding, looking happy dancing at a sparsely attended reception. A few items adorned his dresser and side table: an alarm clock two hours too fast, a watch with a cracked crystal, an empty money clip, and a receipt from a few months prior. The money clip and watch I recognized, gifts from Mom and Jonah and me for Father's Day or his birthday, things Jonah and I had given very little thought to when growing up, but items Dad valued enough to keep throughout the years, even when his health was wavering and he had little room to store his things.

"You can take those, if you want," Jonah said when he caught me staring at them. "He doesn't have a use for them anymore."

Dad stirred and made a noise like he couldn't catch his breath, gasping for air. He inhaled deeply, once, twice, three times, all without exhaling, and then blinked when he spotted us in his room.

"Dad?" Jonah said. "It's me. I brought someone to see you."

He nudged me toward Dad, but I didn't move. As much as I didn't want to admit it, it frightened me to see Dad this feeble, his mind deteriorated and his body wasted. He was pale and frail and his teeth had turned yellow. He looked like he was on the verge of death, and I just thought that couldn't be. Not Dad. He'd always been Herculean, someone larger than life, someone made of gravel and sandpaper and who could take pain after pain after pain and keep on standing, no matter what. He was immovable, my dad. An immovable rock. But there he was, so feeble I doubted he could pull himself out of bed.

"Hi, Dad," I said. "It's been a long time."

Dad blinked at me, nodded, but I wasn't sure what that meant. I couldn't be sure if he recognized me, or if he was just indicating he could hear my voice, a subconscious reaction so he didn't have to admit he didn't understand what was going on.

"You look good," I said. "You look like you're happy here."

He raised a hand and pointed at me, his index finger dangling, and alternated between me and Atchley.

"This is Atchley," I said. "I—uh—well—she's my friend."

"Girlfriend," Atchley said. "I'm your son's girlfriend."

Dad scowled. It wasn't so much out of anger, I thought, but confusion. He was having a hard time following the conversation perhaps, or maybe he just couldn't quite fathom me with a girlfriend, the idea striking him as too unlikely to ever occur.

"You," he said, his voice garbled and deep like he had cotton balls stuffed into his mouth. "And him?" He pointed between Atchley and me, and smiled.

"Yes," Atchley said, laughing. "I'm with him."

"Good," Dad said. "I'm glad."

We talked and we talked. Or I did, mostly, about my place in Oklahoma City and how I was thinking about going back to school, perhaps go into social work to help troubled teens or maybe become a history teacher, about how so much had changed in the past six years, in such a small amount of time I just couldn't believe it, how everyone had cell phones now and was constantly moving, and about how sometimes I just liked to sit, it didn't even matter where, outside a sandwich shop or in the frozen-food section at the grocery store, just watch people, a mother trying to herd her two young twins or a man confused by the incredible plethora of deodorant choices. I talked about how I was thinking about getting a dog and how I found myself binge-watching television reruns from before I'd been incarcerated, shows like *Seinfeld* and *Friends* and *Full House*. I talked about how I was sorry for how things turned out. I talked about how I was sorry I didn't listen to him sooner. I talked about how I would visit more often, and how things would be different from there on out. That he'd see. Things were finally looking up. And Dad just listened. He nodded his head and grimaced and smiled and scooted upright, but after a while, I knew he was tiring. His eyes drooped and his face strained and he kept sucking on his teeth like he was trying to keep from losing focus, and eventually I told him it was time for me to go.

He was too tired and too medicated to say goodbye. He jerked open his eyes, but they slowly drooped closed. He returned to snoring, his face relaxed, and he no longer seemed to be in pain.

STEPPING BACK INTO GROVE WAS difficult. About thirty minutes from town, my skin began to itch and turn red and little bumps formed around my elbows and forearms. My throat constricted. I suffered from a mild case of vertigo. My mouth flooded with saliva and I felt nauseated and for a moment I thought I might be sick, and Atchley kept asking if I wanted to turn around, if I was feeling okay, and I just nodded and pointed forward and held my breath as we crossed the sign denoting city limits. I held my breath until I saw stars and everything looked bulbous and blurry and dark. I held my breath until my lungs hurt and I couldn't hold it any longer, and when I finally exhaled, it came out of me in one fell swoop, and when I did, we were on the other side, and there was no turning back.

Despite only being six years since I'd last been there, the town had changed. A new four-lane bridge brought us into town, and as soon as we crossed, shiny new shopping centers accosted us: Old Navy and Bed Bath & Beyond and a scuba-diving shop. There were seafood and Italian restaurants and a new office-supply store. There was a Chili's and a Best Buy and a brand-new Walmart Superstore. Outlet malls sprawled on both sides of the highway, shaped like a community of teepees. I almost didn't even recognize the place. And I was thankful for that. It made the whole prospect of facing my past that much easier to bear.

The old trailer park looked nothing like it had before. The dozens of tiny homes and Sam's house had been razed, but the barn still stood. It had warped and faded and had fallen into disrepair, its door hanging from its hinge. The fences still stood, but the wood had begun to rot. About sixty or so yards toward the lake, a fire pit smoldered where a large bonfire had recently burned. Dark smoke still wafted up into the air and over the canopy. Where once there were well-manicured, roll-ing fields was now an overgrown underbrush, thick with waist-high Indian grass, dandelion, and blackjack saplings. Cut through that was a gravel driveway, marked by dirt tire tracks, and at the end stood a mobile home, its siding oxidized and turning brown.

We got out of the car and stood on the side of the road, and I pointed out to Atchley where everything once was, telling her how we had services every morning and how we grew soybean and wheat on that side of the farm and corn on the other. How the well was at the back of the property, and how we'd played pickup football games in front of the house and put on Shakespearean plays on a makeshift stage, and how we'd been planning, before everything had gone bad, to build a go-kart track on the eastern side of the property. There were lots of plans we never had the chance to enact, good plans, plans that would've made a difference in the community, like how we'd hoped to start an after-school program for at-risk teens from the town, teach-ing them how to till and work the land, the intricacies of combus-tible-engine repair, carpentry, or how we'd started an environmental program cleaning up litter from the lake strewn about by tourists and drunk, sunburnt youth, how it was funny that nobody ever wanted to talk about those things, the good things. That it was always about the death and the crazy and the brainwashings and the lies and the lies and the lies. That's not what it was all about. That was such a small part of it, actually, if you really, really took the time to understand what had happened. If you got right down to it, all we were trying to do was some good in the world.

"Do you miss it?" she asked.

"I'm sorry?"

"You talk like it was the best time of your life," she said. "It sounds like you miss it."

"There were some good times. In the beginning. Sure. I suppose I miss parts of it."

"But not all of it?"

"No. Definitely not all of it."

We heard a truck engine approaching. The owner of the land was leaving his property, and so we moved off to the side so as not to block the end of the driveway. When he neared, however, we noticed the driver carried a shotgun. He stopped about twenty feet from us and pointed it out the window and yelled for us to get away from his property. His face was wracked with rage, burnt red, and he seethed. He seethed and he cursed and he spat and he waved his gun about, screaming he was tired of everyone always coming out there all the time, that there wasn't anything left to see anymore, that all the crazies had left town years ago; they were gone, dead, adios, gone forever, and we didn't have to be told twice—we turned and got back into the car, figuring sometimes it's best just to run.

When we pulled out onto the highway, the man was still behind us, waving the shotgun above his head, but in front of us we could see for miles. The sky burned a blue I didn't think possible. It was bright, indigo even, iridescent so the whole world lit up. It lit up the corn and the wheat and the soybean. It lit up the lake and the farmhouses, the Indian grass and cattle. It lit up everything like I could see the whole of the earth. It was like it was just one big continent again, and all the world was still connected.

Born and raised in the Bible Belt, Noah Milligan is the author of the novel *An Elegant Theory* and the short-story collection *Five Hundred Poor*. His work has been named a semifinalist for the Horatio Nelson Fiction Prize and a finalist for Foreword Review's 2016 Book of the Year. His short fiction has been published in *Cowboy Jamboree, Orson's Review, Windmill: The Hofstra Journal of Literature and Art*, and elsewhere. He lives in Norman, OK, with his wife and two children.

FIVE HUNDRED POOR

Noah Milligan

Short Stories - 978-1-77168-139-1

From acclaimed author, Noah Milligan, comes a short story collection, Five Hundred Poor. The title comes from Adam Smith's The Wealth of Nations, "Wherever there is great property there is great inequality. For one very rich man there must be at least five hundred poor, and the affluence of the few supposes the indigence of the many. The affluence of the rich excites the indignation of the poor, who are often both driven by want, and prompted by envy, to invade his possessions."

These are ten stories of those five hundred poor, the jaded, the disillusioned, and the disenfranchised.

"Noah Milligan writes about Oklahoma in such an uncanny, dark, compelling way." —Brandon Hobson, author of Where The Dead Sit Talking"